Nine barons had ruled Poictesme under their lord Count Manuel. But Manuel has vanished mysteriously, the Fellowship is broken, and nine wandering adventurers set out to find their fates, fates as diverse, colourful and unusual as the champions themselves. Among them is Miramon the magician, who gets into trouble by reviving a long-retired Divinity, and Gonfal, whose wooing of the Dark Queen of the Isles of Wonder has fateful results.

Coth survives a few exhausting weeks in the harem of Queen Zelee and Guivric the Sage puts a little too much faith in the power of mind over matter. And there is Donander, who, as the result of a celestial error, finds himself in the wrong Paradise, and takes full advantage of it and its inmates.

THE SILVER STALLION continues the loose trilogy begun in FIGURES OF EARTH.

Also by James Branch Cabell
FIGURES OF EARTH
JURGEN

'Now, the redemption which we as yet await (continued Imlac), will be that of Kalki, who will come as a Silver Stallion: all evils and every sort of folly will perish at the coming of this Kalki: true righteousness will be restored, and the minds of men will be made clear as crystal.'

The Silver Stallion

JAMES BRANCH CABELL

Introduction by
James Blish

London
UNWIN PAPERBACKS
Boston   Sydney

First published in Great Britain by The Bodley Head Ltd 1926
First published by Unwin Paperbacks 1983

UNWIN® PAPERBACKS
40 Museum Street, London WC1A 1LU, UK

Unwin Paperbacks
Park Lane, Hemel Hempstead, Herts HP2 4TE, UK

George Allen & Unwin Australia Pty Ltd
8 Napier Street, North Sydney, NSW 2060, Australia

British Library Cataloguing in Publication Data

Cabell, James Branch
    Silver stallion.
I. Title
813'.54[F]   PS3505.A153
ISBN 0-04-823242-4

Set in 10 on 11½ point Imprint by Computape (Pickering) Ltd
and printed in Great Britain by Cox and Wyman Ltd, Reading

Introduction

Of the more than 50 books written by James Branch Cabell (1879–1958), *The Silver Stallion* is the only one ever to be the sole subject (in 1969) of an entire seminar of the Modern Language Association. I don't mention this fact to terrify, for the novel is first and foremost a witty, compassionate and elegantly written book which is a pure delight to read. However, the MLA seminar offers a shorthand way of noting that it is also so rich that it was still being mined by scholars 43 years after it was first published.

It tells its own story, is complete in itself, and needs no explanation. However, it is also a sequel to the story of Dom Manuel, *Figures of Earth* (also published in Unicorn by Unwin Paperbacks). As readers of that novel will remember, and as Cabell makes plain in this one, the 'real' Dom Manuel was something of a scoundrel, who betrayed everybody who ever had anything to do with him, including, in the end, himself. Now, however, we find his actual history in the process of being turned into a myth, and the real Manuel into a religious Redeemer; and *The Silver Stallion* is the story of this process, and of how Manuel's former comrades-at-arms and others fared under it. The theme is one brimming with possibilities for both comedy and tragedy, and Cabell exploits them all.

The highly ambiguous 'moral' of this wholly unedifying tale is pronounced by an ageing pawnbroker named Jurgen, who appeared briefly as a little boy in *Figures of Earth*. In his summary, he mentions a most curious dream which he has had. This dream – almost as outlandish a one as Joyce's *Finnegans Wake* and a great deal easier to read – is the subject of *Jurgen*, which completes this loose trilogy.

Why should scholars, of all people, be interested in such outrageously overt fantasies as this one? Well, one example will suffice: When, in *The Silver Stallion*, Donander is accidentally transported to the Valhalla of Scandinavian myth, and meets many of the familiar gods and goddesses one would expect to find there, Cabell gives all these divine personages new names; and it turns out that Cabell knew enough Old Norse *and* Gothic so that these new names tell you something about the gods that you can't find in the myths themselves.

JAMES BLISH

To

Carl Van Doren

COULD but one luring dream rest dead forever
As dreamers rest at last, with all dreams done,
Redeemers need not be, and faith need never
Lease, for the faithful, homes beyond the sun.

Victoriously that dream—above the sorrow
And subterfuge of living,—still lets fail
No heart to heed its soothing lure. . . . *To-morrow*
Dreams will be true, and faith and right prevail.

Out of the bright—and, no, not vacant!—heavens
Redeemers will be coming by and by,
En route to make our sixes and our sevens
Neat as a trivet or an apple-pie.

In this volume the text of Bülg has not been followed overscrupulously: but it is hoped that, in a book intended for general circulation, none will deplore such excisions and euphemisms, nor even such slight additions, as seemed to make for coherence and clarity and decorum.

The curious are referred to the pages of *Poictesme en Chanson et Légende* for a discussion of the sources of *The Silver Stallion*; and may decide for themselves whether or not Bülg has, in Codman's phrase, 'shown' these legends to be 'spurious compositions of 17th century origin'. But, for myself, I confess to finding the educed evidence equally inadequate and immaterial, since it concerns my present purpose not one button's worth whether Nicolas de Caen or some other person first wrote these stories. These chronicles, such as they are, present the only known record of the latter days of champions whose youthful exploits have long since been made familiar to English readers of Lewistam's *Popular Tales of Poictesme*: authentic or not, and irrespective of whether such legends cannot be quite definitely proved to have existed earlier than 1652, here is the sole account we have anywhere, or are now likely ever to receive, of the changes that followed in Poictesme after the passing of Manuel the Redeemer.

It is as such an account—which for my purpose was a desideratum,—that I have put *The Silver Stallion* into English.

The Lords that Poictesme Had in Dom Manuel's Time

These ten were of the Fellowship of the Silver Stallion:

DOM MANUEL, Count of Poictesme, held Storisende and Belle-garde, the town of Beauvillage and the strong fort at Lisuarte, with all Amneran and Morven.

MESSIRE GONFAL OF NAIMES, Margrave of Aradol, held Upper Naimousin.

MESSIRE DONANDER OF EVRE, the Thane of Aigremont, held Lower Naimousin.

MESSIRE KERIN OF NOINTEL, Syndic and Castellan of Basardra, held West Val-Ardray.

MESSIRE NINZIAN OF YAIR, the High Bailiff of Upper Ardra, held Val-Ardray in the East.

MESSIRE HOLDEN OF NÉRAC, Earl Marshal of St Tara, held Belpaysage.

MESSIRE ANAVALT OF FOMOR, the Portreeve and Warden of Manneville, held Belpaysage Le Bas.

MESSIRE COTH OF THE ROCKS, Alderman of St Didol, held Haut Belpaysage.

MESSIRE GUIVRIC OF PERDIGON, Heitman of Asch, held Piemon-tais.

MESSIRE MIRAMON OF RANEC, Lord Seneschal of Gontaron, held Duardenois.

Likewise there were the fiefs of DOM MEUNIER, *Count of Mon-tors,* DOM MANUEL'S *brother-in-law.* MEUNIER *was not of this fellowship: he held also Giens. Here his wife ruled over Lower Duardenois.*

OTHMAR BLACK-TOOTH, *whom some called Othmar the Lawless, long held Valnères and Ogde, until* MANUEL *routed him: thereafter these villages, with the most of Bovion, stayed masterless.*

HELMAS THE DEEP-MINDED, *after a magic was put upon him in the year of grace 1255, held, in his fashion, the high place at Brunbelois: but the rest of Acaire, once Lorcha had been taken and Sclaug burned, was no man's land. Also upon Upper Morven lived disaffected persons in defiance of all law and piety.*

—POICTESME EN CHANSON ET LÉGENDE, G. J. —*Bülg. Strasburg, 1785*   [pp. 87–88]

Contents

BOOK SEVEN

WHAT SARAIDE WANTED

BOOK EIGHT

THE CANDID FOOTPRINT

BOOK NINE

ABOVE PARADISE

BOOK TEN
AT MANUEL'S TOMB

Author's Note

With *The Silver Stallion* the Biography turns to those who in some sense were – just as Jurgen asserts, – 'Dom Manuel's children in the spirit.' Yet upon that relationship, as actually familiary, I would not insist. Rather, was it my aim in this book to record the growth of the great legend of Manuel as a spiritual Redeemer and in particular to trace the slowly widening influence of this legend among those persons who had known Manuel almost intimately. I agree with Freydis that, for various reasons, nobody ever, quite, know Manuel really well.

The hero of *The Silver Stallion* is, thus, no person, but an idea, – an idea presented at the moment of its conception, and thence passing through its infancy and its little-regarded youth, wholly unhurt by the raging of Coth, and the unregeneracy of Gonfal and of Miramon, to come gradually to full growth and vigor; until at the end of the book this idea, which stays always the book's hero, is, in accordance with the true romantic code, dismissed to live happily ever afterward, in the mind of Donander Veratyr. I mean, of course, the idea that Manuel, who was yesterday the physical Redeemer of Poictesme, will by and by return as his people's spiritual Redeemer.

Upon a planet not often over-fertile in perpetual bliss, to be sure, this ideal protagonist of *The Silver Stallion* did not live happily ever afterward. Instead, the great legend of Manuel was definitely annihilated during the fourteenth century by Manuel's reputed great-grandson: but with that fact we have, as yet, no concern.

We know, in any case, that, if the annals of Poictesme are to be trusted, Dom Manuel for a while flourished quite handsomely as a messiah. He had his vogue and his enthusiasts without ever having much else in common with those hordes of pagan Redeemers who, at odd times, have brought the consolations and ferocities of religion to innumerable millions. For men have looked for the return of other Redeemers than Hammurabi and Krishna and Saoshyant; not merely Bar-Kokebas and Moses of

Crete, not only David Alroy and Sabbatai Sevi, have been revealed as the one true Savior's incarnation in human flesh; Popé and Teuskwa'tawa also have had their compeers in a more civilised form of worship; and the Mahdis, the countless scores of Mahdis since the days of Mohammed Ibn al Hanafiyah, – all those divinely inspired Redeemers whose coming has so frequently justified the faith of Islam, – have been no more numerous than have been the Redeemers gratifyingly untainted by paganism.

So has it come about that this belief in a Redeemer who is to return, tomorrow, is not merely a heathen superstition: it has been found, time and again, wholly consistent with continued membership in many branches of the Christian Church. Dom Manuel, thus, we may assume to have been worshipped well within the confines of the Christian faith, very much as Elkesai was once worshipped by a division of the Ebionites, and St James the Just by the Eucharists, and Hans Böhm by the Taborites, and John of Leyden by the Anabaptists. Dom Manuel, let us say, was for a while as ardently believed, by the most zealous Christians, to be mankind's predestined spiritual Redeemer as, for a while, also, was Venner the Wine Cooper, or Anne Lee, or Savely Kapustin, or that son of Joanna Southcote who rather vexatiously failed ever to be born. Dom Manuel, in fine, according to the annals of Poictesme, was worshipped without any impiety, as a purely Christian messiah, as at other times were Melchior Hoffmann and Arise Evans and Danelo Filopovitch and John Alexander Dowie.

Today, of course, no one of these Christian Redeemers is at all honored, unless the Doukhobors still await the return of Kapustin. I am sure I do not know. But each had once a vogue and a formally organised and endowed church wherein to be worshipped and the enthusiasts who endured persecution and who died for his sake – or, as it might be, for her sake, – very gladly. Each in his day, and within a howsoever limited circle of adherents, awakened that sustaining faith which appears vitally necessary to men's contentment, in the legend of the all-powerful Redeemer who will come again, tomorrow.

The theme of this book, then, is how that legend came to attach itself to Dom Manuel; how, in particular, that legend afterward affected, or did not affect, those persons who had known Dom Manuel almost intimately; and how in the end nobody believed in

it any longer except Donander Veratyr. But Donander Veratyr
was God.

The Silver Stallion was, roughly, planned while I was finishing
Figures of Earth in 1920. Two of the episodes were completed
early in 1922, but not until the autumn of 1924 was the book in
due form begun. It was finished in the September of 1925: and I
may here record that, precisely as happened with *The Certain
Hour*, the exodus of the one existing copy of *The Silver Stallion*
from out of my keeping was closely attended by tragedy.

For it was mailed at Dumbarton. There, I should here explain,
the outgoing mail bag is hanged on a sort of gibbet beside the
railway track, and as the mail train thunders by, it disdainfully
acquires this mail bag with a large iron hook. I have observed the
performance many hundred times; and always, I believe, I was
moved by its petulance. No mail train ever seemed to convey any
of my work toward publication except with frank and even
boisterous distaste.

In any event, when the typescript of *The Silver Stallion* was
mailed, late on a Saturday afternoon, the viciously lunging hook
struck just a little too low. It thus ripped open the mail bag; and,
carrying off the remainder of the mail to the least post card, left
with invidious distinction *The Silver Stallion* lying in the ditch
beside the railway. There it remained all night: and, I must
repeat, this was then the only copy of this book anywhere
existent. No typist can decipher my handwriting, and I cannot
with any retention of equanimity attempt carbon copies upon my
own typewriter, because seven times out of ten I insert the carbon
paper wrong side up.

Sunday, however, was a fine day, the sun shone full upon my
now badly muddied, painstakingly wrapped package, and out of
the scores of persons who crossed the ditch during the forenoon it
was natural enough the first comer should find my typescript. As
it happened, to be sure, the parcel was not discovered by absolutely the first passer-by, nor by the second. Dozens of people had
gone by before, at last, it might be the hundredth person to cross
that ditch upon that bright Sunday glanced casually down to
ensure his foothold and observed my three-and-a-half pound
package not at all. Nobody ever noticed it during the whole day.

And thus *The Silver Stallion* passed yet another night in the mire of a ditch beside a railway track under no surveillance save that of Orion and the Pleiades.

The genius of compassion whispers me to keep you no longer in suspense. Upon Monday morning, when the mail carrier, after his Sabbath holiday, came to hang the outgoing mail bag upon the gibbet to which I have already referred, he quite unavoidably saw the package. So it was retrieved from the ditch, exceedingly soiled but unhurt; and was duly forwarded to McBride's; and in due time was published, in the April of 1926.

All of which constitutes no thrilling tale. My point though, is that anybody who refuses to concede the typescript was, for at least thirty-six hours, protected by heaven, can but, rather impiously, presuppose some supernal slackness somewhere, – when ten minutes' rain could so easily have deleted my entire year's work. My point is that this book did, at the tip-end of a quite showery September, really and directly receive heaven's imprimatur; and that therefore some of the criticism accorded it, later, appeared to me a little rash.

I cite, for example, an uncommonly well-thought-of-English critic who was but one of a largish chorus which has just thus hymned the merits of *The Silver Stallion*: 'The malignity and malevolence of this monstrous literary sacrilege cannot be pardoned. Its banality is no excuse for its brutality. Its stupidity is no extenuation for its blasphemy. Cabell has in this book committed the unpardonable sin of art, – hooliganism. He may not be capable of understanding the vision of good that raises man above the level of vermin. He may not be able to feel the mystery of faith. He may not possess the power of reverence or the grace of humility. But he ought to love his fellow creatures, and to respect their ideals and their dreams. He may find it amusing to hurt and wound the lowly and the simple, but he should not trample on their highest and holiest imaginings, even if he cannot soar out of his literary mire and mud.'

– Yes, howsoever much one may admire alliteration, that seems to me a little rash. I cannot quite imagine heaven protecting just that sort of book. I concede, of course, that *The Silver Stallion* did actually come to its publishers out of the mire and mud of an actual Henrico County ditch. But it came to tell (with, I think, all proper reverence) of a legend in which most men believe instinctively, and believe for mankind's perpetual good, even if this legend be not true about any of the countless Redeemers between Hammurabi and John Alexander Dowie, – and of a very lovely legend which in the end, as I would by no means have you not note, this book dismisses as yet living in the heart of that God whom men adore as the Creator and Preserver of all earthly things.

– JAMES BRANCH CABELL
Richmond-in-Virginia, 30 April, 1927

HEREWITH BEGINS THE HISTORY OF THE BIRTH AND OF THE TRIUMPHING OF THE GREAT LEGEND ABOUT MANUEL THE REDEEMER, WHOM GONFAL REPUDI- ATED AS BLOWN DUST, AND MIRAMON, AS AN IMPOSTOR, AND WHOM COTH REPUDIATED OUT OF HONEST LOVE: BUT WHOM GUIVRIC ACCEPTED, THROUGH TWO SORTS OF POLICY; WHOM KERIN ACCEPTED AS AN HONORABLE OLD HUMAN FOIBLE, AND NINZIAN, AS A PATHETIC AND SERVICEABLE JOKE; WHOM DONANDER ACCEPTED WHOLE- HEARTEDLY (TO THE ETERNAL JOY OF DONANDER), AND WHO WAS ACCEPTED ALSO BY NIAFER, AND BY JURGEN THE PAWNBROKER, AFTER SOME LITTLE PRIVATE RESERVATIONS; AND HEREINAFTER IS RECORDED THE MANNER OF THE GREAT LEGEND'S ENGULFMENT OF THESE PERSONS

Book One

Last Siege of the Fellowship

'They shall be, in the siege, both against Judah and against Jerusalem.'
ZECHARIAH, xii, 2

—Et *la route, fait elle aussi un grand tour?*

—Oh, *bien certainement, étant donné qu'elle circonvient à la fois la destinée et le bon sens.*

—Puisqu'il *le faut, alors! dit Jurgen; d'ailleurs je suis toujours disposé à goûter n'importe quel breuvage au moins un fois.*

—LA HAULTE HISTOIRE DE JURGEN

Chapter I

Child's Talk

They relate how Dom Manuel that was the high Count of Poictesme, and was everywhere esteemed the most lucky and the least scrupulous rogue of his times, had disappeared out of his castle at Storisende, without any reason or forewarning, upon the feast day of St Michael and All the Angels. They tell of the confusion and dismay which arose in Dom Manuel's lands when it was known that Manuel the Redeemer – thus named because he had redeemed Poictesme from the Northmen, through the aid of Miramon Lluagor, with a great and sanguinary magic – was now gone, quite inexplicably, out of these lands.

For whither Manuel had gone, no man nor any woman could say with certainty. At Storisende he had last been seen by his small daughter Melicent, who stated that Father, mounted on a black horse, had ridden westward with Grandfather Death, on a white one, to a far place beyond the sunset. This was quite generally felt to be improbable.

Yet further inquiry had but made more deep the mystery as to the manner of Dom Manuel's passing. Further inquiry had disclosed that the only human eyes anywhere which had, or could pretend to have, rested upon Dom Manuel after Manuel had left Storisende were those of a little boy called Jurgen, the son of Coth of the Rocks. Young Jurgen, after having received from his father an in no way unusual whipping, had run away from home, and had not been recaptured until the following morning. The lad reported that during his wanderings he had witnessed, toward dusk, upon Upper Morven, a fearful eucharist in which the Redeemer of Poictesme had very horribly shared. Thereafter – so the child's tale ran – had ensued a transfiguration, and a prediction as to the future of Poictesme, and Dom Manuel's elevation into the glowing clouds of sunset. . . .

Now, these latter details had been, at their first rendering, blubbered almost inarticulately. For, after just the initiatory passages of this supposed romance, the parents of Jurgen, in their first rapturous relief at having recovered their lost treasure, had, of course, in the manner of parents everywhere, resorted to such moral altitudes and to such corporal corrections as had disastrously affected the putative small liar's tale. Then, as the days passed, and they of Poictesme still vainly looked for the return of their great Dom Manuel, the child was of necessity questioned again: and little Jurgen, after sulking for a while, had retold his story without any detected deviation.

It certainly all sounded quite improbable. Nevertheless, here was the only explanation of the land's loss tendered anywhere by anybody: and people began half seriously to consider it. Say what you might, this immature and spanked evangelist had told a story opulent in details which no boy of his age could well, it seemed, have invented. Many persons therefore began sagely to refer to the mouths of babes and sucklings, and to nod ominously. Moreover, the child, when yet further questioned, had enlarged upon Manuel's last prediction as to the future glories of Poictesme, to an extent which made incredulity seem rather unpatriotic; and Jurgen had amplified his horrific story of the manner in which Manuel had redeemed his people from the incurred penalties of their various sins up to and including that evening.

The suggested inference that there was to be no accounting anywhere for one's unavoidable misdemeanors up to date – among which Dom Manuel had been at pains to specify such indiscretions as staying out all night without your parents' permission – was an arrangement which everybody, upon consideration, found to be more and more desirable. Good-hearted persons everywhere began, with virtually a free choice thus offered between belief and disbelief, to prefer to invest a little, it might well be, remunerative faith in the story told with such conviction by the sweet and unsullied child, rather than in the carping comments of materialists – who, after all, could only say, well out of earshot of Coth of the Rocks, that this young Jurgen was very likely to distinguish himself thereafter, either in the pulpit or upon some gallows.

Meanwhile one woeful facet was, in any case, undeniable: the saga of that quiet, prospering grand thief of a Manuel had ended with the inconsequent, if the not actually incredible, tales of these two little children; and squinting tall gray Manuel of the high head had gone out of Poictesme nobody could say whither.

Chapter II

Economics of Horvendile

And meanwhile too the Redeemer's wife, Dame Niafer, had sent a summoning to each of the nine lords that, with Manuel, were of the Fellowship of the Silver Stallion: and all these met at Storisende, as Niafer commanded them, for a session or, as they more formally called it, a siege of this order.

Now this fellowship took its name from the banner it had fought under so destroyingly. Upon that sable banner was displayed a silver stallion, which was rampant in every member and was bridled with gold. Dom Manuel was the captain of this fellowship; and it was made up of the nine barons who, under Manuel, had ruled Poictesme. Each had his two stout castles and his fine woodlands and meadows, which he held in fealty to Dom Manuel: and each had a high name for valor.

Four of these genial murderers had served, under the Conde de Tohil Vaca, in Manuel's first and utterly disastrous campaign against the Northmen: but all the nine had been with Manuel since the time of the great fighting about Lacre Kai, and throughout Manuel's various troubles with Oribert and Thragnar and Earl Ladinas and Sclaug and Oriander, that blind and coldly evil Swimmer who was the father of Manuel; and in all the other warrings of Manuel these nine had been with him up to the end.

And the deeds of the lords of the Silver Stallion had fallen very little short of Manuel's own deeds. Thus, it was Manuel, to be sure, who killed Oriander: that was a family affair. But Miramon Lluagor, the Seneschal of Gontaron, was the champion who subdued Thragnar and put upon him a detection and a hindrance: and it was Kerin of Nointel – the Syndic and, after that, the Castellan of Basardra – who captured and carefully burned Sclaug. Then, in the quelling of Othmar Black-Tooth's rebellion, Ninzian of Yair, the High Bailiff of Upper Ardra, had killed eleven more of the outlaws than got their deaths by Manuel's sword. It was Guivric of Perdigon, and not Manuel, who put the great Arabian Al-Motawakkil out of life. And in the famous battle with the Easterlings, by which the city of Megaris was rescued, it was Manuel who got the main glory and, people said, a three nights' loan of the body of King Theodoret's young sister; but capable judges declared the best fighting on that day was done by Donander of Évre, then but a boy, whom Manuel thereafter made Thane of Aigremont.

Yet Holden of Nérac, the Marshal of St Tara, was the boldest of them all, and was very well able to hold his own in single combat with any of those that have been spoken of: Coth of the Rocks had not ever quitted any battle-field except as a conqueror: and courteous Anavalt of Fomer and light-hearted Gonfal of Naimes – who had the worst names among his company for being the most cunning friends and coaxers of women – these two had put down their masculine opposers also in gratifyingly large numbers.

In fine, no matter where the lords of the Silver Stallion had raised their banner against an adversary, it was in that place they made an end of that adversary: for there was never, in any time, a hardier gang of bullies than was this Fellowship of the Silver Stallion in the season that they kept earth noisy with the clashing of their swords and darkened heaven with the smoke of the towns they were sacking, and when throughout the known world men had talked about the wonders which these champions were performing with Dom Manuel to lead them. Now they were leaderless.

These heroes came to Storisende; and with Dame Niafer they of course found Holy Holmendis. This saint had lately come out of Philistia, to christen Manuel's recently born daughter, Ettarre, and to console the Countess in her bereavement. But they found with her also that youthful red-haired Horvendile under whom Dom Manuel, in turn, had held Poictesme, by the terms of a contract which was not ever made public. Some said this Horvendile to be Satan's friend and emissary, while others declared his origin to lurk in a more pagan mythology: all knew the boy to be a master of discomfortable strange magics such as were unknown to Miramon Lluagor and Guivric the Sage.

This Horvendile said to the nine heroes, 'Now begins the last siege of the Fellowship of the Silver Stallion.'

Donander of Évre was the youngest of them. Yet he spoke now, piously and boldly enough. 'But it is our custom, Messire Horvendile, to begin each siege with prayer.'

'This siege,' replied Horvendile, 'must nevertheless begin without any such religious side-taking. For this is the siege in which, as it was prophesied, you shall be both against Judah and against Jerusalem, and against Thebes and Hermopolis and Avalon and Breidablik and all other places which produce Redeemers.'

'Upon my word, but who is master here!' cried Coth of the Rocks, twirling at his long mustachios. This gesture was a sure sign that trouble brewed.

Horvendile answered: 'The master who held Poictesme, under my whims, has passed. A woman sits in his place, his little son inherits after him. So begins a new romance; and a new order is set afoot.'

'Yet Coth, in his restless pursuit of variety, has asked a wholly sensible question,' said Gonfal, the tall Margrave of Aradol. 'Who will command us, who now will give us our directions? Can Madame Niafer lead us to war?'

'These things are separate. Dame Niafer commands: but it is I – since you ask – who will give to all of you your directions, and your dooms too against the time of their falling, and after that to your names I will give life. Now, your direction, Gonfal, is South.'

Gonfal looked full at Horvendile, in frank surprise. 'I was already planning for the South, though certainly I had told nobody about it. You are displaying, Messire Horvendile, an uncomfortable sort of wisdom which troubles me.'

Horvendile replied, 'It is but a little knack of foresight, such as I share with Balaam's ass.'

But Gonfal stayed more grave than was his custom. He asked, 'What shall I find in the South?'

'What all men find, at last, in one place or another whether it be with the aid of a knife or of a rope or of old age. Yet, I assure you, the finding of it will not be unwelcome.'

'Well,' – Gonfal shrugged – 'I am a realist. I take what comes, in the true form it comes in.'

Now Coth of the Rocks was blustering again. 'I also am a realist. Yet I permit no upstart, whether he have or have not hair like a carrot, to give me any directions.'

Horvendile answered, 'I say to you –'

But Coth replied, shaking his great bald head: 'No, I will not be bulldozed in this way. I am a mild-mannered man, but I will not tamely submit to be thus browbeaten. I believe, too, that Gonfal was insinuating I do not usually ask sensible questions!'

'Nobody has attempted –'

'Are you not contradicting me to my face! What is that but to call me a liar! I will not, I repeat, submit to these continued rudenesses.'

'I was only saying –'

But Coth was implacable. 'I will take directions from nobody who storms at me and who preserves no dignity whatever in our hour of grief. For the rest, the children agree in reporting that, whether he ascended in a gold cloud or traveled more sensibly on a black horse, Dom Manuel went westward. I shall go west, and I shall fetch Dom Manuel back into Poictesme. I shall, also, candidly advise him, when he returns to ruling over us, to discourage the tomfooleries and the ridiculous rages of all persons whose brains are over-heated by their hair.'

'Let the West, then,' said Horvendile, very quietly, 'be your direction. And if the people there do not find you so big a man as you think yourself, do not you be blaming me.'

These were his precise words. Coth himself conceded the coincidence, long afterward. . . .

'I, Messire Horvendile, with your permission, am for the North,' said Miramon Lluagor. The magician alone of them was upon any terms of intimacy with this Horvendile. 'I have yet upon gray Vraidex my Doubtful Castle, in which an undoubtable and a known doom awaits me.'

'That is true,' replied Horvendile. 'Let the keen North and the cold edge of Flamberge be yours. But you, Guivric, shall have the warm wise East for your direction.'

That allotment was uncordially received. 'I am comfortable enough in my home at Asch,' said Guivric the Sage. 'At some other time, perhaps – But, really now, Messire Horvendile, I have in hand a number of quite important thaumaturgies just at

the present! Your suggestion is most upsetting. I know of no need
for me to travel east.'

'With time you will know of that need,' said Horvendile, 'and
you will obey it willingly, and you will go willingly to face the
most pitiable and terrible of all things.'

Guivric the Sage did not reply. He was too sage to argue with
people when they talked foolishly. He was immeasurably too sage
to argue with, of all persons, Horvendile.

'Yet that,' observed Holden of Nérac, 'exhausts the directions:
and it leaves no direction for the rest of us.'

Horvendile looked at this Holden, who was with every reason
named the Bold; and Horvendile smiled. 'You, Holden, already
take your directions in a picturesque and secret manner, from a
queen –'

'Let us not speak of that!' said Holden, between a smirk and
some alarm.

'And you will be guided by her, in any event, rather than by
me. To you also, Anavalt of Fomor, yet another queen will call
resistlessly by and by, and you, who are rightly named the
Courteous, will deny her nothing. So to Holden and to Anavalt I
shall give no directions, because it is uncivil to come between any
woman and her prey.'

'But I,' said Kerin of Nointel, 'I have at Ogde a brand-new wife
whom I prize above all the women I ever married, and far above
any mere crowned queen. Not even wise Solomon,' now Kerin
told them, blinking, in a sort of quiet scholastic ecstasy, 'when
that Judean took his pick of the women of this world, accom-
panied with any queen like my Saraïde: for she is in all ways
superior to what the Cabalists record about Queen Naäma, that
pious child of the bloodthirsty King of Ammon, and about Queen
Djarada, the daughter of idolatrous Nubara the Egyptian, and
about Queen Balkis, who was begotten by a Sheban duke upon
the person of a female Djinn in the appearance of a gazelle. And
only at the command of my dear Saraïde would I leave home to go
in any direction.'

'You will, nevertheless, leave home, very shortly,' declared
Horvendile. 'And it will be at the command and at the personal
urging of your Saraïde.'

Kerin leaned his head to one side, and he blinked again. He had just Dom Manuel's trick of thus opening and shutting his eyes when he was thinking, but Kerin's mild dark gaze in very little resembled Manuel's piercing, vivid and rather wary consideration of affairs.

Kerin then observed, 'Yet it is just as Holden said, and every direction is pre-empted.'

'Oh, no,' said Horvendile. 'For you, Kerin, will go downward, whither nobody will dare to follow you, and where you will learn more wisdom than to argue with me, and to pester people with uncalled-for erudition.'

'It follows logically that I,' laughed young Donander of Évre, 'must be going upward, towards paradise itself, since no other direction whatever remains.'

'That,' Horvendile replied, 'happens to be true. But you will go up far higher than you think for; and your doom shall be the most strange of all.'

'Then must I rest content with some second-rate and commonplace destruction?' asked Ninzian of Yair, who alone of the fellowship had not yet spoken.

Horvendile looked at sleek Ninzian, and Horvendile looked long and long. 'Donander is a tolerably pious person. But without Ninzian, the Church would lack the stoutest and the one really god-fearing pillar it possesses anywhere in these parts. That would be the devil of a misfortune. Your direction, therefore, is to remain in Poictesme, and to uphold the edifying fine motto of Poictesme, for the world's benefit.'

'But the motto of Poictesme,' said Ninzian, doubtfully, 'is *Mundus vult decipi*, and signifies that the world wishes to be deceived.'

'That is a highly moral sentiment, which I may safely rely upon you alike to concede and prove. Therefore, for you who are so pious, I shall slightly paraphrase the Scripture: and I declare to all of you that neither will I any more remove the foot of Ninzian from out of the land which I have appointed for your children; so that they will take heed to do all which I have commanded them.'

'That,' Ninzian said, looking markedly uncomfortable, 'is very delightful.'

Chapter III

How Anavalt Lamented the Redeemer

Then Madame Niafer arose, black-robed and hollow-eyed, and she made a lament for Dom Manuel, whose like for gentleness and purity and loving kindness toward his fellows she declared to remain nowhere in this world. It was an encomium under which the attendant warriors stayed very grave and rather fidgety, because they recognised and shared her grief, but did not wholly recognise the Manuel whom she described to them.

And the Fellowship of the Silver Stallion was decreed to be disbanded, because of the law of Poictesme that all things should go by tens forever. There was no fighting-man able to fill Manuel's place: and a fellowship of nine members was, as Dame Niafer pointed out, illegal.

It might well be, however, she suggested, with a side glance toward Holmendis, that some other peculiarly holy person, even though not a warrior – At the same instant Coth said, with a startling and astringent decisiveness, 'Bosh!'

His confrères felt the gross incivility of this interruption, but felt, too, that they agreed with Coth. And so the fellowship was proclaimed to be disbanded.

Then Anavalt of Fomor made a lament for the passing of that noble order whose ranks were broken at last, and for Dom Manuel also Anavalt raised a lament, praising Manuel for his hardihood and his cunning and his terribleness in battle. The heroes nodded their assent to this more intelligible sort of talking.

'Manuel,' said Anavalt, 'was hardy. It was not wise for any enemy to provoke him. When that indiscretion was committed, Manuel made himself as a serpent about the city of that enemy, girdling his prey all round: he seized the purlieus of that city, and its cattle, and its boats upon the rivers. He beleaguered that city everywhere, he put fire to the orchards, he silenced the mill-races, he prevented the plowers from plowing the land; and the people of that city starved, and they ate up one another, until the survivors chose to surrender to Dom Manuel. Then Manuel raised his gallows, he whistled in his headsmen, and there were no more survivors of that people.'

And Anavalt said also: 'Manuel was cunning. With a feather he put a deception upon three kings, but the queens that he played his tricks on were more than three, nor was it any feather that he diddled them with. Nobody could outwit Manuel. What he wanted he took, if he could get it that way, with his strong hand: but, if not, he used his artful head and his lazy, wheedling tongue, and his other members too, so that the person whom he was deluding would give Manuel whatever he required. It was like eating honey, to be deluded by Manuel. I think it is no credit for a private man to be a great rogue; but the leader of a people must know how to deceive all peoples.'

Then Anavalt said: 'Manuel was terrible. There was no softness in him, no hesitancy, and no pity. That, too, is not a virtue in a private person, but in the leader of a people it may well be a blessing for that people. Manuel so ordered matters that no adversary ever troubled Poictesme the second time. He lived as a tyrant over us; but it is better to have one master that you know the ways of than to be always changing masters in a world where none but madmen run about at their own will. I do not weep for Manuel, because he would never have wept for me nor for anybody else; but I regret that man of iron and the protection he was to us who are not ruthless iron but flesh.'

There was a silence afterward. Yet still the heroes nodded gravely. This was, in the main, a Manuel whom they all recognised.

Dame Niafer, however, had risen up a little way from her seat, when the pious gaunt man Holy Holmendis, who sat next to her, put out his hand to her hand. After this she said nothing: yet it was perfectly clear the Countess thought that Anavalt had been praising Manuel for the wrong sort of virtues.

A fire was kindled with that ceremony which was requisite. The banner of the great fellowship was burned, and the lords of the Silver Stallion now broke their swords, and they cast these fragments also into this fire, so that these swords might never defend any other standard. It was the youth of these nine men and the first vigor and faith of their youth which perished with the extinction of that fire: and they knew it.

Thereafter the heroes left Storisende. Each rode for his own home, and they made ready, each in his own fashion, for that new order of governance which with the passing of Dom Manuel had come upon Poictesme.

Chapter IV

Fog Rises

Now Guivric and Donander and Gonfal rode westward with their attendants, all in one company, as far as Guivric's home at Asch. And as these three lords rode among the wreckage and the gathering fogs of November, the three talked together.

'It is a pity,' said Gonfal of Naimes, 'that, while our little Count Emmerick is growing up, this land must now be ruled by a lame and sallow person, who had never much wit and who tends already to stringiness. Otherwise, in a land ruled over by a widow, who is used to certain recreations, one might be finding amusement, and profit too.'

'Come now,' said loyal Donander of Évre, 'but Madame Niafer is a chaste and good woman who means well!'

'She has yet another quality which is even more disastrous in the ruler of any country,' returned Guivric the Sage.

'And what hook have you found now to hang a cynicism on?'

'I fear more from her inordinate piety than from her indifferent looks and her stupid well-meaningness. That woman will be reforming things everywhere into one gray ruin.'

'Indeed,' said Gonfal, smiling, 'these rising fogs have to me very much the appearance of church incense.'

Guivric nodded. 'Yes. Had it been possible, I believe that Madame Niafer would have preserved and desecrated the fellowship by setting in Dom Manuel's place that Holy Holmendis who is nowadays her guide in all spiritual matters; and who will presently, do you mark my prophesying, be making a sanctimonious hash of her statecraft.'

'He composed for her, it is well known,' said Gonfal, 'the plaint which she made for Dom Manuel.'

'That was a cataloguing of ecclesiastic virtues,' Guivric said, dryly, 'which to my mind did not very immediately suggest the tall adulterer and parricide whom we remember. This Holmendis has, thus, already brought hypocrisy into fashion.'

'He will be Niafer's main counselor,' Gonfal speculated. 'He is a pushing, vigorous fellow. I wonder now – ?'

Guivric nodded again. 'Women prefer to take counsel in a bedchamber,' he stated.

'Come, Guivric,' put in pious young Donander of Évre. 'Come now, whatever his over-charitable opinion of our dead master, this Holmendis is a saint: and we true believers should speak no ill of the saints.'

'I have nothing against belief, nor hypocrisy either, within reason, nor have I anything against saints, in their proper place. It is only that should a saint – and more particularly, a saint conceived and nurtured and made holy in Philistia – ever come to rule over Poictesme, and over the bedchamber of Dom Manuel,' said Guivric, moodily, 'that saint would not be in his proper place. And our day, my friends, would be ended.'

'It is already ended,' Gonfal said, 'so far as Poictesme is concerned: these fogs smell over-strongly of church incense. But these fogs which rise about Poictesme do not envelop the earth. For one, I shall fare south, as that Horvendile directed me, and as I had already planned to do. In the South I shall find nobody so amusing as that fine great squinting quiet scoundrel of a Manuel. Yet in the South there is a quest cried for the hand of Morvyth, the dark Queen of Inis Dahut; and, now that my wife is dead, it may be that I would find it amusing to sleep with this young queen.'

The others laughed, and thought no more of the light boastfulness of this Gonfal who was the world's playfellow. But within the month it was known that Gonfal of Naimes, the Margrave of Aradol, had in truth quitted his demesnes, and had traveled southward. And he was the first of this famous fellowship, after Dom Manuel, to go out of Poictesme, not ever to return.

Book Two

The Mathematics of Gonfal

'He multiplieth words without knowledge.'
                    JOB, XXXV, 16

Chapter V

Champion at Misadventure

Now the tale is of how Gonfal fared in the South, where the people were Fundamentalists. It is told how the quest was cried; and how, in the day's fashion, the hand of Morvyth, the dark Queen of Inis Dahut and of the four other Isles of Wonder, was promised to the champion who should fetch back the treasure that was worthiest to be her bridal gift. Eight swords, they say, were borne to the altar of Pygé-Upsízugos, to be suitably consecrated, after a brief and earnest address, by the Imaun of Bulotu. Eight appropriately ardent lovers raised high these swords, to swear fealty to Queen Morvyth and to the quest of which her loveliness was the reward. Thus all was as it should be, until they went to sheathe these swords. Then, one champion among the company, striking his elbow against his neighbor, had, rather unaccountably, the ill luck to drop his sword so that it pierced his own left foot.

The horns sounded afterward, through the narrow streets and over the bronze and laquer roofs, and seven of Queen Morvyth's suitors armed and rode forth to ransack the world of its chief riches for a year and a day.

He who did not ride with the others was Gonfal of Naimes. It was three months, indeed, before his wound was so healed that Gonfal could put foot to stirrup. And by that time, he calculated regretfully, the riches of the world must have been picked over with such thoroughness that it would hardly be worth while for a cripple to be hobbling out to make himself ridiculous among unsympathetic strangers. His agony, as he admitted, under this inclement turn of chance, was well-nigh intolerable; yet nothing was to be gained by blinking the facts: and Gonfal was, as he also admitted, a realist.

Gonfal, thus, remained at court through the length of a year, and lived uneventfully in the pagan Isles of Wonder. Gonfal sat unsplendidly snug while all his rivals rode at adventure in the meadows that are most fertile in magic and ascended the mountains that rise beyond plausibility in the climates most favorable to the unimaginable. But Gonfal's sufficing consolation appeared to be that he sat, more and more often, with the Queen.

However, the Margrave of Aradol, alone of Morvyth's suitors, had overpassed his first youth; the aging seem to acquire a sort of proficiency in being disappointed, and to despatch the transaction with more ease; and so, Queen Morvyth speculated, the Margrave of Aradol could perhaps endure this cross of unheroic tranquility – even over and above his natural despair, now he had lost all hope of winning her – with an ampler fortitude than would have been attainable by any of the others.

Besides, their famousness was yet to be won, their exploits stayed, as yet, resplendent and misty magnets which drew them toward the future. But this Gonfal, who had come into Inis Dahut after so much notable service under Manuel of Poictesme and the unconquerable banner of the Silver Stallion, had in his day, the young Queen knew, been through eight formal wars, with any amount of light guerrilla work. He had slain his satisfactory quota of dragons and usurpers and ogres, and, also some years ago, had married the golden-haired and starry-eyed and swan-throated princess who is the customary reward of every champion's faithful attendance to derring-do.

Now, in the afternoon of Gonfal's day, with his princess dead, and with the realms that he had shared with her all lost – and with his overlord Count Manuel too departed from this world, and with the banner of the Silver Stallion no longer followed by anyone – now this tall Gonfal went among his fellows in Inis Dahut a little aloofly. Yet the fair-bearded man went smilingly, too, as one who amuses himself at a game which he knows to be not very important: for he was, as he said, a realist, even in the pagan Isles of Wonder.

And Morvyth, the dark Queen of the five Isles of Wonder, was annoyed by the bantering ways of her slow-spoken lover; she did not like these ways: she would put out of mind the question whether this man was being bitterly amused by his own hopeless infatuation or by something – incredible as that seemed – about her. But that question would come back into her mind: and

Morvyth, with an habitual light lovely gesture, would tidy the hair about her ears, and would go again to talk with Gonfal, so that she might, privately and just for her own satisfaction, decide upon this problem. Besides, the man had rather nice eyes.

Chapter VI

The Loans of Power

Now, when the year was over, and when the bland persistent winds of April had won up again out of the South, the heroes returned, each with his treasure. Each brought to Morvyth a bridal gift as miraculous as the adventures through which it had been come by: and all these adventures had been marvelous beyond any easy believing.

Indeed, as the Queen remarked, in private, their tales were hardly credible.

'And yet, I think, these buoyant epics are based upon fact,' replied Gonfal. 'Each of these men is the shrewd, small and ill-favored third son of a king. It is the law that such unprepossessing midgets should prosper, and override every sort of evil, in the Isles of Wonder and all other extra-mundane lands.'

'But is it fair, my friend, is it even respectful, to the august and venerable powers of iniquity, that these whipper-snappers – ?'

Gonfal replied: 'Nobody contends, I assure you, that such easy conquests are quite sportsmanlike. Nevertheless, they are the prerogatives of the third son of a king. So, as a realist, madame, I perforce concede that fortune, hereabouts, regards these third sons with a fixed grin of approval. Even foxes and ants and ovens and broomsticks put aside their customary taciturnity, to favor these royal imps with invaluable advice: all giants and three-headed serpents must, I daresay, confront them with a half-guilty sense of committing felo-de-se: and at every turn of the road waits an enamored golden-haired princess.'

Now not every one of these truisms appeared, to the dark eyes of Morvyth, wholly satisfactory.

'Blondes do not last,' said Morvyth, 'and I am a queen.'

'That is true,' Gonfal admitted. 'I am not certain every third prince prospers with a queen. I can recall no authority upon the point.'

'My friend, there is not any doubt that these dauntless champions have prospered everywhere. And it is another trouble for me now to decide which one has fetched back the treasure that is worthiest to be my bridal gift.'

Gonfal pursed up his remarkably red and soft-looking lips. He regarded the young Queen for a brief while, and throughout that while he wore his odd air of considering an amusing matter which was of no great importance.

'Madame,' Gonfal then said, 'I would distinguish. To be worthiest, a thing must first be worthy.'

At this the slender brows of Morvyth went up. 'But upon that ebony table, my friend, are potent magics which control all the wealth of the world.'

'I do not dispute that. I merely marvel – as a perhaps unpractical realist – how such wealth can be termed a gift, when it at utmost is but a loan.'

'Now do you tell me,' commanded Morvyth, 'just what that means!'

But Gonfal before replying considered for a while the trophies which were the increment of his younger, smaller and more energetic rivals' heroism. These trophies were, indeed, sufficiently remarkable.

Here, for one thing – tetched from the fiery heart of the very dreadful seven-walled city of Lankha, by bustling little Prince Chedric of Lorn, after an infinity of high exploits – was that agate which had in the years that are long past preserved the might of the old emperors of Macedon. Upon this strange jewel were to be seen a naked man and nine women, portrayed in the agate's veining: and this agate assured its wearer of victory in every battle. The armies of the pagan Isles of Wonder would be ready, at the first convenient qualm of patriotism or religious faith, to lay waste and rob all the wealthiest kingdoms in that part of the world, should Morvyth choose that agate as her bridal gift.

And yet Gonfal, as he now put it aside, spoke rather sadly, and said only, 'Bunkhum!' in one or another of the foreign tongues which he had acquired during his mundivagant career of knight-errantry.

Gonfal then looked at an onyx. It was the onyx of Thossakan. Its wearer had the power to draw out the soul of any person, even of himself, and to imprison that soul as a captive inside this hollowed onyx; and its wearer might thus trample anywhither resistlessly. Beyond the somber gleaming of this onyx showed the green lusters of an emerald, which was engraved with a lyre and three bees, with a dolphin and the head of a bull. Misfortune and failure of no sort could enter into the house wherein was this Samian gem. But the brightest of all the ensorcelled stones arrayed upon the ebony table was the diamond of Luned, whose wearer might at will go invisible: and to this Cymric wonder Gonfal accorded the tribute of a shrug.

'This diamond,' said Gonfal then, 'is a gift which a well-balanced person might loyally tender to his queen, but hardly to his prospective wife. I speak as a widower, madame: and I assure you that Prince Duneval of Orc we may dismiss from our accounting, as a too ardent lover of danger.'

Morvyth thought this very clever and naughty and cynical of him, but smilingly said nothing. And Gonfal touched the offering of pompous little Thorgny of Vigeois. This was the gray sideritis, which, when bathed in running waters and properly propitiated, told with the weak voice of an infant whatever you desired to learn. The secrets of war and statecraft, of all that had ever happened anywhere, and of all arts and trades, were familiar to the wearer of the gray sideritis. And Gonfal touched, more gingerly, the moonstone of Naggar Tura, whose cutting edge no material substance could resist, so that the strong doors of an adversary's treasure house, or the walls of his fortified city, could be severed with this gem just as a knife slices an apple.

Yet equally marvelous, in another fashion, was this moonstone's neighbor, a jewel of scarlet radiancy streaked with purple. All that was needed to ensure a prosperous outcome of whatsoever matter one had in hand could be found engraved upon this stone, in the lost color called tingaribinus. For the wearer of this stone – a fragment, as the most reputable cantraps attested, of the pillar which Jacob raised at Beth-El – it was not possible to fail in any sort of worldly endeavor.

Yet Gonfal put this too aside, speaking again in a foreign language unfamiliar to Morvyth, and saying, 'Hohkum!'

And then, but not until then, Gonfal answered Queen Morvyth.

'I mean,' he said, 'that with my own eyes I have seen that sturdy knave Dom Manuel attain to the summit of human estate, and thence pass, bewilderingly, into nothingness. I mean that, through the virtues of these amulets and periapts and other very dreadful manifestations of lithomancy, a monarch may retain, for a longer season than did Manuel, much money and acreage and all manner of power, and may keep all these fine things for a score or for two-score or even for three-score of years. But not for four-score years, madame: for by that time the riches and the honors of this world must fall away from every mortal man; and all that can remain of the greatest emperor or of the most dreadful conqueror will be, when four-score years are over, picked bones in a black box.'

And Gonfal said also: 'Such is now the estate of Alexander, for all that he once owned this agate. Achilles, who wore the sideritis and was so notable at Troy, is master of no larger realm. And to Augustus and Artaxerxes and Attila – here to proceed no further in the alphabet – quite similar observations apply. These men went very ardently about this earth, the vigor of their misconduct was truly heroic, and the sound of their names is become as deathless as is the sound of the wind. But once that four-score years were over, their worldly power had passed as the dust passes upon the bland and persistent wind which now is come up out of the South to bring new life into Inis Dahut, but to revive nothing that is dead. Just so must always pass all worldly honors, as just such dust.'

Then Gonfal said: 'Just so – with my own eyes – I have seen Dom Manuel tumbled from the high estate which that all-overtrampling rogue had purchased and held so unscrupulously; and I have seen his powerfulness made dust. These occasional triumphs of justice, madame, turn one to serious thinking. . . . Therefore it seems to me that these questing gentlemen are offering you no gift, but only a loan. I perforce consider – as a realist, and with howsoever appropriate regret – that the conditions of the quest have not been fulfilled.'

The Queen deliberated his orotundities. And she regarded Gonfal with a smile which now was like his smiling, and which appeared not very immediately connected with the trituration they were speaking of.

Morvyth said then: 'That is true. Your mathematics are admirable, in that they combine resistlessly the pious and the platitudinous. There is no well-thought-of Fundamentalist in Inis Dahut, nor in any of the Isles of Wonder, who will dare dispute that the riches of this world are but a loan, because that is the doctrine of Pygé-Upsízugos and of all endowed religions everywhere. These over-busy, pushing ugly little pests that ride impertinently about the world, and get their own way in every place, have insulted me. By rights,' – the Queen said, rather hopefully – 'by rights, I ought to have their heads chopped off?'

'But these heroic imps are princes, madame. Thus, to pursue your very natural indignation, would entail a war with their fathers: and to be bothered with seven wars, according to my mathematics, would be a nuisance.'

Morvyth saw the justice of this; and said, with ever so faint a sighing: 'Very well, then! I approve of your mathematics. I shall pardon their impudence, with the magnanimity becoming to a queen; and I shall have the quest cried for another year and another day.'

'That,' Gonfal estimated, still with his odd smiling, 'will do nicely.'

'And, besides,' she added, 'now you will have a chance with the others!'

'That,' Gonfal assented, without any trace of a smile or any other token of enthusiasm, 'will be splendid.'

But Morvyth smiled as, with that habitual gesture, she tidied her hair: and she sent for her seven heroic lovers, and spoke to them, as she phrased it, frankly.

Chapter VII

Fatality the Second

Thus all was to do again. The champions pulled rather long faces, and the lower orders were disappointed in missing the gratis entertainments attendant on a royal marriage. But the clergy and the well-thought-of laity and the leading tax-payers applauded the decision of Queen Morvyth as a most glorious example in such feverish and pleasure-loving days of soulless materialism.

So again the eight lovers of Morvyth met in the cathedral, to have their swords appropriately consecrated by the Imaun of Bulotu. And that beneficent and justly popular old prelate, after he had cut the throats of the three selected children, began the real ceremony with a prayer to Pygé-Upsízugos, as to Him whose transformations are hidden in all temples patronised by the best-thought-of people, and saying, as was customary and polite:

'The height of the firmament is subservient unto thee, O Pygé-Upsízugos! thy throne is very high! the ornaments upon the seat of thy blue trousers are the bright stars which never diminish! Every man makes offering unto that portion of thee which is revealed, and thou art the Sedentary Master commemorated in heaven and upon earth. Thou art a shining noble seated above all nobles, permanent in thy high station, established in thy stern sovereignty, and the callipygous Prince of the Company of Gods.'

Nobody quite believed this, of course, but in Inis Dahut, as in all other places, the Fundamentalists took a proper pride in their tribal deity, and, whenever they could spare time for religious matters, made as much of him as possible. So they now tendered to Pygé-Upsízugos a fine offering of quails and cinnamon and bullocks' hearts, and they raised the Hymn of the Star-Spangled Buttock in the while that the two ewers containing the blood of the children were placed upon his altar.

Thus everything at first went nicely enough. But when the company of Morvyth's lovers, with all their swords drawn, had approached the altar, for the consecrating, and in the while that they ascended the smooth porphyry steps, then limping Gonfal stumbled or else he slipped. He thus dropped his sword. The tall champion, clutching hastily at this sword as it fell, caught up the weapon by the newly sharpened blade; and he grasped it with such rather unaccountable vigor that he cut open his right hand to the bone, and cut also the muscles of his fingers.

'Decidedly,' said Gonfal, with a wried smile, 'there is some fatality in this; and the quest of Morvyth is not for me.'

He spoke the truth, for his sword-bearing days were over. Gonfal must seek for a physician and bandages, while his rivals' swords were being consecrated. The Queen noted his going, and, from a point midway between complacence and religious scruples, said under her breath, 'One must perforce somewhat admire this realist.'

She heard, from afar, a dwindling resonance of horns and knew that once more the seven heroic lovers of Queen Morvyth had ridden forth to ransack the world of its chief riches. But fair-bearded Gonfal stayed in the pagan Isles of Wonder, and beneath the same roof that covered Morvyth, and cared for no riches except the loveliness of Morvyth, whom he saw daily. And with time the hurt in his hand was cured, but the fingers on that hand he could not ever move again. And for the rest, if people whispered here and there, the susurrus was a phenomenon familiar enough to the economy of court life.

Chapter VIII

How the Princes Bragged

Now, when the year was over, and the south wind was come again into Inis Dahut, the seven lovers returned, bringing with them yet other prodigies acquired by heroic exploits.

Here, for example, was the effigy of a bird carved in jade and carnelian.

'With the aid of this inestimable bird,' explained Prince Chedric of Lorn – who, upon a very dreadfully inhabited peninsula, if one elected to believe him, had wrested this talisman from Morskoï of the Depths – 'you may enter the Sea Market, and may go freely among a folk that dwell in homes builded of coral and tortoise-shell, and tiled with fishes' scales. Their wisdom is beyond the dry and arid wisdom of earth: their knowledge derides the fictions which we call time and space: and their children prattle of mysteries unknown to any of our major prophets and most expert geomancers.'

'Ah, but,' cried Prince Balein of Targamon, 'but I have here a smoke-colored veil embroidered with tiny gold stars and inkhorns; and it enables one to pass through the ardent gateway of Audela, the country that lies behind the fire. This is the realm of Sesphra: there is no grieving in this land, and happiness and infallibility are common to everybody there, because Sesphra is the master of an art which corrodes and sears away all error, whether it be human or divine.'

Prince Duneval of Ore said nothing. His mutely tendered offering was a small mirror about three inches square. Morvyth looked into this mirror: and what she saw in it was very like a sumptuous dark young girl. She hastily put aside that gleaming and over-wise counselor: and the Queen's face was troubled, because there was no need to ask what mirror Duneval had fetched to her from out of Antan.

But Thorgny of Vigeois did not love silence. And he was the next suitor.

'Such knickknacks as I notice at your feet, my princess,' stated Thorgny of Vigeois, 'have their merits. Nobody denies their merits. But I, who may now address you with the frankness which ought to exist between two persons already virtually betrothed, I bring that sigil which gave wisdom and all power to Apollonious, and later to Merlin Ambrosius. It displays, as you observe, an eye encircled with scorpions and stags and' – he coughed – 'with winged objects which do not ordinarily have wings: and it controls the nine million spirits of the air. I need say no more.'

'I need to,' said Prince Gurguint. 'I say that I have here the shining triangle of Thorston. And to say that, is to say a great deal more than Thorgny has said. For this triangle is master of the wisdom of the Duergar and of all peoples that dwell underground. Moreover, madame, when this triangle is inverted – thus – it enables you to bless and curse at will, to converse with dead priests, and to control the power and the seven mysteries of the moon.'

'To such hole and corner wisdom, to such caveman devices, and more especially to your lunar vaporings, I cry out like a bird upon the house-tops, and I cry, Cheap, cheap!' observed Prince Clofurd. 'For I have here, in this shagreen case, the famous and puissant and unspeakably sacrosanct ring of Solomon, to whose wearer are subject the Djinns and the ass-footed Nazikeen and fourteen of Jahveh's most discreet and trustworthy seraphim.'

Prince Grimauc said: 'Solomon had, in his archaic way, his wisdom, a good enough sort of workaday wisdom, but yet a limited wisdom, as it was meted out to him by the god of Judea: but I have here an altar carved from a block of selenite. Within this altar you may hear the moving and the dry rustlings of an immortal. Let us not speak of this immortal: neither the sun's nor the moon's light has ever shone upon him, and his name is not lovable. But here is the Altar of the Adversary; and the owner of this little altar may, at a paid price, have access to the wisdom that defies restraint and goes beyond the bounds permitted by any god.'

Such were the gifts they brought to Morvyth. And, for reasons of not less than two kinds, the Queen found difficulty in saying which of these offerings was the worthiest to be her bridal gift.

Chapter IX

The Loans of Wisdom

But Gonfal, when the Queen consulted him in private, as she was now apt to do about most matters, tall handsome Gonfal shrugged. He said that, to his finding – as a, no doubt, un-practical realist – her lovers had, once more, fetched back no gifts, but only loans of very dubious value.

'For I have seen Dom Manuel purchase a deal of just such wisdom from unwholesome sources: and I have seen too what came of it when the appointed season was at hand for the gray knave to be stripped of his wisdom. Just so, madame, must every sort of wisdom be reft away from everybody. These wise men that had all this knowledge in the old time, do they retain it now? The question is absurd, since the dirt that once was Solomon keeps no more sentiency than does the mud which formerly was Solomon's third underscullion. Indomitable persons have, before today, won to the wisdom of Audela or of the Sea Market; and that Freydis with whom Dom Manuel lived for a while in necromantic iniquity, and that unscriptural Herodias who was Tana's daugh-ter, these women, once, attained to the wisdom of Antan: but might they carry any of this wisdom into the grave?'

'I see,' said Morvyth, reflectively; and she smiled.

'Equally,' Gonfal continued, 'where now is your Thorston or your Merlin? All which today remains of any one of these thaumaturgists may well, at this very instant, be passing us as dust in that bland and persistent wind which now courses over Inis Dahut: but the mage goes undiscerned, unhonored, im-potent, and goes as the wind wills, not as he elects. Ah, no, madame! These quaint archaic toys may for a little while lend wisdom and understanding: but, none the less, within four-score of years – '

'Oh, have done with your arithmetic!' she begged of him. 'It serves handily, and I approve of your mathematics. I really do consider it is perfectly wonderful, sweetheart, how quickly you realists can think of suitable truisms. But, just the same, I begin to dislike that wind: and I would much rather talk about something else.'

'Let us talk about, then,' Gonfal said, 'the different way I feel concerning you, as compared with all other women.'

'That is not a new topic. But it is invariably interesting.'

So they discussed the matter at some length. Then they went on to other matters. And Morvyth asked Gonfal if he was sure that he respected her just as much as ever, and Morvyth tidied her hair, and she summoned the Imaun of Bulotu, and sent also for Masu the prime minister.

'The wisdom of this world is as a dust that passes,' said Morvyth. 'The wise men that had wisdom in the old time, do they retain it now?'

She then repeated the rest of Gonfal's observations with applaudable accuracy.

And her hearers did applaud, in unfeigned emotion. 'For this prying into matters which Pygé-Upsízugos has not seen fit to reveal has always seemed to me unwholesome,' remarked the prime minister.

'In fact, the claims of science, so-called – ' began the Imaun; and spoke for the usual twenty minutes.

All was thus settled edifyingly. The offerings of the kings' sons were decreed to be no true gifts; the quest was cried again; and once more the seven champions rode forth. There was no thought of tall Gonfal going with the little heroes, for a cripple who could not bear a sword was not fitted to ransack the treasures of the world. Instead, fair-bearded Gonfal stayed in Inis Dahut, and lived uneventfully in the pagan Isles of Wonder. And if people now talked outright, a queen can never hope to go wholly free of criticism.

Chapter X

Relative to Gonfal's Head

It followed through the two mischances already recorded that, when spring came again, and when once more the south wind was coursing over Inis Dahut, Gonfal of Naimes sat, as it happened, with his handsome head in Morvyth's lap, and waited for less ill-starred lovers to return.

'What gifts, I wonder, will they be bringing me,' Queen Morvyth said, 'at about this time tomorrow?'

And Gonfal, without moving, sighed stupendously, and answered: 'To me, madame, they will be bringing bitter gifts. For, whosoever wins in this quest, I lose: and whatsoever he may bring to you, to me he brings disseverance from content, and to me he brings a poignant if brief period of loneliness before you decide to have my head off.'

Now she caressed that head maternally. 'Why, but what a notion!' said Morvyth, now that the man himself spoke of the nearing social duty whose imminence had for some while been fretting her. 'As if, sweetheart, I would ever think of such a thing!'

'Undoubtedly, that will happen, madame. Marriage entails many obligations, not all of them pleasant. Queens in particular have to preserve appearances, they have to ensure the discretion of those whom they have trusted.'

'That,' she said, sorrowfully, 'is what the dear old Imaun has been telling me – lately, you know. And Masu talks about what a married woman owes to religion and setting a fine moral example.'

Then Gonfal, still smiling up at her, went on: 'And yet it seems an odd thing, delight of my delights, that I shall leave you – for the headsman – without any real regret. For I am content. While my shrewd fellows rode about the world to seek and to attain to power and wisdom, I have elected, as an unpractical realist, to follow after beauty. I have followed, to be sure, in the phrase of that absurd young Grimauc, at a paid price. Yet, at that price, I have won, maimed and fore-doomed, to beauty. And I am content.'

The Queen put on the proper air of diffidence. 'But what, my friend, what, after all, is mere beauty?'

And he replied with the neatness which she always rather distrusted. 'Beauty, madame, is Morvyth. It is not easy to describe either of these most dear and blinding synonyms, as how many reams of ruined paper attest!'

She waited, still stroking him: and in her mind was the old question, whether it was possible that, even now, this man was laughing at her?

She said: 'But would it not grieve you unendurably, sweetheart, to see me the wife of another man? And so, would it not be really a kindness – ?'

But the obtuse fellow did not chivalrously aid in smoothing her way to that nearing social duty. Instead, he replied, oddly enough:

'The Morvyth that I see, and in my manner worship, can be no man's wife. All poets learn this truth in their vexed progress to becoming realists.'

For yet another while the young Queen was silent. And then she said:

'I do not quite understand you, my dear, and probably I never shall. But I know that through your love of me you have twice maimed yourself, and have, as though it were a trifle, put aside your chance of winning honor and great wealth and all that gentle persons most prize – '

'I am,' he replied, 'a realist. To get three utterly pleasant years one pays, of course. But realists pay without grumbling.'

'My dearest,' the Queen continued – now breathing quicklier, and with the sort of very happy sobbing which she felt the occasion demanded – 'you alone of all the men who have talked and postured so much, you alone have given me whole-hearted and undivided love, not weighing even your own knightly honor and worldly fame against the utterness of that love. And while of course, just as the Imaun says, if I were ever to marry anybody else, as I suppose I did promise to do – in a way, that is – still, it is not as if I cared one snap of my fingers about appearances, and I simply will not have it cut off! For such utterly unselfish love as yours, dear Gonfal, is the gift which is worthiest to be my bridal gift: and, no matter what anybody says, it is you who shall be my husband!'

'Ah, but the quest, madame!' he answered, 'and your promise to those seven other idiots!'

'I shall proclaim to these detestable third sons, and to the Imaun, and to Masu, and to everybody,' the Queen said, 'a very weighty and indeed a sacred truth. I shall tell them that there is no gift more great than love.'

But the tall man who now stood before her shared in nothing in the exaltedness of her sentiments: and his dismay was apparent. 'Alas, madame, you propose an enormity! for we are all so utterly the slaves of our catchwords that everybody would agree with you. There is no hope in "what anybody may say". Imbeciles everywhere will be saying that you have chosen wisely.'

Morvyth now sat peculiarly erect upon the ivory couch. 'I am sure, I am really quite sure, Gonfal, that I do not understand you.'

'I mean, madame, that – while of course your offer is all that is most kind and generous – that I must, here again, in mere honesty, I must distinguish. I mean that I think you know, as well as I do, love is not a gift which any man can give nor any person hope long to retain. Ah, no, madame! we shrug, we smilingly allow romanticists their catchwords: meanwhile it remains the veriest axiom, among realists like you and me, that love too is but a loan.'

'So you have come back,' the Queen remarked, with an approach to crossness, 'to your eternal loans!'

He slightly flung out both hands, palms upward. 'Love is that loan, my dear, which we accept most thankfully. But at the same time let us concede, as rational persons, the impermanence of all those materials which customarily provoke the erotic emotions.'

'Gonfal,' the young Queen said, 'now you talk stupidly. You talk with a dangerous lack of something more important than discretion.'

'My love, I talk, again, as a widower.' Then for a while he said nothing: and it appeared to Morvyth that this incomprehensible ingrate had shivered. He said: 'And still, still, I talk of mathematical certainties! For how can you hope to remain in anything a lovable object? In a score of years, or within at most two-score, you will have become either fat or wrinkled, your teeth will rot and tumble out, your eyes will blear; your thighs will be most unenticingly mottled, your breath will be unpleasant, and your breasts will have become flabby bags. All these impairments, I repeat, my dear are mathematical certainties.'

To such horrid and irrelevant nonsense the Queen replied, with dignity, 'I am not your dear; and I simply wonder at your impudence in ever for one moment thinking I was.'

'Then, too,' the ill-mannered wretch had gone on, meditatively, 'that you have not much intelligence. That is very well for the present, because intelligence in youth, for some reason or another, is bad for the hair and muddies the complexion. Yet an aging woman who is stupid, such as Madame Niafer or such as another woman whom I remember, is also quite unendurable.'

'But what,' she asked him, rationally, 'have I to do with stupid old women? I am Morvyth, I am Queen of the Isles of Wonder. I have the secrets which control all wealth and – if I should ever take a fancy to such things – all wisdom too. There is no beauty like my beauty, nor any power like my power – '

'I know, I know!' he returned – 'and for the present I of course adore you. But nevertheless, did I fall in with your very dreadful suggestion, and permit you to place me, quite publicly at your dear side, upon the terraced throne of Inis Dahut – why, then, within a terribly brief while, I would not mind your being stupid, I would not actually notice your dilapidated looks, I would accept all your shortcomings complacently. And I would be contented enough with you, who now are the despair and joy of my living. No, Morvyth, no, my child! I, who was once a poet of sorts, could not again endure to live in contentment with a stupid and querulous woman who was unattractive to look at. And, very certainly within two-score of years – '

But a queenly gesture had put a check to such wild talk, and Morvyth too had arisen, saying:

'Your arithmetic becomes tiresome. One can afford to honor truisms in their proper place, and about suitable persons: but there is, and always must be, a limit to the scope of such trite philosophy. Your audience is over, Messire Gonfal. And it is your last audience, because I consider you quite unutterably a beast.'

He kissed the imperious little hand which dismissed him. 'You at all events, my dear,' he stated, 'arc quite unutterably human.'

Chapter XI

Economics of Morvyth

Thus it came about, to the Imaun's vast relief – and, as it seemed to the pious, kindly old man, perhaps in direct answer to his prayers that this matter might be settled agreeably all round and without any unpleasantness – that the next day at noon, just as the seven champions were returning with their gifts, an attendant brought to Queen Morvyth the severed head of Gonfal.

This was in the vaulted hall of Tothmes, whose building was a famous tale, and of whose splendors travelers, come homeward, spoke without real hope to be believed. There Morvyth waited, crowned, upon the terraced throne: and without, on that bright April morning, the trumpets sounded through the narrow streets and over the bronze and lacquer roofs, proclaiming that the mightiest and most shrewd of champions were riding toward Inis Dahut from all kingdoms of the earth, through their desire of the young Queen of the Isles of Wonder whose beauty was the marvel of the world, and a legend in far lands not known to her even by their names.

Thus Morvyth sat: and at her feet one placed the severed head of Gonfal. There was blood on the fair beard: but still the lips were smiling, pallidly, over something of no great importance. And in her mind was the old question, whether it was possible that – even now – this man was laughing at her? Or, was it possible, she wondered (as she of a sudden recollected that first talk of theirs), that blondes did sometimes last very damnably? and that some little washed-out fly-by-night princess of nowhere in particular might thus get, in one way or another, even from her grave, the better of a great queen?

Well, but there was no need for a great queen to think as yet about graves, and their most unpleasant contents. For Morvyth say high, as yet, superb and young and all powerful, in this fine palace of hers, about which so many lovers sighed, and the bland winds of April went caressingly. . . . Nobody denied that this very tiresome wind would every year be coming up from the South – the lovely girl reflected, as she fell meditatively to prodding with her toe at what remained of Gonfal – nor that, just so, this most persistent wind would be coursing over Inis Dahut, when there was no Morvyth and no palace in this place any longer. . . . Nobody denied, and nobody except insane and very rude persons thought at all seriously about, such truisms.

It was enough, for really pious people, that in youth one had the loan of a bright sheltering against the ruthless and persistent wind which bore everything away as dust: if one felt a bit low-spirited now and then, it was not for any special cause: and Morvyth – that, as yet, for her permitted season, was Queen of the five Isles of Wonder – could hear the trumpets and the heralds proclaiming the entry of Prince Chedric of Lorn. . . .

He, then, was the first to return of those perfectly detestable little meddlers who out of love for her had, now for a third time, ransacked the riches of the world: and he had rather nice eyes. Morvyth tidied her hair.

Book Three

Toupan's Bright Bees

'*The bee that is in the land of Assyria
shall rest upon all bushes.*'
ISAIAH, vii, 18

Chapter XII

The Mage Emeritus

Now the tale is no more of Gonfal, who was the first to perish of the lords of the Silver Stallion. The tale instead tells that, in the while of Gonfal's adventuring in Inis Dahut, yet three other champions of the fellowship had left the Poictesme which under Dame Niafer's rule was altering day by day. Coth of the Rocks, indeed, had ridden westward within the same month that Gonfal departed for the South. There was never any profitable arguing with Coth: and so, when he declared his intention of fetching back Dom Manuel into the Poictesme which women and holy persons and lying poets – as Coth asserted – were making quite uninhabitable, nobody did argue. Coth blustered westward, unmolested and unreasoned with: and for that while no more was heard of him.

And it was in the May of this year that Kerin of Nointel, the Syndic and Castellan of Basardra, disappeared even more unaccountably than Dom Manuel had done, for about Kerin's passing there were not even any rumors. Kerin, so far as anybody could learn, had vanished in the darkness of the night season just as unaidedly as that darkness itself had vanished in turn, and with just as slight vestigial traces of his passing. The desolation of Kerin's young wife, Dame Saraïde, was such that dozens upon dozens of lovers might not content her for her widowhood, as was immediately shown: and of Kerin also, for that while, no more was heard.

And Miramon Lluagor, too, that under Manuel had been the Lord Seneschal of Gontaron, had now gone out of Poictesme – sedately and unmysteriously departing, with his wife and child seated beside him upon the back of an elderly and quite tame dragon, for his former home in the North. It was there that Miramon had first encountered Dom Manuel in the days when Manuel was only a swineherd. And it was there that Miramon

Lluagor hoped to pass the remainder of as long a life as his doom permitted him, in such limited comfort as might anywhere be possible for a married man.

Otherwise, he could foresee, upon the brighter side of his appointed and appalling doom, nothing which was likely to worry him. For Miramon Lluagor had very wonderfully prospered at magic, he was, as they say, now blessed with more than any reasonable person would ask for: and the most clamant of these superfluities appeared to him to be his wife.

They tell how Miramon was one of the Léshy, born of a people that was neither human nor immortal, telling how his ancestral home was built upon the summit of the mountain called Vraidex. To Vraidex Miramon Lluagor returned, after the Fellowship of the Silver Stallion had been disbanded, and Miramon had ceased to amuse himself with the greatness of Manuel and with the other notions of Poictesme.

They narrate that this magician dabbled no more in knight-errantry, for which the Seneschal of Gontaron – who through his art was also lord of the nine kinds of sleep and prince of the seven madnesses – had never shown any real forte. He righted no more wrongs, in weather as often as not unsuited to a champion subject to rheumatism, and he in no way taxed his comfort to check the prospering of injustice. Instead, he now maintained, upon the exalted scarps of Vraidex, the sedate seclusion appropriate to a veteran artist, in his ivory tower carved out of one of the tusks of Behemoth; and maintained also a handsome retinue of every sort of horrific illusion to guard the approaches to his Doubtful Palace; wherein, as the tale likewise tells, this mage resumed his former vocation, and once more designed the dreams for sleep.

Thus it was that, upon the back of the elderly and quite tame dragon, Miramon returned to his earlier pursuits and to the practice of what he – in his striking way of putting things – described as art for art's sake. The episode of Manuel had been, in the lower field of merely utilitarian art, amusing enough. That stupid, tall, quiet posturer, when he set out to redeem Poictesme, had needed just the mere bit of elementary magic which Miramon had performed for him, to establish Manuel among the great ones of earth. Miramon had, in consequence, sent a few obsolete gods to drive the Northmen out of Poictesme, while Manuel waited

upon the sands north of Manneville and diverted his leisure by
contemplatively spitting into the sea. Thereafter Manuel had
held the land to the admiration of everybody but more particularly of Miramon – who did not at all agree with Anavalt of
Fomor in his estimation of Dom Manuel's mental gifts.

Yes, it had been quite amusing to serve under Manuel, to play
at being lord of Gontaron and Ranec, and to regard at close
quarters this tall, grave, gray, cockeyed imposter, who had
learned only not to talk.... For that, thought Miramon, was
Manuel's secret: Manuel did not expostulate, he did not explain,
he did not argue; he, instead, in any time of trouble or of
uncertainty kept quiet: and that quiet struck terror to his ever-
babbling race; and had earned for the dull-witted but shrewd
fellow – who was concealing only his lack of any thought or of
any plan – a dreadful name for impenetrable wisdom and for
boundless resource.

'Keep mum with Manuel!' said Miramon, 'and all things shall
be added to you. It is a great pity that my wife has not the knack
for these little character analyses.'

Yes, the four years had been an amusing episode. But dreams
and the designing of dreams were the really serious matters to
which Miramon returned after his holiday outing in carnage and
statecraft.

And here, too – as everywhere – his wife confronted him.
Miramon's personal taste in art was for the richly romantic
sweetened with nonsense and spiced with the tabooed. But his
wife Gisèle had quite other notions, a whole set of notions, and
her philosophy was that of belligerent individualism. And the
magician to keep peace, at least in the intervals between his
wife's more mordantly loquacious moments, must of necessity
design such dreams as Gisèle preferred. But he knew that these
dreams did not express the small thoughts and fancies which
harbored in the heart of Miramon Lluagor, and which would
perish with the falling of his doom unless he wrought these
fancies into dreams that, being fleshless, might evade carnivor-
ous time.

He was pre-eminent among the dream-makers of this world,
he was the dreaded lord (because of his retinue of illusions) over
all the country about Vraidex: but in his own home he was not

dreaded, he, very certainly, was not pre-eminent. And Miramon hungered for the lost freedom of his bachelorhood.

His wife also was discontent, because the ways of the Léshy appeared to this mortal woman indecorous. The dooms that were upon the Léshy seemed not entirely in good taste, to her who had been born of a race about whom destiny appeared not to bother. In fact, it was a continual irritation to Gisèle that her little boy Demetrios was predestinate to kill his father with the charmed sword Flamberge. This was a doom Gisèle found not the sort of thing you care to have imminent in your own family: and she felt that the sooner the gray Norns, who weave the fate of all that live, were spoken to quite candidly, the better it would be for everybody concerned.

She was irritated by the mere sight of Flamberge. So her thinking was not of silk and honey when, after polishing the sword as was her usage upon Thursday morning, she came into Miramon's ivory tower to hang the fatal weapon in its right place.

With Miramon under the green tasseled canopy sat one whom Gisèle was not unsurprised to see there. For closeted with Miramon today was Ninzian, the High Bailiff of Yair and Upper Ardra, who was the most famous for his piety of all the lords of the Silver Stallion. The dreadful need and the peculiar reason which Ninzian had for being pious and philanthropic were matters not known to everybody: but Miramon Lluagor knew about these things, and therefore he made appropriate use of Ninzian. Indeed, upon this very afternoon, the two were looking at that which Ninzian had fetched out of the land of Assyria, and had procured for the magician, at a price.

Chapter XIII

Economics of Gisèle

Now Madame Gisèle also was looking at that which Ninzian had procured for her husband at a price. She looked at it – upon the whole – with slightly less disfavor than she afterward looked at the two men.

'A good day and a grand blessing to you, Messire Ninzian!' said Madame Gisèle: and she extended her hand, along with her scouring-rag, for him to kiss, and she inquired about his wife Dame Balthis, pleasantly enough. She spoke then, in a different tone, to Miramon Lluagor. 'And with what are you cluttering up the house now?'

'Ah, wife,' replied Miramon, 'here, very secretly fetched out of the land of Assyria, are those bees about whom it is prophesied that they shall rest upon all bushes. Here are the bright bees of Toupan, a treasure beyond word or thinking. They are not as other bees, for theirs is the appearance of shining ice: and they crawl fretfully, as they have crawled since Toupan's downfall, about this cross of black stone –'

'That is a very likely story for you to be telling me, who can see that the disgusting creatures have wings to fly away with whenever they want to! And, besides, who in the world is this Toupan?'

'He is nobody in this world, wife, and it is wiser not to speak of him. Let it suffice that in the time of the Old Ones he made all things as they were. Then Koschei came out of Ydalir, and took the power from Toupan, and made all things as they are. Yet three of Toupan's servitors endure upon earth, where they who were once lords of the Vendish have now no privilege remaining save to creep humbly as insects: the use of their wings is denied them here among the things which were made by Koschei, and the charmed stone holds them immutably. Oho, but, wife, there is a cantrap which would free them, a cantrap which nobody has as yet discovered, and to their releaser will be granted whatever his will may desire –'

'This is some more of your stuff and nonsense, out of old fairy tales, where everybody gets three wishes, and no good from any of them!'

'No, my love, because I shall put them to quite practical uses. For you must know that when I have found out the cantrap which will release the bees of Toupan –'

Gisèle showed plainly that his foolishness did not concern her. She sighed, and she hung the sword in its accustomed place. 'Oh, but I am aweary of this endless magic and piddling with vain dreams!'

'Then, wife,' said Miramon, 'then why are you perpetually meddling with what you do not understand?'

'I think,' Ninzian observed at once, for Ninzian too was married, 'I think that I had best be going.'

But Gisèle's attention was reserved for her husband. 'I meddle, as you so very politely call it, because you have no sense of what is right and proper, and no sense of morals, and no sense of expediency, and, in fact, no sense at all.'

Miramon said, 'Now, dearest – !'

Ninzian was hastily picking up his hat.

And Gisèle continued, with that resistless and devastating onflow which is peculiar to tidal waves and the tongue of her who speaks for her husband's own good.

'Women everywhere,' Gisèle generalised, 'have a hard time of it: but in particular do I pity the woman that is married to one of you moonstruck artists. She has not half a husband, she has but the tending of a baby with long legs –'

'It is so much later than I thought, that really now –' observed Ninzian, ineffectively.

'– And I might have had a dozen husbands –'

Miramon said, 'But, surely, no woman of your well-known morality, my darling –'

'– I might, as you very well remember, have married Count Manuel himself –'

'I know. I can recall how near you came to marrying him. He was a dull, a cold-blooded and a rather dishonest clod-hopper: but the luck of Manuel Pig-Tender did not ever desert him,' said

Miramon, sighing, 'not even then!'

'I say, I might have had my pick of a dozen really prominent and looked-up-to warriors, who would have had the decency to remember our anniversary and my birthday, and in any event would never have been in the house twenty-four hours a day! Instead, here I am tied to a muddle-head who fritters away his time contriving dreams that nobody cares about one way or the other! And yet, even so –'

'And yet, even so – as you were no doubt going on to observe, my dearest – even so, since your soliloquy pertains to matters in which our guest could not conceivably be interested –'

'– And yet,' said Gisèle, with a heavier and a deadlier emphasis, 'even so, if only you would be sensible about your silly business I could put up with the inconvenience of having you underfoot every moment. People need dreams to help them through the night, and nobody enjoys a really good dream more than I do when I have time for it, with the million and one things that are put upon me. But dreams ought to be wholesome –'

'My darling, now, as a matter of aesthetics, as a mere point of fact –'

'– But dreams ought to be wholesome, they ought to be worth while, they ought to teach an uplifting moral, and certainly they ought not to be about incomprehensible thin nonsense that nobody can half way understand. They ought, in a word, to make you feel that the world is a pretty good sort of place, after all –'

'But, wife, I am not sure that it is,' said Miramon, mildly.

'Then, the more shame to you! and the very least you can do is to keep such morbid notions to yourself and not be upsetting other people's repose with them!'

'I employ my natural gift, I express myself and none other. The rose-bush does not put forth wheat, nor flax either,' returned the magician, with a tired shrug. 'In fine, what would you have?'

'A great deal it means to you – you rose-bush! – what I prefer! But if I had my wish your silly dream-making would be taken away from you so that we might live in some sort of reputable and common-sense way.'

All the while that she reasoned sensibly and calmly with her husband for his own good. Gisèle had feverishly been dusting things everywhere, just to show what a slave she was to him, and because it irritated Miramon to have his personal possessions thus dabbed at and poked about: and now, as she spoke, Gisèle slapped viciously with her scouring-rag at the black cross. And a thing happened, to behold which would have astonished the innumerable mages and the necromancers and the enchanters who had given over centuries to searching for the cantrap which would release the bees of Toupan. For now without any exercise of magic the scouring-rag swept from the stone one of the insects. Koshchei, who made all things as they are, had decreed, they report, that these bright perils could be freed only in the most obvious way, because he knew this would be the last method attempted by any learned person.

Then for an instant the walls of the ivory tower were aquiver like blown veils. And the bee passed glitteringly to the window and through the clear glass of the closed window, leaving a small round hole there, as the creature went to join its seven fellows in the Pleiades.

Chapter XIV

The Changing That Followed

Now when this eighth bright bee had joined its seven fellows in the Pleiades, then Toupan, afloat in the void, unclosed his ancient unappeasable eyes. Jacy returned to his aforetime estate in the moon: all plants and trees everywhere were withered, and the sea also lost its greenness, and there were no more emeralds. And the Star Warriors and the Wardens of the Worlds were troubled, and They cried out to Koshchei who had devised Them and who had placed Them in Their stations to remain in eternal watchfulness over all things as they are.

Koshchei, for reasons of his own, did not reply.

Then Jacy whispered to Toupan: 'Now is the hour of thy release, O Toupan! now is the hour that Koshchei falls. For among the things that are there stays no verdancy anywhere, and without green things nobody can keep health and strength.'

Toupan answered: 'I am diminished. My bones have become like silver, and my members have turned into gold, and my hair is like lapis-lazuli.'

'Thine eyes remain unchanged,' said the slow whispering of Jacy. 'Send forth thine eyes, O Toupan, against the work of Koshchei, who has blasphemed against the Old Ones, and who has created things as they are.'

'Though he acknowledge both of these misdoings, why need my eyes be troubled – as yet?'

Then Jacy said: 'Send forth thine eyes, O Toupan, so that we Old Ones may rejoice in the dreadfulness of thy over-looking!'

Toupan answered: 'I was before the Old Ones. My soul was before thought and time. It is the soul of Shu, it is the soul of Khnemu, it is the soul of Heh: it is the soul of Night and of Desolation, and there is a thinking about my soul which looks out of the eyes of every serpent. My soul alone keeps any knowledge of that dark malignity which everywhere encompasses the handiwork of Koshchei who made things as they are. Why need my soul be troubled, therefore – as yet?'

But Jacy said again: 'Give aid now to the Old Ones! Already thy bees go forth, that shall rest upon all bushes, and already no verdancy remains. Send forth thine eyes now, also, in which there is the knowledge denied to Koshchei!'

And Toupan answered: 'The time of my release is not yet at hand. Nevertheless, between now and a while, when yet another bee is loosed, I shall bestir my soul, I will send forth my eyes, so that all may perceive the dreadfulness of my overlooking.'

At that the Star Warriors and the Wardens of the Worlds cried out again to Koshchei.

Then Koshchei answered Them: 'Have patience! When Toupan is released I perish with You. Meanwhile I have made all things as they are.'

Chapter XV

Disastrous Rage of Miramon

Now also, when this eighth bright bee had joined its fellows in the Pleiades, in that same instant Miramon Lluagor, as he stood appalled in his ivory tower, was aware of a touch upon his forehead, as if a damp sponge were passing over it. Then he perceived that, with the petulant voicing of his damnable wife's desire, he had forthwith forgotten the secret of his pre-eminence.

Something he could yet recall, they say, of the magic of the Purin and the cast stones, of the Horse and the Bull of the Water, and most of the lore of the Apsarasas and the Faidhin remained to him. He could still make shift, he knew, to control the roving Lamboyo, to build the fearful bridge of the White Ladies, or to contrive the dance of the Korred. He retained his communion with Necksa and Paralda, those sovereign Elementaries. He kept his mastery of the Shedeem who devastate, of the Shehireem who terrify, and of the Mazikeen who destroy. Nor had he lost touch with the Stewards of Heaven – of whom at this period Och had the highest power and was customarily summoned by Miramon Lluagor, for a brief professional consultation, every Sunday morning at sunrise.

But such accomplishments, as Miramon despairingly knew, were the stock in trade of mere hedge wizards, they were the rudiments of any fairly competent sorcerer anywhere: and that supreme secret which had made Miramon Lluagor the master of all dreams was gone away from him completely.

He was very angry. He was the angrier for that he saw, just for an instant, a sort of frightened and bewildered remorse in his wife's foolish face, and he desperately fore-knew himself to be upon the brink of comforting her.

'Accursed woman!' Miramon cried out, 'now indeed has your common-sense completed what your nagging began! This is the doom of all artists that have to do with well-conducted women.

Truly has it been said that the marriage bed is the grave of art. Well, I have put up with much from you, but this settles it, and I will not put up with your infatuation for a reputable and common-sense way of living, and I wish you were in the middle of next week!'

With that he caught the soiled scouring-rag from the hand of Gisèle, and he slapped at one of the remaining bees, and he brushed it from the black cross. And this bee departed as the other had done.

Chapter XVI

Concerns the Pleiades and a Razor

When this bright bee had departed as the other had done before him, then Toupan moved his wings, and he made ready to overlook the work of Koshchei: and in the instant that Toupan moved, the worlds in that part of the universe were dislodged and ran melting down the sky. It was Gauracy who swept all the fragments together and formed a sun immeasurably larger than that which he had lost, and an obstreperous mad conflagration which did not in anything conform with the handiwork of Koshchei.

And Gauracy then shouted friendlily to Toupan, 'Now is the hour of thy release, O Toupan! now is the hour of the return of the Old Ones, now is the hour that Koshchei falls!'

Toupan answered: 'The hour of my release is not yet come. But this is the hour of my overlooking.'

Then Gauracy bellowed, as he swept yet other worlds into the insatiable flaming of his dreadful sun, 'I kindle for you a fine light to see by!'

And now the gods who were worshiped in those worlds which remained, these also cried out to Koshchei. For now, in the intolerable glare of Gauracy's malefic sun, they showed us flimsy and incredible inventions. And the gods knew, moreover, that, if ever the last remaining bee were freed from the cross, the dizain of the Pleiades would be completed, and Toupan would be released, and the power of the Old Ones would return; and that a day foretold by many prophets, the day upon which every god must shave with a razor that is hired, would be at hand; and that, with the falling about of this very dreadful and ignominious necessity, the day of the divine contentment of all gods in any place would be over, forever.

Meanwhile the eyes of Toupan went forth, among the Star Warriors and the Wardens of the Worlds. It was They who, under Koshchei, had shaped the earths and the waters, and who had knit together the mountains, and who had fashioned all other things as they are. It was They who had woven the heavens, and who had placed the soul of every god within him. They were the makers of the hours and the creators of the days and the kindlers of the fires of life, and They were powers whose secret and sustaining names were not known to any of the gods of men. Yet now the eyes of Toupan went among the Star Warriors and the Wardens of the Worlds, and Toupan regarded them one by one; and wheresoever the old eyes of Toupan had rested there remained no world nor any Warden watching over it, but only, for that instant, a very little spiral of thin sluggish vapor.

And those of Them who were not yet destroyed cried piteously to Koshchei, who had devised Them and who had placed Them in Their stations to keep eternal watchfulness over all things as they are.

Now there is no denying that, in the manner of artists, Koshchei had cleared his throat, and had fidgeted a little, in the while that Toupan was overlooking Koshchei's handiwork. But when the Wardens and the Star Warriors cried out to him for aid, then Koshchei, lifting never a finger, said only:

'Eh, sirs, have patience! For I made all things as they are; and I know now it is my safeguard that I made them in two ways.'

Chapter XVII

Epitome of Marriage

But Miramon, in his ivory tower upon Vraidex, knew only that his wish had been granted, for Gisèle had gone just as a bubble breaks, and she was now somewhere in the middle of next week.

'And a good riddance, too!' said Miramon. He turned to Ninzian, that smiling large philanthropist. 'For did you ever see the like of such outrageousness as her outrageousness!'

'Oh, very often,' replied this Ninzian, who too was married. Then Ninzian asked, 'But what will you do next?'

Said Miramon, 'I shall wish to have back the secret and the solace of my art.'

But to Ninzian this seemed less obvious. 'You can do that, readily enough, by releasing the third bee which my devices have procured for you out of the land of Assyria. Yes, Miramon, you can in this manner get back your art, but thus also you will be left defenseless against the doom which is appointed. So, friend, by my advice you will, instead, employ the cantrap as you at first intended, and you will secure for yourself eternal life by wishing that Flamberge may vanish from this world of men.'

And Ninzian waved toward the sword with which according to the foreordainment of the Norns great Miramon Lluagor was to be killed by his own son.

The fallen magician answered, 'Of what worth is life if it breed no more dreams?' And Miramon said also, 'I wonder, Ninzian, just where is the middle of next week?'

Sleek Ninzian spoke, secure in his peculiar erudition. 'It will fall upon a Wednesday, but nobody knows whence. Olybrius states it is now in Aratu, where all that enter are clothed like a bird with wings, and have only dust and clay to eat in the unchanging twilight —'

'She would not like that. She had always a delicate digestion.'

'Whereas Asinius Pollio suggests, not unplausibly, that it waits beyond Slid and Gjold, in the blue house of Nostrand, where Sereda bleaches the unborn Wednesdays, under a roof of plaited serpents –'

'Dear me!' said Miramon, disconsolately rubbing at his nose, 'now that would never suit a woman with an almost morbid aversion to reptiles!'

'– But Sosicles declares it is in Xibalba, where Zipacna and Cabrakan play at handball, and the earthquakes are at nurse.'

'She would be none the happier there. She does not care for babies, she would not for one moment put up with a fractious young earthquake, and she would make things most uncomfortable for everybody, Ninzian,' – and Miramon cleared his throat – 'Ninzian, I begin to fear I have been a little hasty.'

'It is the frailty of all you artists,' the man of affairs replied. 'So my advice, about Flamberge, is not to the purpose?'

'Well, but, you see,' said Miramon, very miserably, 'or perhaps I ought to say that, while of course, still, when you come to look at it more carefully, Ninzian, what I really mean is that the fact is, as it seems to me –'

'The fact is,' Ninzian returned, with a depressed but comprehending smile, 'you are a married man. So am I. Well, then, you have one wish remaining, and no more. You can at will desire to have back again the control of your lost magics or you can have back your wife to control you –'

'Yes,' Miramon agreed, forlornly.

'And indeed,' sleek Ninzian went on, with that glib optimism reserved for the dilemmas of one's friends, 'indeed it is in many ways a splendid thing for you to have the choice clear cut. Nobody can succeed alike at being an artist and a husband. I hold no brief for either career, because I think that art is an unreasonable mistress, and I think also that a wife is amenable to the same description. But I am certain no man can serve both.'

Miramon sighed. 'That is true. There is no marriage for the maker of dreams, because he is perpetually creating finer women than earth provides. The touch of flesh cannot content him who has arranged the shining hair of angels and modeled the breasts of the sphinx. The woman that shares his bed is there of course, much as the blanket or the pillow is there, and each is an aid to comfort. But what has the maker of dreams, what has that troubled being who lives inside the creature which a mirror reveals to him, to do with women? At best, these animals provide him with models to be idealised beyond the insignificant truth, somewhat as I have made a superb delirium with only a lizard to start on. And at worst, these animals can live through no half-hour without meddling where they do not understand.'

Now Miramon kept silence. He was fingering the magic colors with which he blazoned the first sketches of his dreams. Here was his white, which was the foam of the ocean made solid, and the black he had wrung from the burned bones of nine emperors. Here was the yellow slime of Scyros, and crimson cinnabaris composed of the mingled blood of mastodons and dragons, and here was the poisonous blue sand of Puteoli. And Miramon, who was no longer an all-accomplished magician, thought of that loveliness and horror which, but a moment ago, he had known how to evoke with these pigments, he who had no longer any power to lend life to his designs, and who kept just skill enough, it might be, to place the stripings on a barber's pole.

Then Miramon Lluagor said: 'It would be a sad happening if I were never again to sway the sleeping of men, and grant them yet more dreams of distinction and clarity, of beauty and symmetry, of tenderness and truth and urbanity. For whether they like it or not, I know what is good for them, and it affords to their starved living that which they lack and ought to have.'

And Miramon said also: 'Yet it would be another sad happening were my poor wife permitted eternally to scold the shivering earthquakes in the middle of next week. What does it matter that I do not especially like her? There is a great deal about myself that I do not like, such as my body's flabbiness and the snub nose which makes ludicrous the face I wear: but do I hanker to be transformed into a sturdy man-at-arms? Do I view the snout of an elephant with covetousness? Why, but, Ninzian, I am astonished at your foolish talking! What need have I of perfection? What would I have in common with anybody who was patient with me and thought highly of my doings?'

Miramon shook his head, with some sterness. 'No, Ninzian, it is in vain that you pester me with your continuous talking, for I am as used to her shortcomings as I am to my own shortcomings. I regard her tantrums with the resignation I extend to inclement weather. It is unpleasant. All tempests are unpleasant. Ah, yes, but if life should become an endless clear May afternoon we could not endure it, we who have once been lashed by storms would cross land and sea to look for snow and pelting hail. Just so, to have Gisèle about keeps me perpetually fretted; but now that she is gone I am miserable. No, Ninzian, you may spare your talking, you need say no more, for I simply could not put up with being left to live in comfort.'

Ninzian had heard him through without impatience, because they were both married men. Now Ninzian, shrugging, said, 'Then do you choose, Miramon, for your wife and no more dreams, or for your art and loneliness?'

'Such wishing would be over-wasteful,' Miramon replied, as he dusted away the third bee. 'Since I can bear to give up neither my wife nor my art, no matter how destroyingly they work against each other, I wish for everything to be put back just where it was an hour ago.'

The third bee flew in a wide circle, and returned to the cross. The knowledge which Miramon had lost was put back into his mind.

Chapter XVIII

Koshchei is Vexed

Even as the knowledge which Miramon had lost was put back into his mind, just so did life reawaken in all else which had perished in that hour. Gauracy's baleful sun was gone, and the dislodged and incinerated worlds, with all their satellites, were revolving trimly in their proper places, undamaged. And the gods who were worshiped in these worlds now made a celestial rejoicing, because once more there were only seven Pleiades. The Old Ones had sunk back into their sleeping; things, for the while, stayed as they are; and even Toupan now seemed harmless enough. . . .

For the eyes were closed wherein lurked tireless and unappeasable malignity, and a remembrance of all that which was before Koshchei's time, and an undivulged foreknowledge which withered Toupan shared with brisk little Koshchei alone. Nobody could speak certainly about this: yet it was whispered that both of these well knew that, in the end, the Old Ones would return, and that only Toupan knew in what manner and at what hour. . . .

But above the gods who in the multitudinous heavens and paradises were now rejoicing over their regained omnipotence, far higher than these junketing gods stood the Star Warriors and the Wardens of the Worlds, each in the appointed place, and each once more set in eternal watchfulness over all things as they are. And the Star Warriors and the Wardens of the Worlds said, soberly, to Koshchei:

'Sir, your protection is established. You are protected as the guide of the things which exist and of the things which are not yet created. You are protected as a dweller in the realm which goes round about Those who are over Hidden Things. For now the Old Ones sleep again, and not any new thing anywhere shall ever gain the mastery over you, who are our only master: and all things as they are stay yours forever.'

Koshchei replied, rather absent-mindedly: 'What need was

there to worry? Did I not make my creatures male and female? and did I not make the tie which is between them, that cord which I wove equally of love and of disliking? Eh, sirs, but that is a strong cord, and though all things that are depend upon it, my weaving holds.'

They answered him, 'Your weaving holds, sir, assuredly: yet you do not rejoice, as we rejoice.'

'Why, but,' said Koshchei, 'but I do so hate flat incivility! And after overlooking my handiwork, the fellow might very well have said something intelligent. Nobody minds an honest criticism. Just to say nothing – and in that rather marked way, you know – is stupid!'

For Koshchei also, they relate, was, in his fashion, an artist.

Chapter XIX

Settlement: in Full

But that lesser artist, Miramon Lluagor – once more a highly competent magician, in his ivory tower, and once more pre-eminent among the dream-makers of this world – knew nothing about how he had played havoc with the handiwork of Koshchei who made things as they are. Miramon only knew that upon the black stone cross were buzzing three bees, who had now no luster and no power to grant wishes to anybody; and that his wife Gisèle also was making noises, not fretfully but in a tearing rage.

'A pretty trick that was to play on me!' she said. 'Oh, but I pity the woman that is married to an artist!'

'But why do you perpetually meddle without understanding?' he replied, as fretful as the accursed bees, as angry as the intolerable woman. . . .

And they went on very much as before. . . .

They went on very much as before, because, as Miramon put it, the Norns, for all their strength, had not been able to contrive for him any doom more inflexible than he, like every other married man who holds his station unmurderously, had contrived out of his weakness. The way of Miramon Lluagor's death, said he, was set and inescapable, because he was one of the Léshy: but the way of his life he blushed to find quite equally set and inescapable, because he was also a husband. In brief, he detested this woman; she pestered his living, she hampered his art, and with her foolish notions about his art she had, now, frittered away his immortality: but he was rather fond of her, too, and he was used to her.

Miramon, in any event, fell back upon his famous saying that the secret of a contented marriage is to pay particular attention to the wives of everybody else; and from this axiom he derived what comfort he could. He might, he reflected, have been married to that sallow, crippled, flat-faced Niafer, who in the South was upsetting all the familiar customs of Poictesme with her unrelenting piety, and who was actually imposing upon her associates that sort of reputable and common-sense way of living which Gisèle at worst only talked about. Niafer, indeed, seemed to be becoming wholly insane; for very curious tales reached Miramon as to the nonsense which this woman, too, was talking, about – of all mad fancies! – how that cock-eyed husband of hers was to return by and by, in another incarnation. . . . Or Miramon, instead of his lost comrade Kerin of Nointel, might have been married to that chit of a Saraïde who had managed so artfully to dispose of her husband, in some undetected manner or another, and who was now providing poor Kerin with such a host of extra-legal successors. . . . Yes, Miramon would reflect (in Gisèle's absence), he might – conceivably at least – have been worse off. Yet, a bit later, with her return, this possibility would seem more and more dubious.

And – in fine – they went on very much as before. And Miramon Lluagor was pre-eminent among the dream-makers of this world, and he was a dreaded lord: but in his own home he was not dreaded, and he, very certainly, was not pre-eminent.

Then, when the time was due, fell the appointed doom of Miramon, and he was slain by his son Demetrios with the charmed sword Flamberge. For this thing, people say, had long ago been agreed upon by the Norns, who weave the fate of all that live: to them could not matter that Miramon Lluagor was pre-eminent among the dream-makers of this world, because the Norns do not ever sleep: and no magician, through whatsoever havoc and upsetment of Koshchei's chosen economy, has, in the end, power to withstand the Norns.

Then Demetrios went far overseas into Anatolia; and he married Calliston there, and in yet other ways he won a fine name for his hardihood and shrewdness. And in the years that followed, he prospered (for a while) without any check, and, because of a joke about Priapos, he pulled down one emperor of heathenry, to raise up in his stead another emperor with superior taste in humor. Demetrios held wide power and much land, and was a ruthless master over all the country between Quesiton and Nacumera. He was supreme there, as upon Vraidex Miramon Lluagor had been supreme. It was the boast of Demetrios that he feared nobody in any of the worlds beneath or above him, and that boast was truthful.

Yet none of these pre-eminencies could avail Demetrios, when the time was due, and when the doom of Demetrios fell in that manner and that instant which the Norns had agreed upon, and when he who had put his father out of life with the great sword was, in his turn, put out of life with a small wire. For this thing also, people say, had been appointed by Urdhr and Verdandi and Skuld as they sat weaving under Yggdrasill beside the carved door of the Sylan's House: and to this saying the didactic like to add that no warrior, through whatsoever havoc and upsetment of human economy, has, in the end, power to withstand the Norns.

Now it was this Demetrios who married, among many other women, Dom Manuel's oldest daughter Melicent, as is narrated in her saga.

Book Four

Coth at Porutsa

*'Their land also is full of idols: they
worship the work of their own hands.'*
ISAIAH, ii, 8

Chapter XX

Idolatry of an Alderman

Now the tale is again of Coth, and of how Coth went blustering westward to fetch back Dom Manuel into his Poictesme, which, as Coth asserted, skinny women and holy persons and lying poets were making quite uninhabitable. It is probable that Coth thus more or less obliquely referred to the Countess Niafer herself, as well as to Holy Holmendis and to pious Ninzian and to the most virtuous but not plump Madame Balthis, the wife of Ninzian, since these three nowadays were the advisers of Dame Niafer in everything. It is certain that, even in these early days, Dom Manuel had already become a legend; and the poets everywhere were rehearsing his valor and his wisdom and his noble excellencies in all the affairs of this life.

But Coth of the Rocks twirled his mustachios, and he disapprovingly shook his great bald head, and he went very quickly away from all these reformings of Poictesme and of the master whom his heart remembered and desired. Coth of the Rocks traveled westward, without any companion, faring alone by land and sea. Coth broke his journeying, first, at Sorcha, and he companioned there with Credhê of the Red Brown Hair: he went thence to the Island of Hunchback Women, and it was in that island (really a peninsula) he had so much pleasure, and deadly trouble too, with a harlot named Bar, the wife of Ögir. But in neither of these realms did Coth get any sure news of Dom Manuel, although there was a rumor of such a passing. Then, at Kushavati, in a twilit place of rustling leaves and very softly chiming little bells, Coth found, with the aid of Dame Abonde, the book of maps by which he was thereafter to be guided.

Coth journeyed, in fine, ever westward, with such occasional stays to rest or copulate or fight as were the natural concomitants of travel. In some lands he found only ill-confirmed reports that such a person as Dom Manuel had passed that way before him: in other lands there was no report. But Coth had reason, after what Abonde had showed him in that secluded place under the rustling leaves, to put firm faith in his maps.

So he went on, always westward, with varied and pleasant enough adventures befalling him, at Leyma, and Skeaf, and Adrisim. He had great sorrow at Murnith, in the Land of Marked Bodies, on account of a religious custom there prevalent and of the girl Felfel Rhasif Yedua; and – at Ran Reigan – the one-legged Queen Zélélé held him imprisoned for a while, in her harem of half a hundred fine men. Yet, in the main, Coth got on handily, in part by honoring the religious customs everywhere, but chiefly by virtue of his maps and his natural endowments. These last enabled him amply to deal with all men who wanted a quarrel and with all women whom he found it expedient to placate and to surprise: and as far as to Lower Yarold, and even to Khaikar the Red, his maps served faithfully to guide him, until Coth perforce went over the edge of the last one, into a country which was not upon any map; and in this way approached, though he did not know it, to the city of Porutsa.

Thus, it was near Porutsa that Coth found a stone image standing in a lonely field which was overgrown with pepper plants. Among these plants, charred thigh-bones and ribs and other put-by appurtenances of mankind lay scattered every-whither rather dispiritingly: and before the image were the remnants of yet other burnt offerings, upon a large altar carved everywhere with skulls.

This image represented a seated and somewhat scantily clothed giant carved of black stone: from its ears hung rings of gold and silver; its face was painted with five horizontal yellow stripes; and a great gleaming jewel, which might or might not be an emerald, was set in its navel. Such was the limited apparel of this giant's person. But in the right hand of the image were four arrows, and the left hand held a curious fan made of a mirror surrounded by green and yellow and blue feathers. Coth had never before seen such an idol as this.

'However, in this unknown region,' Coth reflected, 'there are, doubtless, a large number of unknown gods. They may not amount to much, but Dame Abonde has taught me that in religious matters a traveler loses nothing by civility.'

Coth knelt. He tendered fealty, and he prayed to this image for protection in his search for his lost liege-lord. Coth heard a voice saying:

'Your homage is accepted. Your prayers are granted.'

Coth looked upward, still kneeling. Coth saw that the huge black image regarded him with living eyes, and that the mouth of this image was now of moving purple flesh.

'Your prayers are granted, full measure,' the image continued, 'because you are the first person of your pallid color and peculiar clothing to come over the edge of the map and worship me. Such enterprise in piety ought to be rewarded: and I shall reward it, prodigally. Bald-headed man with long mustaches, I promise you, upon the oath of the Star Warriors, even by the Word of the Tzitzi-Mimé, that you shall rule over all the country of Tollan. So that is settled: and now do you tell me who you are.'

'I am Coth of the Rocks, the Alderman of St Didol. I followed Dom Manuel of Poictesme, about whom the poets nowadays are telling so many outrageous lies. I followed him, that is, until he rode westward to a far place beyond the sunset. Now I still follow him, since to do that was my oath: and I have come into the West, not to rule over this outlandish place, but to get news of my master, and to fetch him back into Poictesme.'

'You will get no such news from me, for I never heard of this Manuel.'

'Why, then, whatever sort of deity can you be!'

'I am Yaotl, the Capricious Lord, the Enemy upon Both Sides. This is my Place of the Dead: but I have everywhere power in this land, and I shall have all power in this land when once I have driven out the Feathered Serpent.'

'Then let me tell you, Messire Yaotl, you might very profitably add to this power at least such knowledge as is common to the run of civilised persons. It is not becoming in any deity never to have heard of my liege-lord Dom Manuel, who was the greatest of all captains, and who founded the Fellowship of the Silver Stallion, of which I had the honor to be a member. Such ignorance appears strange in anybody. In a deity it is perfectly preposterous.'

'I was only saying – '

'Stop interrupting me! What sort of god are you, who break in upon the devotional exercises of people when they are actually upon their knees! It is my custom, sir, whenever I go into a foreign country, to be civil to the gods of that country; and I am thus quite familiar with the behavior appropriate to a deity in such circumstances. When people pray to you, you ought to exhibit more repose of manner and a certain well-bred reticence.'

'Oh, go away!' said the image of Yaotl, 'and stop lecturing me! Go up into Porutsa yonder, where the Taoltecs live, and where it may be they have heard of your Dom Manuel, since the Taoltecs also are fools and worship the Feathered Serpent. And when you are emperor over the country of Tollan, do you come back and pray to me more civilly!'

Coth rose up from his kneeling, in strong indignation. 'I tendered fealty in the liberal sense appropriate to religious matters. It was but a bit of politeness recommended by Dame Abonde, and I did not mean a word of it – '

The image replied: 'Nobody cares what you meant, it matters only what you have sworn. I have accepted your sworn homage; and the affair is concluded.'

' – And upon no terms,' Coth continued, 'would I consent to be emperor of this outlandish place. For the rest, do you instantly tell me what you meant by saying "the Taoltecs also are fools," because I do not understand that "also".'

'But,' said the image, wearily, 'but you will have to be emperor, now that I have sworn it upon the oath of the Star Warriors. I do not deny that I spoke hastily: even so, I did say it, with an unbreakable oath; and, here likewise, the affair is concluded.'

Coth replied, 'Stuff and nonsense!'

'You are now,' continued the image of Yaotl, 'under my protection: and as a seal of this, I must put upon you three refrainments. We will make them very light ones, since this is but a matter of form. I will order you to refrain from such things as no sane person would ever dream of doing in any event; and thus nobody will be discommoded.'

Coth cried out, 'Bosh!'

'So you must not infringe upon divine privileges by going naked in public; you must avoid any dealings with green peppers such as you see over yonder, for the reason that they are sacred to my worthless stepson, the Flower Prince; and the third refrainment which I now put upon you I shall not bother to reveal, because you are certain to find this abstinence even more easy to observe than the others. I have spoken.'

'I know well enough that you have spoken! But you have spoken balderdash. For if you for one moment think I am going to be bullied by you and your idiotic refrainments – !'

But Coth saw that the image had closed its eyes, and had tranquilly turned back in all to stone, and was not heeding him any longer.

Chapter XXI

The Profits of Pepper Selling

Coth was goaded, by such incivility, from indignation into a fine rage. He addressed the idol at some length, in terms which no person, whether human or divine, could have construed as worshipful. He gathered from the plants about him an armful of green peppers, he took off all his clothes, and he left them there in a heap upon the altar that was carved with skulls. He went up into the city of Porutsa stark naked and sat down in the market-place, crying, 'Who will buy my green peppers!'

None of the Taoltecs hindered him, because the hill people, from Uro and Hipal and Thiapas, were used to come into Porutsa almost thus lightly clad; and it was evident enough that this fair-skinned stranger, with the bare, great, round, pink head, came unarmed with anything except the equipments of nature.

Coth sold his peppers, and went striding about the market-place inquiring for news of Dom Manuel, but none of these charcoal- and copper-colored persons seemed ever to have heard of the gray champion. When the market for that day was over, Coth went up into the hills about Tzatzitepec, in company with a full-bosomed, brown-eyed, delicious girl who had been selling water-cresses in the market-place: she proved brisk; and Coth spent four days with her to their mutual contentment.

On the fifth day he returned, still naked as his mother bore him, to the market-place in Porutsa; and there he again sold green peppers, so that his brow-beating Yaotl might have no least doubt as to the value which Coth set on this god's patronage.

And all went well enough for a while. But by and by seven soldiers came into the market-place, and so to where Coth had just disposed of the last bunch of peppers; and the leader of these soldiers said, 'Our Emperor desires speech with you.'

'Well,' Coth returned, 'I am through with my day's work, and I can conveniently spare him a moment or two.'

He went affably with these soldiers, and they led him to the Emperor Vemac. 'Who are you?' said the Emperor, first of all, 'and what is your business in Porutsa?'

'I am an outlander called Coth of the Rocks, a dealer in green peppers, and I came hither to sell my green peppers.'

'But why do you come into my city wearing no blanket and no loin-cloth and, in fact, nothing whatever except a scowl?'

'That is because of a refrainment which was put upon me by an impudent black rascal who carried arrows and a fan with a mirror in it, and who called himself Yaotl.'

'Blessed be the name of that god!' said the pious Emperor Vemac, 'although we worship the Feathered Serpent and not the Capricious Lord.'

Then Vemac went on to explain that he had an only daughter, who five days earlier had observed Coth, first from the windows of the palace, and later had gone down veiled into the market-place in order to regard at close quarters this virtually pink person. She had returned, astounded and in some excitement, to demand of her father that he give her this queerly colored and greatly gifted seller of peppers to be her husband. Vemac granted her request, because he never denied his daughter anything, and ardently desired a grandson: but when they sent to look for the pink-colored pepper vendor with the great and hairless, pink-colored head, he was nowhere to be found.

The Princess Utsumé had taken this disappointment, with its attendant delay of her nuptials, rather hard. In fine, said Vemac, the girl had fallen sick with love, six physicians had been able to do nothing for her, and nobody could heal her, she declared, except that beautifully tinted and in all ways magnificent pepper vendor.

'Well, you must tell the poor girl that I already have a wife,' said Coth, 'even over and above an understanding with a seller of water-cresses.'

'I do not,' Vemac submitted, 'see what that has to do with it. In Tollan a man is permitted as many wives as he cares to have, within, of course, reason.'

'Marrying does not come under the head of reason,' said Coth.

'Then, as the husband of my only child,' said Vemac, 'you will rule over Tollan along with me.'

'Oh! Oh!' said Coth. For, since he had punctiliously disobeyed Yaotl in everything, he knew this must be a coincidence, and seemed a very strange coincidence.

'And, finally,' said Vemac, 'if you are hard-headed about this really excellent opening in life for a green pepper vendor, we shall have to persuade you.'

'But how,' asked Coth, reservedly, 'how would you persuade me?'

Vemac raised his brown hand. His persuaders came, masked, and bringing with them their implements and a stalwart male slave. They demonstrated their methods of persuasion; and after what remained of the slave was quiet at last, Coth also for a while remained quiet.

'Of two evils,' Coth said then, 'one should choose the more familiar. I will marry.'

He let them take him and bathe him and trim his long mustachios and dye his body black and perfume him and set upon his great bald head a coronal of white hens' feathers. A red cloth was wrapped about his loins, upon his feet a priest put painted sandals with little golden bells fastened to them, and about Coth's scented body was placed a mantle of yellow netting very beautifully fringed.

'Now,' said Vemac, 'when you have had supper, do you go in there and comfort my daughter in her sickness!'

Coth obeyed, and found the Princess – who proved to be in an unmitigatedly brunette fashion a most charming girl – recumbent and weeping in a solidly built double-bed. Coth hung upon a peg in the wall his coronal of white hens' feathers, he coughed, and he looked again at the weeping Princess.

Coth said: 'By such an attachment to me, my dear, I am touched. An attachment to me, in this land of half-men, is indicative of sound sense.' He coughed again, perhaps to hide his emotion, and he added: 'An attachment to me is moving. So do you move over!'

She, still weeping, made room for him. He sat down upon the bed and began to comfort her. She in turn began to express her appreciation of this comforting. He hung upon a peg in the wall a mantle of yellow netting, and a red loin-cloth.

In the morning no trace whatever remained of the Princess Utsumé's illness except a great and agreeable fatigue. And in the forenoon Coth was married to the Princess Utsumé and escorted to the temple of the Feathered Serpent, and there given the imperial name Toveyo, and he was crowned as the co-ruler along with Vemac over all Tollan.

Yet afterward a rather curious ceremony – called, as his brown loving bride informed Toveyo, the Feast of Brooms – was enacted by the clergy and the entire populace of Porutsa, in order to ensure for the marriage of their Princess fertility.

'I feel that this ceremony is superfluous,' Utsumé said, still yawning. 'But this ceremony was divinely ordained by the Goddess of Dirt; and I feel, too, my wonderful pink darling, that it is becoming for persons of our exalted rank to encourage all true religious sentiment, and generally to consent that the will of the gods be done.'

Meanwhile these rites had opened with the beheading of a quite handsome young woman, from whose body the skin was then removed, in two sections, like a horrid corselet and trousers. As such they were worn each by a priest during the rest of the ceremony: and about this Feast of Brooms the less said, the better, but to the newly christened Toveyo a great deal of it seemed morbid and even a bit immodest.

Chapter XXII

Toveyo Dances

Toveyo's first official act was to send ambassadors to the kings in that neighbourhood – to Cocox and Napaltzin and Acolhua, the second of that name – but none of these could give him any news of Dom Manuel. Meanwhile Coth cherished his wife and dealt with other persons also according to his nature.

Of his somewhat remarkable behavior in the war with Cacat and Coöt, of how in one of his rages he destroyed a bridge with all the people on it, and of how he killed ten of his subjects with a gardener's hoe, there is in this place no need to speak. But it came about unavoidably that, before Coth's honeymoon was over, a deputation from the Taoltecs was beseeching Vemac to have this son-in-law of his unostentatiously assassinated.

'For there is really,' they said, 'no standing him and his tantrums.'

'Such,' Vemac replied, 'has been my own experience. I am afraid, though, that if we kill him my daughter will be put out, for she seems to have discovered about him some feature or another feature of great and unfailing attractiveness.'

'It is better, majesty, that she should weep than that we all be driven mad. The man's pride and self-conceit are unbearable.'

'Nobody knows that better than I do. He hectors me in my own palace, where I am not accustomed to be overrun by anybody except my daughter. In such a position we must be politic. We must first see that this Toveyo is belittled in my daughter's eyes. Afterward, if I know her as well as I think I do, she will consent to let us get rid of him.'

One of the darker Taoltecs, who called himself Tal-Cavêpan, said then: 'This all-overbearing Toveyo is now in the market-place. Follow me, and you shall see him belittled in his wife's eyes and in the eyes of everybody!'

They followed, inquiring among themselves who might be this

huge Tal-Cavêpan, that he spoke so boldly. Nobody remembered having seen him before. Meanwhile Tal-Cavêpan went up to where Coth and his royal wife Utsumé were chaffering with a Yopi huckster over some melons. Tal-Cavêpan clapped his hand to Coth's shoulder and bore down his hand. Coth became smaller and smaller, so that presently Tal-Cavêpan stooped and picked up the nuisance whom they called Toveyo, and thus displayed to the Taoltecs their blustering oppressor as a pink midget not more than four inches high, standing there in the palm of Tal-Cavêpan's black hand.

'Dance, majesty! dance, dreadful potentate!' said Tal-Cavêpan. And Coth danced for them. All the while that he danced, he swore very horribly, and his little voice was like the cheeping of a young bird.

The people crowded about him, because no such wonder-working had ever before been seen in Porutsa. Tal-Cavêpan cried merrily to Vemac the Emperor, 'Is not this capering son-in-law of yours belittled in his wife's eyes and in the eyes of everybody?'

Vemac called out to his guards, 'Kill this sorcerer!'

His soldiers obeyed the Emperor. But the Princess Utsumé caught up her tiny husband and thrust him into the bosom of her purple gown, out of harm's way, the while that Tal-Cavêpan was being enthusiastically despatched.

Chapter XXIII

Regrettable Conduct of a Corpse

Now the huge body of Tal-Cavêpan lay where it had fallen, and it instantly began to corrupt, and from it arose a most astounding stench. 'Take that devil carrion out of my city!' Vemac commanded his guards, 'lest it breed a pestilence in Porutsa.'

But when they attempted again to obey the Emperor, they found the body was so heavy that no force could raise it from the ground. So the Taoltecs of necessity left the corpse in their market-place. And a pestilence, in the form of a small yellow whirlwind, went stealthily about the city; and many hundreds died.

Those who yet remained in life, now that they were not able to help themselves, prayed for help from the Feathered Serpent, and, at each of the seven holy stations, sacrificed to him suckling children decked with bands and streamers of properly colored paper. But the pestilence continued.

The Taoltecs then made a yet handsomer oblation, of plump and really valuable slaves and of captive warriors, each one of whom had been duly painted with blue-and-gilt stripes; and they offered the hearts of all these to their older and somewhat outmoded gods, to the Slayer with the Left Hand and to the Maker of Sprouts. Then, as the pestilence grew worse, they became desperate, and they experimentally decapitated and flayed eight of the lesser nobility in honor of the new god called Yaotl, the Capricious Lord, the Enemy upon Both Sides.

Forthwith the dead Tal-Cavêpan raised up what was left of his countenance, and he said: 'Fasten to me ropes woven of black and red cords, you worshipers of the Feathered Serpent! and when fifty of you have done so-and-so' – he stipulated very exactly what they were to do, each to the other – 'then do you drag my body to the Place of the Dead, which is Yaotl's place; and there let my body be burned upon his altar. So shall this pestilence be ended.'

The Taoltecs obeyed. Fifty of them, forming a circle, shamefacedly did the abomination which was required, and fifty of them tugged at the parti-colored ropes: but still the corpse could not be moved. Tal-Cavêpan spoke again, saying, 'Fetch Vemac, that Emperor who decreed my death!'

Vemac came, and along with him came his daughter.

'Hail, Vemac, son of Imos, of the line of Chán, and of the race of Chivim!' said the corpse. 'It appears that these puny sons of nobodies, enfeebled by their long worship of the Feathered Serpent, are not able – after one little act of homage to the Capricious Lord – to remove me from this city. It is therefore necessary that their broad-shouldered and heavenly descended Emperor draw my body to the Place of the Dead, and there burn my body upon the altar of Yaotl.'

'What will become of me in the Place of the Dead?' Vemac asked.

The corpse smiled. 'From that holy place the Emperor will depart on a long journey. His son-in-law will thereafter reign, as was foretold, over all Tollan. For the Emperor Vemac will be traveling afar, he will be journeying between two mountains and beyond the lair of the snake and the crocodile, even to the Nine Waters, which he will cross upon the back of a red dog. Nor will the Emperor Vemac ever return from that journeying.'

Vemac shivered a little. But he said:

'It is right that an emperor should die rather than his people perish. I will not degrade my body, but your body I will draw to the Place of the Dead; and I will abide what follows.'

Now Coth cried out, like the cheeping of a bird, from where he sat in the bosom of his wife's gown. 'This sort of talk is very well, but what assurance have we that this dungpile is speaking the truth?'

The corpse answered: 'To you, Toveyo, I swear that when the Emperor of Tollan has drawn my body to the Place of the Dead, the pestilence will cease: and I swear too that the Emperor will never return. Thus shall his son-in-law reign in his stead, precisely as was foretold.'

'Oho!' said Coth, 'so it is as I thought, and nobody guarantees the affair but you! Well, now, upon my word, do you take us for buzzards or for scavengers, that we should in any way be bothering about what emanates from you! By what oath can garbage swear, that anybody should heed it!'

The great corpse stirred restively under the midget's piping taunts. But the voice of Tal-Cavêpan said only, 'I swear by the oath of the Star Warriors, even by the Word of the Tzitzi-Mimé.'

'Ah, ah!' said Coth. 'Put me down, dear little wife!' Then Coth, the very tiny pink mannikin, strutted toward the evil-smelling black corpse, and brown Utsumé followed fondly after him. Coth posed in a majestic attitude, resting one elbow upon his wife's instep, and twirling at his mustachios. Coth said:

'You have sworn to these things, Yaotl, by that unbreakable oath of yours which first started all this trouble. Very well! I am co-emperor of Tollan. I am as much emperor as Vemac is: and it is I who will draw you to the burning you have richly earned; and it is I whom your oath will prevent from ever returning into this infernal Porutsa, where such uncalled-for liberties are taken with a person's size, and the people are very much too fond of dancing.'

'But,' said the corpse, 'I meant the other emperor!'

Coth answered: 'Bosh! Nobody cares what you meant, it matters only what you have sworn.'

'But,' said the corpse, 'but, you pernicious pink shrimp – !'

Coth replied, 'I do not deny that you spoke lightly: even so, you did swear it, by an unbreakable oath; and the affair is concluded.'

Coth caught at the parti-colored ropes with tiny fingers. But as he tugged, Coth began to grow. The harder he pulled, the greater became his stature, in order that the honor of the Capricious Lord might stay undisgraced, and Yaotl not be evicted from Porutsa by a midget. And now the corpse moved. Now the Taoltecs saw hauling doggedly at those black and red ropes a full-grown if somewhat short-legged champion, with a remarkably large and glistening pink head: before him went a little yellow whirlwind, and behind him dragged a dreadful black corruption. Thus Coth passed through the east gate of their city.

'The will of the gods be done!' said Vemac – 'especially when it is in every way a very good riddance.' Nobody dissented from his pious utterance. 'Let the city gates be closed!' said Vemac then. 'Put new bolts on them, lest that son-in-law of mine be coming back to us against the will of the gods. And you, my dear Utsumé, since you alone are losing anything, howsoever happily, by this business, you shall have another husband, of less desultory dimensions, and, in fact, you may have as many husbands as you like, my darling, to raise up an heir for us in Porutsa and an emperor to come after me and rule over all Tollan.'

Utsumé replied: 'I have reason to believe, my revered father, that the matter of an heir has been attended to. I shall regret my pink Toveyo and his great natural gifts, which were to me as a tireless fountain of delights. And I shall honor his memory by always marrying somebody as near like him as it may be possible to find in this degenerate country. Meanwhile I quite agree with you that it is becoming for persons of our exalted rank to encourage all true religious sentiment, and generally to consent that the will of the gods be done.'

Chapter XXIV

Economics of Yaotl

In the Place of the Dead, Yaotl sat up and scratched his nose reflectively. The Capricious Lord had put off the putrid appearance of Tal-Cavêpan. He now had the seeming which is his in the heaven called Tamo-Anchan: and as he sat opposite the black stone idol there was no difference between Yaotl and the image of Yaotl. At the god's navel also shone a green jewel, his face was striped with yellow, and from his ears hung rings of gold and silver. Otherwise he wore nothing at all, but in one hand he carried arrows, and in his other hand was the scrying-stone with long feathers of three differing colors set about it.

'I will now,' said Yaotl, 'reveal to you the third refrainment which was put upon you. It was that you must never obey my commands in anything.'

'That,' Coth replied, hotly, 'is not a fair refrainment. It gives me no chance to treat you as you deserve. It is a refrainment which strikes directly at the doctrine of free will. It is a treacherous and vile refrainment! For if you will consider just for a moment – you black and very dull-witted dancing-master! – even you will see that, by commanding any self-respecting person to do the exact contrary of your most absurd and tyrannical wishes – '

'I had considered that,' said Yaotl, dryly. 'It was quite necessary I should retain some little protection for my real wishes in the lands over which I exercise divine power.' Now the Capricious Lord fell into a silence, out of which by and by bubbled a chuckle. 'Well, you tricked me neatly enough, just now, when I was in train to make you the sole ruler over this country. And I was going to have a rather pleasant afternoon, too, with that Vemac! Still, I did make you an emperor: and I have kept in everything the oath of the Star Warriors. So the affair is concluded: I am released from my oath: and you may now return to that home of yours, where people have, in some unimaginable fashion, learned how to put up with you.'

'I shall not give over my searching of the West,' Coth answered stubbornly, 'until I have found my liege-lord, whom I intend to fetch back into Poictesme.'

'But that will never do, because we really must preserve hereabouts some sort of order and rule! And no man nor any deity can hope for actual ease in Tollan as long as you are blustering about like a bald-headed pink hornet. . . . So do you let me think the thought of the Most High Place of the Gods, and take counsel with the will of Teotex-Calli. About this Dom Manuel of yours, for instance – '

Yaotl sat quite still for a moment, thinking and looking into the scrying-stone. And his thought, which was the thought of the Most High Place of the Gods of Tollan, took form there very slowly as a gray smoke; and a little by a little this pallid smoke assumed the appearance of a tall gray man, clad all in silvery gray armor, and displaying upon his shield the silver emblem of Poictesme: and Coth knelt before his master, in Yaotl's Place of the Dead.

Chapter XXV

Last Obligation upon Manuel

'Coth,' said the voice of Manuel, 'most stubborn and perverse of all that served me! Coth, that must always serve me grudgingly, with so much of grumbling and of ill grace and of more valor! So, is it you, Coth, is it you, bald-headed, gruff growler!'

Coth answered: 'It is I, master, who am come to fetch you back into Poictesme. And I take it very ill, let me tell you quite frankly, sir, that you should be expressing any surprise to see me in my place and about my proper duty! I follow, as my oath was, after the captain of the Fellowship of the Silver Stallion. They tell me that the fellowship is dissolved by your wife's orders. Well, we both know what wives are. We know, moreover, that my oath was to follow you and to serve you. So I take it that such surprise in the matter comes from you most unbecomingly: and that much, master or not, I wish you distinctly to understand.'

And Manuel said: 'You follow me across the world and over the world's rim because of that oath, you pester these gods into summoning me from my last home, and then you begin forthwith to bluster at me! Yes, this is Coth, who serves me just as he did of old. What of the others who swore with you, Coth?'

'They thrive, master. They thrive, and they listen to small poets caterwauling about you, in those fine fiefs and castles which you gave them.'

'But you only, the least honored and the most rebellious of my barons, have followed me even to this far Place of the Dead! Coth, yet you also had your lands and your two castles.'

'Well, they will keep! What do you mean by hinting that anybody will dare in my absence to meddle with my property!

Did I not pick up an empire here with no trouble at all! You are casting reflections, sir, upon my valor and ability, which, I must tell you quite frankly, and for your own good – '

But Manuel was speaking, rather sadly. 'Coth, that which you have done because of your given word was very nobly done, and with heroic unreason. Coth, you are heroic, but the others are wise.'

'Master, there was an oath.' Coth's voice now broke a little. 'Master, it was not only the oath. There was a great love, also, in a worsening land, where lesser persons ruled, and there remained nobody like Manuel.'

But Manuel said: 'The others are wise. You follow still the Manuel who went about Poictesme. Now in Poictesme all are forgetting that Manuel, and our poets are busied with quite another Manuel, and my own wife has builded a large tomb for that other Manuel . . . Coth, that is always so. It is love, not carelessness, which bids us forget our dead, so that we may love them the more whole-heartedly. Unwelcome memories must be recolored and reshaped, the faults and blunders and the vexing ways which are common to all men must be put out of mind, and strange excellencies must be added, until the compound in nothing resembles the man that is dead. Such is love's way, Coth, to keep love immortal. . . . Coth, oh, most bungling Coth!' said Manuel, very tenderly, 'you lack the grace even to honor your loved dead in a decorous and wise fashion!'

'I follow the true Manuel,' Coth replied, 'because to do that was my oath. There was involved, I cannot deny it, sir, some affection.' Coth gulped. 'I, for the rest, am not interested in these new-fangled, fine lies they are telling about you nowadays.'

Then there was silence. A small wind went about the pepper plants; and it seemed to whisper of perished things.

Now Manuel said: 'Coth, I repeat to you, the others are wise. I have gone, forever. But another Manuel abides in Poictesme, and he is nourished by these fictions. Yearly he grows in stature, this Manuel who redeemed Poictesme from the harsh Northmen's oppression and lewd savagery. Already this Manuel the Redeemer has become a most notable hero, without fear or guile or any other blemish: and with each generation he will increase in virtue. It is this dear Redeemer whom Poictesme will love and emulate: men will be braver because this Manuel was so very brave; and men, in one or another moment of temptation, will refrain from folly because his wisdom was so well rewarded; and at least now and then, a few men will refrain from baseness, too, because all his living was stainless.'

'I,' Coth said, heavily, 'do not recall this Manuel.'

'Nor do I recall him either, old grumbler. I can remember only one who dealt with each obligation as he best might, and that was always rather inefficiently. I remember many doings which I would prefer not to remember. And I remember a soiled struggler who reeled blunderingly from one half-solved riddle to another, thwarted and vexed, and hiding very jealously his hurt. . . . Well, it is better that such a person should be forgotten! And so I come from my last home to release you from your oath of service. I release you now, forever, dear Coth, and I now bid you do as all the others have done, and I now lay upon you my last orders. I order that you too forget me, Coth, as those have forgotten who might have known me better than you did.'

Coth said, with a queer noise which was embarrassingly like a sob: 'I cannot forget the most dear and admirable of earthly lords. You are requiring, sir, the impossible.'

'Nevertheless, it is necessary that you too – bald realist! – should serve this other Manuel; and should forget, as your fellows have forgotten, that muddied and not ever quite efficient bull-necked struggler who has gone out of life and vigor and out of all persons' memory. For now is come upon me my last obligation: it is that the figure which I made in the world shall not endure anywhere in any particle; and I accept this obligation also, and I submit to the common lot of all men, without struggling any longer.'

Coth said, 'Return to us, dear master! return, and with the brave truth do you make an end of your people's bragging and vain lies!'

But Manuel said: 'No. For Poictesme has now, as every other land must have, its faith and its legend, to lead men more nobly and more valorously than ever any living man may do. I, who was strong, had not the strength to beget this legend: but it has been created, Coth, it has been created by the folly of a woman and the wild babble of a frightened child; and it will endure.'

Coth replied, brokenly: 'But, master, we are men of this world, a world made of dirt. Oh, my dear master, we pick our way about that dirt as we best can! The results need surprise nobody. The results are rather often, in a pathetic fashion, very admirable. Should this truth be disregarded for a vain-glorious dream!'

And Manuel answered: 'The dream is better. For man alone of animals plays the ape to his dreams.'

Chapter XXVI

The Realist in Defeat

Here Yaotl ended thinking, and put aside the scrying-stone. And his thought was no longer of Manuel, and nothing was apparent in the Place of the Dead save Yaotl and the image of Yaotl and Coth standing there, in the apparel of an emperor, alone and small and remarkably subdued looking, between the vast black naked twins.

'It would appear,' said Yaotl, 'that some men are no more tractable than are the gods when the affair concerns a keeping of oaths. And so Toveyo will be remembered in this land for a long while.'

And Coth answered, rather drearily: 'Yes; it is such fools as you and I, Messire Yaotl, who create unnecessary trouble everywhere. Well, I also am now released from my oath! And my master has spoken bitter good sense. The famousness of Manuel is but a dream and a loud jingling of words which happen to sound well together; it is a vanity and a great talking by his old wife and my gray peers: and yet, this nonsense, it may be, will hearten people, and will serve all people always, better than would the truth. And my faith is a foolishness, in that, because of a mere oath – like your Star Warriors' Word of the Thingumajigs, sir – I have followed after the truth, across this windy planet upon which every person is nourished by one or another lie.'

'Each to his creed,' said Yaotl. 'So do men choose between hope and despair.'

'Yet creeds mean very little,' Coth answered the dark god, still speaking almost gently. 'The optimist proclaims that we live in the best of all possible worlds; and the pessimist fears this is true. So I elect for neither label. I merely know that, at the end of all my journeying, there remains for me only to settle down, in my comfortable castles yonder in Poictesme, and to live contentedly with my fine-looking wife Azra and with my son Jurgen – that innocent dear lad, whom his old hypocrite of a father will by and by, beyond any doubt, be exhorting to imitate a Manuel who never lived! And I know, too, that this is not the ending which I would have chosen for my saga. For I also, I suppose, must now decline into fat ease and high thinking, and I would have preferred the truth.' Coth meditated for a while: he shrugged: and he laughed without hilarity. 'Capricious Lord, I pray you, what sort of creatures do men seem to the gods?'

'Let us think of more pleasant matters,' Yaotl replied. 'For one, I am already thinking of the way in which I can most speedily get you, O insatiable grumbler, again to your far home, and out of my too long afflicted country.'

He turned his naked huge back toward Coth, as Coth supposed, to indulge in meditation. Coth was, however, almost instantly disabused, by a miracle.

Book Five

'Mundus Vult Decipi'

'*Not only in this world, but also in that which is to come.*'
EPHESIANS, i, 21

Chapter XXVII

Poictesme Reformed

Now the tale, for one reason and another, does not record the miracle which Yaotl performed. The Gods of Tollan were always apt to be misled by their queer notions of humor. Instead, the tale is of that Poictesme to which – borne by that favorable if malodorous wind which Yaotl provided and aimed – Coth now perforce returned alone.

During the years of Coth's absence there had been many changes. Nominally it was the Countess Niafer who ruled over this land, but she in everything seemed to be controlled by St Holmendis of Philistia. About the intimacy between the Countess and her lean but sturdy adviser there was now no longer any gossip nor shrugging: people had grown used to this alliance, just as they were becoming reconciled to the reforms and the prohibitions which were its fruitage.

For now that Manuel was gone, Coth found, the times were changing for the better at a most uncomfortable rate. To Coth of the Rocks these days seemed to breed littler men, who, to be sure, if you cared about such kickshaws, lived more decorously than had lived their fathers, now that this overbearing St Holmendis had come out of Philistia with his miracles: for this sacrosanct person would put up with no irregularity anywhere, and would hardly so much as tolerate the mildest form of wonder-working by anybody else. Even Guivric the Sage, who in the elder and more candid times had attended to all of Dom Manuel's conjuring, now found it expedient to restrict his thaumaturgies to a wholly confidential practice.

For the rest, you could go for days now without encountering a warlock or a fairy; the people of Audela but rarely came out of the fire to make sport for and with mankind; and, while many persons furtively brewed spells at home, all traffic with spirits had to be conducted secretly. In fine, Poictesme was everywhere upon its most sedate behavior, because there was no telling when Holy Holmendis might be dealing with you for your own good; and the cowed province, just as Guivric had prophesied, stayed subject nowadays to a robustious saint conceived and nurtured and made holy in Philistia.

But yet another unsettling influence was abroad, nefariously laboring to keep everybody sanctimonious and genteel – Coth said – for over the entire land Coth found, and fretted under, the all-enveloping legend of Manuel the Redeemer. Coth found the land's most holy place, now, to be that magnificent tomb which, in Coth's absence, the Countess Niafer had reared at Storisende to the memory of her husband. And that this architectural perjury was handsome enough, even Coth admitted.

The intricately carved lower half of the sepulchre displayed eight alcoves in each of which was sealed the relic of one or another saint. The upper portion was the pedestal of a very fine equestrian statue of Dom Manuel with his lance raised, and in full armor, but wearing no helmet, so that the hero's face was visible as he sat there, waiting, it seemed, and watching the North. Thus Manuel appeared to keep eternal guard against whatever enemy might dare molest the country which he had once redeemed from the Northmen. And there was never a more splendid looking champion than was this mimic Manuel, for the armor of this effigy was everywhere inset with jewels of every kind and color.

How Madame Niafer, who was, moreover, by ordinary standards a notably parsimonious person, had ever managed to pay for all these gems nobody could declare with certainty, but it was believed that Holy Holmendis had provided them through one or another pious miracle. Coth of the Rocks voiced an exasperated aspersion that they were paste; and declared paste gems to be wholly appropriate to the mortuary imposture. In any event, the Redeemer of Poictesme had been accorded the most magnificent sepulchre these parts had ever known.

And Coth found all this jewelry and tortured stonework, as a piece of art, to be wholly admirable, if you cared for such kickshaws. But as a tomb he considered it to lack at least one essential feature, in that it was empty.

Yet to most persons the emptiness of the great tomb was its peculiar sanctity. This spacious and proud glittering void was, to most persons, a perpetual reminder that Dom Manuel had ascended into heaven while yet alive, uncorrupted by the ignominy of death, and taking with him every heroic bone and bit of flesh, and every tiniest sinew, unmarred. That miracle – no more, to be sure, than the great Redeemer's just due – most satisfactorily and most awfully accounted for the lack of any corpse, as surely as the lack of a corpse was the firm proof of the miracle; sublime verities here interlocked: and that miracle had been set above cavil when it was first revealed, by Heaven's wisdom, through the unsullied innocence of a little child, lest in this world, men and women being what they are, by any scoffer the testimony of an adult evangelist might be suspected.

Coth, after hearing these axioms – so unshakably established as axioms during the seven years of Coth's absence – would look meditatively at his young Jurgen, to whose extreme youth and comparative innocence this revelation had been accorded. The boy was now nearing manhood, he fell short in many respects of the virtues appropriate to an evangelist, and he confessed to remembering very faintly now that tremendous experience of his infancy. That hardly mattered, though, Coth would reflect, when Poictesme at large was so industriously preserving and embroidering the tale which the dear brat had brought down from Upper Morven to explain an overnight truancy from home.

'There is but one Manuel,' Coth would remark, to himself, 'and – of all persons! – my Jurgen is his prophet. That kickshaw creed seems to content everybody, now that the rogue no longer bothers to provide an excuse for staying out all night.'

Chapter XXVIII

Fond Motto of a Patriot

Everywhere, indeed, during the while of Coth's vain adventuring after the real Manuel, the legend had grown steadily. Coth found it wholly maddening to hear of the infallible and perfect Redeemer with whom he had formerly lived in daily converse of a painstakingly quarrelsome and uncivil nature: and he found too that, of his confrères of the Silver Stallion who yet remained in Poictesme, Ninzian and Donander at least were beginning to lie about Manuel with as pious a lack of restraint as anybody. Guivric the Sage, of course, would chillily assent to whatsoever the best-thought-of people affirmed, because the self-centered old knave did not ever really bother about what other persons thought: whereas Holden and Anavalt sought rather markedly, to turn the conversation to other topics. These aging champions had, in fine, encountered, in this legend as to their former glories and privileges, an unconquerable adversary with which they, each according to his nature, were of necessity compromising.

For Manuel the great Redeemer, who had first carnally redeemed Poictesme in battle with the Northmen, and later had redeemed Poictesme in more exalted fields, when at his passing he had taken all his people's sins upon his proud gray head – this Manuel was to return and was to bring again with him the golden age which, everybody now asserted, had existed under Manuel's ruling of Poictesme. That was the sweet and reason-drugging allure of the legend, that was the prediction transmitted by Coth's young scapegrace, who nowadays had averted so whole-heartedly from prophecy to petticoats. There was no sense in arguing against such vaticinatory fanfaronade, since it promised to all inefficient persons that which they preferred to believe in. Everywhere in the world people were expecting the latter coming of one or another kickshaw messiah who would remove the discomforts which they themselves were either too lazy or too incompetent to deal with; and nobody had anything whatever to gain by electing for peculiarity among one's fellow creatures and a gloomier outlook.

Even Coth saw that. So the bald realist looked over his cellar and the later produce among his vassals in the way of likely girls; he gave such orders as seemed best in the light of both inspections; and he settled down as comfortably as might be to the task of making old bones in this land of madmen. He might at least look forward to the requisite creature comforts to be derived from these bins and amiable spry bedfellows. His Azra was no more trying than most wives; and his young Jurgen, after all, might turn out better than seemed probable.

So Coth in the end let maudlin imbeciles proclaim whatsoever they elected about the glorious stay upon earth and the second coming of Manuel the Redeemer, and Coth answered them at worst with inarticulate growlings. But that the old bear's love for Poictesme remained unchanged was evinced by the zeal with which he now caused his two homes superabundantly to be adorned with the arms of Poictesme, so that at every turn your eye fell upon the rampant silver stallion and the land's famous motto, *Mundus vult decipi*. Such patriotism showed, said everybody, that for all his fault-finding, Coth's heart was in the right place.

Chapter XXIX

The Grumbler's Progress

And the tale is still of Coth, telling how he avoided Niafer's court, and the decorums and the pieties which were in fashion there, and how he debauched reasonably in his own citadels.

He fought no more, but he did not lack for other pleasures. He hunted in the Forest of Acaire; and, in his rich coat of fox fur, he rode frequently with hounds and falcons about the plains of the Roigne. He maintained an excellent pit in which wild boars and bears contended and killed one another for his diversion. When the weather was warm he drank, and he amused himself at dice and backgammon, in his well-ordered orchard: in winter he sat snug under the carved hood of his huge fireplace; and it was thus that for his health's sake he was cozily cupped and bled, while the Alderman of St Didol drank quietly and insatiably.

Then, too, it amused Coth now and then to execute a vassal or so upon his handsome gallows – that notorious gallows supported with four posts, although his rank as Alderman entitled him to only two posts – because this bit of arrogance, in the matter of those two extra posts, was a continuous great source of anger to his nominal sovereign, Madame Niafer. But his main recreation, after all, Coth found in emulating those very ancient and most famous monarchs Jupiter and David in a constant change of women; and the fine girls of Poictesme remained as always a lively joy to him.

And daily, too, the Alderman of St Didol squabbled with his wife and son; and, since he could discover profuse grounds everywhere for fault-finding, was comfortable enough.

To his sardonic bent it was at this period amusing to note how staidly Poictesme thrived by virtue of the land's faith in Poictesme's Redeemer, who had removed all troubles and obligations in the past, and who by and by would be coming again, no doubt to wipe similarly clean the moral slate; so that there was no real need to worry about the future, nor about any little personal misdemeanor (which had not become embarrassingly public), since this would of course be included in the general amnesty when Manuel returned to take charge of his people's affairs.

And yet there was another and more troubling side. The younger, here and there, were beginning, within moderation, to emulate that Manuel who had never lived. For Coth saw that too. He saw young persons – here and there – displaying traits and customs strange if not virtually unknown to the old reprobate's varied experience. Civility, for one thing, was rather sickeningly pandemic: you saw fine strapping lads, differing in opinion about this, that or the other, who, instead of resorting sensibly to a duel, stopped – who positively sat down side by side – to examine each the other's point of view, and after that, as often as not, talked themselves out of fighting at all. That was because of the fame of Manuel's uniform civility, which, indeed, the rogue had displayed, and had made excellent profit of.

But you saw, too, people pardoning and even befriending persons who had affronted or injured them, and doing this because of the fame of Manuel's loving kindliness toward his fellows: everywhere you saw that wholly groundless notion flowering also into a squeamishness about taking any other person's property away from him, even when you really wanted it. You saw bodily sound young men avoiding, or at any rate stinting, the normal pleasures of youth, alike among their peers and in bed, because of the famousness of Dom Manuel's sobriety and chastity: and you saw milksops, in fine, giving up all the more intelligent vices because of that slanderous rumor about Manuel's addiction to the virtues.

It was not, either – not altogether – that the young fools thought they had much to gain by these eccentricities. They had, somehow, been tempted into emulation by this nonsense about Manuel's virtues. And then they had – still somehow, still quite unexplainably – found pleasure in it. Coth granted this rather forlornly: these young people were getting a calm and temperate, but a positive, gratification out of being virtuous. There must, then, lurk somewhere deep hidden in humanity a certain trend to perverse delight in thus denying and curbing its own human appetites. And since the comparatively intelligent and unregenerate persons were all profiting by their fellows' increased forbear-ance, altogether everybody was reaping benefit.

This damnable new generation was, because of its insane aspiring, happier than its fathers had been under the reign of candor and common-sense. This moon-struck legend of Manuel was bringing, not to be sure any omnipresent and unendurable perfection, but an undeniable increase of tranquillity and con-tentment to all Poictesme. Coth saw that too.

He remembered what his true liege-lord had said to him in the Place of the Dead: and Coth admitted that, say what you might as to the Manuel who had really lived, the squinting rascal did as a rule know what he was talking about.

Chapter XXX

Havoc of Bad Habits

News as to court affairs and the rest of the province came now to Coth, in his two lairs at Haut Belpaysage, belatedly and rarely. Yet at this time he heard that Anavalt the Courteous had gone out of Poictesme with as little warning as the other lords of the Silver Stallion had accorded their intimates when Gonfal and Kerin and Miramon, and Coth himself, had each gone out of the land after Manuel's passing.

These overnight evasions appeared to be becoming a habit, Coth said to his wife Azra, so you had best cherish me in the night season while you may, instead of shrieking out nonsense about my hands being so cold. She replied with an uxorial generality as to sore-headed bears and snapping-turtles and porcupines, which really was not misplaced. And it was not for a long while that any tidings were had of Anavalt the Courteous, and the riddle of his evasion was unraveled,* but by and by came news as to the end which Anavalt had found near a windmill in the Wood of Elfhame, in his courtship of the mistress of that sinister and superficial forest.

'At his age, too! and with a woman too thin to keep him warm!' said Coth. 'It simply shows you, my dear son, what comes of lecherous habits, and I trust you may profit by it, for the world is very full of such deceits.'

And Coth, for his Jurgen's benefit, piously indicated the motto which you encountered at well-nigh every turn in Coth's two homes, along with the stallion rampant in every member.

Nevertheless, Coth was unhappier than he showed. He had loved Anavalt in the days when these two had served together under the banner of the Silver Stallion. It seemed to Coth that in dark Elfhame a handsome and fine-spoken and kindly rascal had

---

* Among other places, in a volume called *Straws and Prayer Books*.

been trapped and devoured rather wastefully. Nor was it cheering to consider that, now, but five of the great fellowship remained alive. . . . Meanwhile, in rearing a son judiciously, one must preserve the proper moral tone.

And Coth heard also, at about this time, of the magic which had been put upon King Helmas the Deep-minded, that monarch whom, as people said, Dom Manuel in the old days had bamboozled into giving Manuel a fine start in life. At first, to be sure, the tale ran that Helmas had been murdered, and his treasury rifled, by one of his attendants: and his Perion de la Forêt, after his escape from prison, was sought for everywhere. Later, the truth was known: and Coth heard of how a magic had been put upon Helmas, by his own daughter Mélusine, and of the notable transfer on the king's castle of Brunbelois and the king's person and entire entourage, from out of Albania to that high place in the great Forest of Acaire, where, people said, the ill-fated court of Helmas now stayed, enchanted.

And Coth drew the moral. 'It shows you what parents may expect of their children,' he remarked, with a malevolent glance toward his adored Jurgen. 'It shows you what comes of this habit of indulging children.'

'Now, Father – ' said the boy.

'Stop storming at me! How dare you attempt to bulldoze me, sir! Do you take me for another Helmas!'

'But, Father, I was only – '

'Get out of my sight, you quarrelsome puppy! I will not be thus deafened. Get back to that Dorothy of yours! You care for nobody else,' said jealous old Coth.

'But, Father – '

'And must you still be arguing with me! Do you think there is no end to my patience? What is there to argue about? The puppy follows the bitch. That is natural.'

'But, Father, how can you – !'

'Get out of my sight before I break every bone in your body! Get back to that cold sanctimonious court and to your hot wench!' said Coth.

Yet all the while that he spoke with such fluency Coth's heart was troubled. Of course, in rearing a son judiciously, one must preserve the proper moral tone. Nevertheless, Coth felt, at heart, that he might be taking the wrong way with the boy, and was being almost brusque.

But Coth was Coth. That was his doom. He had only one way.

Chapter XXXI

Other Paternal Apothegms

Now Jurgen went very often to court, since the boy at twenty-one was fathoms deep in love with Count Manuel's second daughter, whom they called Dorothy la Désirée. Coth saw her but once: and, even over and above his rage at the thought of sharing Jurgen with anybody, Coth was honestly moved, in the light of his considerable boudoir experience, to uncivil prophecy. He was upon this occasion, in the main hall at Bellegarde, with dozens of persons within earshot, most embarrassingly explicit with Jurgen, alike as to the quality of Jurgen's intelligence and the profession which Coth desired no daughter-in-law of his to practice.

The two quarreled. That nowadays was no novelty. The difference was that into this quarrel Jurgen put all his heart. So the insolent, overbearing, bull-dozing young scoundrel was packed off to serve under the Vidame de Soyecourt: and before the year was out Coth heard that this Dorothy la Désirée was married to Guivric's son Michael.

'This Michael is but the first served at an entertainment preparing for the general public,' was Coth's epithalamium.

And many rumors came back to Haut Belpaysage as to Jurgen's doings in Gâtinais, and, while they all seemed harmless enough, not all were precisely what a father would have elected to hear. Coth considered, for example, that Jurgen had acted with imprudence in thus hastily making Coth a grandfather with the assistance of the third wife of the Vidame de Soyecourt. Husbands had a sad way of being provoked by such offspring, upon the wholly illogical ground that the provocation was not mutual. Still, young people needed their diversions, and husbands, to Coth's experience, were not a dangerous tribe. What really fretted a somewhat aging Alderman, however, was that such stories reached him casually, and that from Jurgen himself he heard nothing.

Yet other gossip came too from the court of Bellegarde and
Storisende, as to how Manuel's oldest daughter, Madame Melicent, was now betrothed to King Theodoret, and how upon the
eve of her marriage she had disappeared out of Poictesme: and
she was next heard of as living in unchristian splendor far
oversea, as – if you elected to put it more gracefully than Coth
did – as the wife of Miramon Lluagor's son and murderer,
Demetrios.

'Why not?' said Coth. 'Why should not snubnosed Miramon's
swarthy lad be having his wenches when convenient? Parricide
is no bar to fornication. They are sins committed with quite
different weapons. And, for the rest, all sons are intent to do
what this one has succeeded in doing. How, for that matter, did
Dom Manuel, that famous Redeemer of yours, deal with his
own father Oriander the Swimmer?'

That, it was hastily explained to Coth by his wife Azra, was
but a part of the great Redeemer's abnegation and self-denial.
That was the atonement, and the immolation of his only beloved
father, in order to expiate the gross sins of Poictesme –

"To expiate the sins of one person by killing another person,'
replied Coth, 'is not an atonement. It is nonsense.'

Well, but, it was furthermore explained, this atonement was a
great and holy mystery; and, as such, it should be approached
with reverence rather than mere rationality. Yet this high mystery of the atonement must undoubtedly symbolise the fact that,
in order to attain perfection, Manuel had put off the ties of his
flesh –

To which Coth answered, staring moodily at his wife Azra: 'I
saw that fight. He put off those ties of his flesh and Oriander's
head from his body, with such pleasure as Manuel showed in no
other combat. And all sons are like him. Have we not a son?
Why do you keep pestering me?'

'I only meant – '

'Stop contradicting me!' But very swiftly Coth added, with a
sort of gulp, ' – my dear.'

For Coth was changing. He hunted no more, he had closed up
his bear-pit. He seemed to prefer to be alone. Azra would very
often find him huddled in his chair, not doing anything, but
merely thinking: and then he would glare at her ferociously,

without speaking; and she would go away from him, without speaking, because she also thought too frequently about their son for her own comfort.

Chapter XXXII

Time Gnaws at All

Then Emmerick came of age, and Madame Niafer's rule was over, men said, because the Count would be swayed in all things by his cousin, the Bishop Ayrart of Montors, the same that afterward was Pope.

'The young church rat drives out the old one,' said Coth. 'Now limping Niafer must learn to do without a night-light and to sleep without a halo on her pillow.'

But Ayrart's supremacy was not for long, and Holy Holmendis remained about the court, after all, because, at just this time, lean Holden the Brave appeared at Storisende with a beautiful young gray-eyed stranger whom he introduced as the widow of Elphànor, King of Kings. People felt that for this Radegonde thus to be surviving her husband by more than thirteen centuries was a matter meritorious of explanation, but neither she nor Holden offered any.

The history of the love which had been between Radegonde and Holden is related elsewhere*: at this time it remained untold. But now, at this love's ending, Radegonde found favor in the small greedy eyes of Count Emmerick, and she married him, nor was there ever at any season thereafter during the lifetime of Radegonde a question as to what person, howsoever flightily, ruled over Poictesme and Emmerick. And Radegonde – after a very prettily worded but frank proviso as to the divine right of princes, which rendered them and their wives responsible to Heaven directly, and to nobody else, as she felt sure dear Messire Holmendis quite understood – Radegonde thereafter favored Holmendis and his wonder-working reforms, among the appropriate class of people, because she considered that his halo was distinctly decorative, and that a practicing saint about the court lent it, as she phrased the matter, an air.

* See note upon page 123.

Coth heard of these things; and he nodded his great dome-shaped head complacently enough. 'A tree may be judged by its fruit. Now in England Dom Manuel's long-legged bastard by Queen Alianora has returned his young wife to the nursery. He is today, they tell me – in the approved fashion of all sons – junketing about foreign courts with the Lord of Bulmer's daughter. He, in brief, while the Barons steal England from him, is intent upon begetting his own bastards – '

'But you also, my husband – '

'Do you stop deafening me with your talk about irrelevant matters! In Philistia, Dom Manuel's most precious bantling by Queen Freydis is working every manner of pagan iniquity, and has brought about the imprisonment, in infamous Antan, of his own mother, after having lived with her for some while in incest – '

'Nevertheless – '

'Azra, you have, as I tell you for your own good, a sad habit, and a very ill-bred habit also, of interrupting people, and that habit is quite insufferable. A tree I repeat to you, may be judged by its fruit! Everybody knows that. Now, in our Poictesme, the increase of Dom Manuel's body has, thus far, produced two strumpets and a guzzling cuckold – '

'But, even so – '

'You are talking nonsense. A tree, I say to you, may be judged by its fruit! I consider this exhibit very eloquently convincing as to the true nature of our Redeemer.'

Azra now answered nothing. And Coth fell to looking at his motto, rather gloomily.

'It was not that I meant,' he said, heroically, by and by, 'to be rude, my dear. But I do hate a fool, and, in particular, an obstinate fool.'

Here too it must be recorded that upon the night of Radegonde's marriage old Holden had the ill taste to die. That it was by his own hand, nobody questioned, but the affair was hushed up: and Count Emmerick's married life thus started with gratifyingly less scandal than it culminated in.

Coth heard of this thing also. He looked at his motto, he recalled the love which he had borne for Holden in the times when Coth had not yet given over loving anybody: and he mildly wondered that Holden, at his age, should still be clinging to the fallacy that one wench was much more desirable than another. By and large, thought Coth, they had but one use, for which any one of them would serve, if you still cared for such kickshaws. For himself, he was growing abstemious; and as often as not, found it rather a nuisance when any of his vassals married, and the Alderman of St Didol was expected to do his seignorial duty by the new made wife. Things everywhere were dwindling and deteriorating.

Even the great Fellowship of the Silver Stallion was wearing away, thus steadily, under the malice and greed of time. Donander of Évre was today the only one of Manuel's barons who yet rode about the world, now and then, in search of good fighting and fine women. All the best of the fellowship were gone from life: the hypocrites and the fools alone remained, Coth estimated modestly. For he and that boy Donander were, at least, not hypocrites. . . .

And very often, too, Coth would look at his wife Azra, and would remember the girl that she had been in the times when Coth had not yet given over loving anybody. He rather liked her now. It was a felt loss that she no longer had the spirit to quarrel with anything like the fervor of their happier days: not for two years or more had Azra flung a really rousing taunt or even a dinner plate in his direction: and Coth pitied the poor woman's folly in for an instant bothering about that young scoundrel of a Jurgen, who had set up as a poet, they said, and – in the company, one heard, of a grand duchess – was rampaging everywhither about Italy, with never a word for his parents. Coth, now, did not worry over such ingratitude at all: not less than twenty times a day he pointed out to his wife that he, for one, never wasted a thought upon the lecherous runagate.

His wife would smile at him, sadly: and after old Coth had been particularly abusive of Jurgen, she would, without speaking, stroke her husband's knotted, stubby, splotched hand, or his tense and just not withdrawing cheek, or she would tender one or another utterly uncalled-for caress, quite as though this illogical and broken-spirited creature thought Coth to be in some sort of trouble. The woman, though, had never understood him. . . .

Then Azra died. Coth was thus left alone. It seemed to him a

strange thing that the Coth who had once been a fearless champion and a crowned emperor and a contender upon equal terms
with the High Gods, should be locked up in this quiet room,
weeping like a small, punished, frightened child.

Chapter XXXIII
Economics of Coth

In the months that followed, Coth wore a puzzled and baffled look. His servants reported that he talked to himself almost incessantly. But it was incoherent, uncharacteristic stuff, without any quarreling in it, they said. . . . Coth at the last had well-nigh given over fault-finding. He was merely puzzled.

For life, somehow, in some as yet undetected fashion, seemed to have cheated him. It was not possible that, with fair play everywhere, life would be affording you, as the sum and harvest of all, no more than this. No sort of pleasure remained: girls left, and for that matter found, you wholly frigid; wine set you to vomiting. You wanted, as if in a cold cemetery of desires, one thing alone, nowadays.

Yet the son Jurgen whom Coth's tough heart remembered and desired was still frolicking about the pleasant and famous places of the world, with no time to waste in sedate Poictesme: and Coth rather suspected that, even now, in this sick unimaginable loneliness, were Jurgen to return, a feebly raging Coth would storm at the lad and turn him out of doors. For that was Coth's way. He had only one way. . . . He reflected, now, Jurgen was no longer a lad: it well might be, indeed, that pockmarked, greasy-headed roisterer had ended living, with some husband's dagger in his ribs. The last news heard of Jurgen, though, was that he was making songs in Byzantium with the aid of a runaway abbess, who at least had no husband. And in any event, Jurgen would not ever return, because Coth had come between the boy that had been and the leering, high-nosed strumpet at Asch, who was reported to be rivaling even that poor Kerin's widow, Saraïde, in the great number of her co-partners in lectual exercise.

'A pert pirate in all men's affairs, a mere cockboat sailing under the Jolly Roger!' was Coth's verdict, as repeated by an eaves-dropping page. 'This Madame Dorothy has had in her more' – he mumbled so that something was lost – 'than there are trees in Acaire. All the trees in Acaire are judged by their fruits. This Dorothy is a very betraying fruit from the rank tree of the Redeemer. This Dorothy has inherited from Dom Manuel such lewdness as is advantageously suited to a warrior, but misbecomes a young woman. It seems rather a pity that this light wagtail should ever have come between me and Jurgen.'

Coth said this without any raging. He was merely puzzled.

For all, everywhere, appeared to have failed and deserted him. This Coth had been in his day a hero: and none of that far-off adventuring seemed much to matter now, nor could he quite believe that these things had happened to the tired old fellow who went muttering about the lonely Château des Roches, and was kept alive with slops of gruel and barleywater. This tremulous frail wreckage was not, assuredly, the Coth who had killed single-handed the three Turks at Lacre Kai, and who had kidnapped the fat King of Cyprus and in the sight of two armies had hung the crown of yet another king on the thorn-bush at Piaja, and who had been himself an emperor, and who had held the White Tower at Skeaf against the Comprachos, and who had put that remarkable deception upon the enamored one-legged tyrant of Ran Reigan, and who had shared in so many other splendid rough-and-tumble happenings.

There had been a host of women in these happenings, fine women, not to be had at anybody's whistle like the two-headed Dorothys whom these sanctimonious times were spawning everywhere to come between a father and a boy with no real harm in him. And none of these dear women mattered now. . . . Besides, it was not true to say that Jurgen had no real harm in him. Jurgen had been violent and headstrong from the very first: that was another pity, but Jurgen had taken after his mother in this, old Coth reflected, and his mother had always been injudicious alike in pampering and in rebuking Jurgen, with the result that Jurgen was nowadays a compendium of all iniquity.

And the Manuel too whom Coth had loved was gone now, and was utterly ousted from every person's memory by that glittering tomb at Storisende, where a Manuel who had never lived was adored as a god is worshiped. Yet that, also, seemed not to matter. It was preposterous. But all the world was preposterous: and nothing whatever could be done about it, by a tired muttering old man.

People, no doubt, were living more quietly and more decorously because of this fictitious Manuel whom they loved and this gaunt ranting Holmendis whom they feared. But that too, to Coth, seemed not to matter. People nowadays were such fools that their doings and the upshot of these doings were equally unimportant, Coth estimated. If they succeeded in worming their way into heaven by existing here as spiritlessly as worms, Coth had not any objection, since he himself was bound for hell and for the company of his peers in a more high-hearted style of living.

Coth fell a little complacently to thinking about hell, and about the fine great sinners who would make room for him there, on account of the Coth that had been, and about the genial flames in which nobody was pestered by milksops prattling about their damned Redeemer. And Manuel – the real Manuel, that squinting swaggering gray rogue whose thefts and bastards and killings had been innumerous – that Manuel would be there too, of course; and he and Coth would make very excellent mirth over those reforms which had ensnared all the milksops into heaven, even at the high price of spoiling the Poictesme of Coth's youth.

For those elder heroic days were quite over. Of the great fellowship there remained, beside the hulk that was Coth, only Guivric and Donander and Ninzian. Donander of Évre was now, they said, in the far kingdom of Marabon, combining the pleasures of knight-errantry with a pious pilgrimage to the tomb of St Thomas. And while Coth had always admired Donander as a fighting-machine, in all other respects Coth considered him a deplorable young fool, nor, after holding this opinion steadfastly for twenty-five years, was Coth prepared to change it. Ninzian was a sleek hypocrite, a half-hearted fellow who had stinted himself to one poor pale adultery with a pawnbroker's wife; and who flourished in the sanctimonious atmosphere of these abominable times because he truckled to Holmendis nowadays just as formerly he had toadied to Manuel. That prim and wary Guivric whom people called the Sage, Coth had always most cordially detested: and when Coth heard – from somebody, as he cloudily remembered, but it was too much trouble to recall from whom – that old Guivric too was now departed from Poictesme, it seemed not to matter.

Perhaps, Coth speculated, one of those troubled-looking servants had told him Guivric was dead. Almost everybody was dead. And in any event, it did not matter about Guivric. Nothing really mattered any longer. . . .

All that Coth had ever loved was gone out of life. Gray Manuel, the most superb and admirable of earthly lords (howsoever often the man had needed a little candid talking to, for his own good), and peevish tender-hearted wise Miramon, and courteous Anavalt, and pedantic innocent Kerin (who had been used to blink at you once or twice, like the most amiable of owls, before he gave his opinion upon any subject), and Holden, the most brave where all were fearless, and indolent gay Gonfal, whom you might even permit, within limits, to rally you, because Gonfal was the world's playmate – all these were gone, the dearest of comrades that any warrior had ever known, in that lost, far-off season when the Fellowship of the Silver Stallion had kept earth noisy with the clashing of their swords, and had darkened heaven with the smoke of the towns they were sacking, and when throughout the known world men had talked about the wonders which these champions were performing with Dom Manuel to lead them.

And so many splendid women too were gone: these days produced only your flibbertigibbet Melicents and Dorothys and such trash. There were no women nowadays like Azra, nor like Gunnhilda, nor like Muirnê of the Marshes – or like plump, ardent, brown Utsumé, or like Orgeleuse, that proud lady of Cyprus, who had yet yielded in the end, or like Azra. . . . And Coth, chewing meditatively at nothingness, with sunken and toothless lips, thought also about greathearted Dame Abonde, and about little Fleurette, and about Azra, and about Credhê, that jolly if remarkably exigent Irish girl, and about tall Asgerda, and about Azra, and about Bar, the treacherous but very lovely sea-wife, and about Oriande, and about poor Felfel Rhasif Yedua, who had given all the hair of her body and afterward her life, to preserve his life, and about Azra.

He remembered the girl that Azra had been, and he thought

without any joy about the scores of other delectable persons which Coth had known, amorously and intricately, so very long ago. All these women were gone out of living: one or two of them might perhaps as yet pretend to survive in the repulsive skins of shriveled old lean ugly hags, and in some remote chimney corner or another might as yet be mumbling – with sunken and toothless lips, like his own lips – over nothingness; for nothingness was now their portion too; and those close-kissing, splendid, satiated, half-swooning girls whom Coth remembered, with indelicate precision, now no longer existed anywhere.

And Jurgen, the unparalleled of babies, and that cuddling little lad prattling his childish lies about Dom Manuel and ascents into heaven and other nonsense to ward off a spanking, and that fine upstanding boy just graduating into pimples in whom Coth had so exulted when Coth returned from Tollan and the throne of Tollan – his Jurgen in dozens upon dozens of stages of growth – now every one of these dear sons was gone. There remained only a dissolute and heartless wastrel bellowing rhymed nonsense and rampaging about the world wherever the grand duchesses and the abbesses made most of him. Coth looked at his motto.

Life then, at utmost, after all the prizes of life had been gained, and you were a looked-up-to and prosperous alderman, amounted to just this. It profited nothing that you had been a tender and considerate father, or a dutiful and longsuffering son who had boxed your father's jaws, when you last parted from him, only after considerable provocation – or a loving and faithful husband to the full extent of human frailty, or a fearless champion killing off brawny adversaries like flies, or even an emperor crowned with that queer soft gold of Tollan and dragging black corrupted gods about the public highways. In the end you were, none the less, a withered hulk, with no more of pride nor any hope of pleasure nor any real desire alive in you; and you felt cold always, even while you nodded here beside the fire; and there was not anybody to talk to, except those perturbed-looking servants who never came very near you. . . .

If you had only had a son, now, matters might be different. . . . Then Coth recollected that he did, in point of fact, have a son, somewhere. It had slipped his mind for the instant. But old people forget things, and he was very old. Yes, a fine lad, that:

and he would be coming in for supper presently – extremely late for supper, with his hat shoved a great way back on his black head, and with his boots all muddy – and Azra would scold him. . . . Only, it seemed to Coth that Azra, or somebody, was dead. That was a pity, but it was too much trouble to remember all the pity and the dying that was in the world; it was a great deal too much trouble for an old man to keep these wearying matters quite straight in his mind. And, besides, everybody died; there was for all an end of all adventuring: and nothing whatever could be done about it.

Well, but at least one more adventure was yet to come, for the Coth who could make no wheedling compromise with the fictions by which fools live and preserve alike their foolish hopes and their smirking amenities. He had, he felt, been sometimes rather brusque with these fools. But all that was over, too. They went their way; and he was going his. And, once that last adventure had been achieved, you might hope to settle down comfortably with the swaggering and greathearted sinners, and to be stationed not too far from the gray squinting sinner who had been the most dear and admirable of earthly lords; and to foregather with all such fine rogues eternally among the genial and robustious flames, in which there was no more loneliness and no more cold and no more pettifogging talk about some Redeemer or another paying your scot, and where no more frightened servants would be spying on you always. . . .

The adventure came unheralded, for Coth died in his sleep, having outlived the wife of his youth by just four months.

Book Six

In the Sylan's House

*'Is it time for you to dwell in your ceiled
houses, and this house lie waste?'*

HAGGAI, i, 4

Chapter XXXIV

Something Goes Wrong: and Why

Now the tale is of Guivric of Perdigon, more generally called the Sage, who in the days after Anavalt went into Elfhame was chief of the lords of the Silver Stallion who yet remained in Poictesme. And the tale tells how it appeared to Guivric of Perdigon that something was going wrong.

He had not anything tangible to complain of. There was, indeed, no baron in Poictesme more powerful and honored than was Guivric the Sage. He had no need to bother over any notions about Manuel which in no way affected the welfare of Guivric of Perdigon, and he had no quarrel with the more staid and religious ordering of matters which now prevailed in Poictesme. Guivric had, howsoever frostily, adapted himself to these times, and in them a reasonably staid and religious Guivric had, thus, thrived.

As Heitman of Asch, he still held as rigorously as he had held in Manuel's heyday, the fertile Piemontais between the Duardenez river and Perdigon. He had money and two castles, he lived in comeliness and splendor, he had wisdom and a high name and the finest vineyards anywhere in those regions. He had every reason to be proud of his tall prospering son Michael, a depressingly worthy young warrior, whose superabundant virtues, modeled with so much earnestness after the Manuel of the legend, caused Guivric to regard the amours of Michael's wife (and Manuel's daughter) with quiet and unregenerate amusement. And Guivric got on with his own wife as well, he flattered himself, as any person could hope to do upon the more animated side of deafness.

Yet something, this prim and wary Guivric knew, was somewhere going wrong. Things, even such prosaic common things as the chair he was seated in, or his own hands moving before him, were becoming dubious and remote. People spoke with thinner voices: and their bodies flickered now and then, as if these bodies were only appearances of colored vapor. The trees of Guivric's flourishing woodlands would sometimes stretch and flatten in the wind like trails of smoke. The walls of Guivric's fine home at Asch, and of his great fort at Perdigon also, were acquiring, as their conservative owner somewhat frettedly observed, a habit of moving, just by a thread's width, when you were not quite looking at them; and of shifting in outline and in station as secretively as a cloud alters.

Instability and change lurked everywhere. Without any warning well-known faces disappeared from Guivric's stately household: the men-at-arms and the lackeys who remained seemed not to miss them, nor indeed ever to have known of those vanished associates.

And Guivric found that the saga which the best-thought-of local bards had compiled and adorned, under his supervision, so as to preserve for posterity's benefit the glorious exploits and the edifying rewards of Guivric the Sage, was dwindling alike in length and in impressiveness. Overnight a line here and there, or a whole paragraph, would drop out unaccountably, an adventure would lose color, or an achievement would become less clear-cut: and the high and outrageous doings in which Guivric had shared as a lord of the Silver Stallion, these began, in particular, to become almost unrecognisable. At this rate, people would soon have no assurance whatever that Guivric the Sage had lived in unexampled heroism and respectability and had most marvelously prospered in everything.

And it was all quite annoying. It was as though Guivric, or else each one of his possessions and human ties, were wasting away into a phantom: and neither alternative seemed pleasant to consider.

Guivric locked fast the doors of the brown room in which now for so many years he had conducted his studies and his thaumaturgies. He set out a table, the top of which was inscribed with three alphabets. He put on a robe of white: about his withered neck he arranged a garland of purple vervain such as is called herb-of-the-cross. From seven rings he selected – because this day was a Sunday – the gold ring inset with a chrysolite upon which was engraved the figure of a lion-headed serpent.

When this ring had been hung above the table, with a looped red hair plucked long ago from the tail of a virgin nightmare, and when the wan Lady of Crossroads had been duly invoked, then Guivric lighted a taper molded from the fat of Saracen women and of unweaned dogs, and with the evil flaming of his taper he set fire to the looped hair. The red hair burned with a small spiteful sizzling: the gold ring fell. The ring rolled about upon the table, it uncoiled, it writhed, it moved glitteringly among the characters of three alphabets, passing like a tortured worm from one ideograph to another, and it revealed to Guivric the dreadful truth.

The Sylan whom people called Glaum-Without-Bones was at odds with Guivric. This was not a matter which anybody blessed with intelligent self-interest could afford to neglect.

Chapter XXXV

Guivric's Journey

Certainly Guivric the Sage, who cared only for himself, did not neglect this matter. The prim and wary man armed, and rode eastward, beyond Megaris; and fared steadily ever further into the East, traveling beyond the Country of Widows and the fearful Isle of the Ten Carpenters. Then, at Oskander's Well, Guivric put off material armor. He put off even his helmet, and in its stead he assumed a cap of owl feathers. He passed through arid high pastures, beyond the wall of the Sassanid, he rubbed lemon juice upon his horse's legs and rode unmolested through the broad and shallow lake, and thus came to the Sylan's House. And all went well enough at first.

Guivric had feared, for one thing, that the Norns would forbid his entering into the mischancy place: but when he had tethered safely the fine horse which Guivric was never again to ride upon, he found that the gray weavers did not hinder him. They had not ever, they said, planned any future for Guivric: and it was all one to them whether he fared forward to face his own destruction or intrepidly went back to living with his wife.

'But do you not weave the sagas and the dooms of all men?' he asked of them.

'Not yours,' lean Skuld replied, looking up at him with pallid little cold bright eyes.

Guivric thus passed the haggard daughters of Dvalinn; and the proud man went onward, disquieted but unhindered. And in the gray anteroom beyond, were the progenitors of Guivric disporting themselves, each in the quaint manner of his bygone day, and talking with uneager and faded voices about the old times.

Since none of these ancestors had ever heard or thought of Guivric, they gave scant attention to him now. And to see them was upsetting, somehow. One of these strangers had Guivric's high thin nose, and another just his long thin hands, and another his prim mouth, and another his excellent broad shoulders. Guivric could recognise all these fragments of himself moving at random about the gray room. He knew that, less visibly but quite as really, his tastes and his innate aversions – his little talents and failings and out-of-date loyalties, his quickness at figures, his aptitude for drawing, his tendency to catch cold easily, and his liking for sweets and highly seasoned foods – were all passing about this gray room.

A compost of odds and ends had been patched together from these unheeding persons; that almost accidental patchwork was Guivric; the thought was humiliating. There was, he reflected, in this gray room another complete Guivric, only this other Guivric was not entire, but moved about in scattered fragments. That thought appeared, to a peculiarly self-centred person like Guivric, rather uncomfortable.

So Guivric went beyond his ancestors. Without delay the proud man passed stiffly by the inconsiderate people whose casual amours had created him, and had given him life and all his qualities, without consulting his preference or his convenience, or even thinking about him.

Chapter XXXVI

The Appointed Enemy

He came to a door beside which a saturnine castrato sat drowsing over a scythe. Guivric caught him intrepidly by the forelock; and tugging at it, thus forced the gaunt warden in his pain to cry out, 'Enough!'

'For time enough is little enough,' said Guivric, 'and when you are little enough, I can go safely by without killing time here. And that I shall certainly do, because to spare time is to lengthen life.'

'Come, come now,' grumbled the ancient warden, 'but these tonsorial freedoms and this foolish talking seem very odd – '

'Time,' Guivric answered him, 'at last sets all things even.'

Then Guivric walked widdershins in a complete circle about the old eunuch; and so went on into a room hung with black and silver: and in this place was a young and beautifully fashioned boy, with the bright unchanging gaze of a serpent.

The boy arose; and, putting aside a rod upon which grew black poppies, each with a silver-colored heart, he said to Guivric, 'It is needful that you should hate.'

Now, at the sight of this stranger, Guivric was filled with an inexplicable wild rapture; and after shaping the sign of the River Horse and of the Writing of Lo, he demanded of this young man his name.

But the other only answered: 'I am your appointed enemy. There is between us an eternal hatred; and should our bodies encounter we would contend as heroes. But something has gone wrong, our sagas have been perverted, and our spirits have been ensnared into the Sylan's House, and all our living wears thin.'

'Come, come, my enemy!' cried Guivric, 'hatred – since, as you tell me, this is hatred – is throbbing in me now as a drum beats: and I would that we two might encounter!'

'That may not be,' replied the young man. 'I am only a

phantom in the Sylan's House. I live as a new-born child in Denmark, I drowse as yet in swaddling cloths, dreaming at this instant about my appointed enemy. Yet in the life which you now have you will not ever go to Denmark: and by the time that I am grown, and am able to wield a sword and to contrive mischief against you, and to beset you everywhere with my lewd perversities, the body which you now have will have been taken away from you.'

'I am sorry,' Guivric said, 'for in all my life, even in the rough old times of that blundering Manuel – I mean, of course, that, although I was privileged to share in the earthly labors of the Redeemer, in all my life I have never hated before today. I have merely disliked some persons, somewhat as I dislike cold veal or house-flies, without real ardor. And very often these persons could be useful to me, so that, through many little flatteries and small falsehoods, I must keep on their good side. But I perceive now that, throughout the living which my neighbors applaud and envy, I have needed some tonic adversary to exalt my living with a great heroic loathing.'

'I know, dear adversary! And I know too that all the life which I now have must run slack because of an unfed lusting for my appointed enemy. But affairs will go more grandly by and by, if ever we get out of the Sylan's House.'

'Heyday,' said Guivric, masterfully, 'I am not going out! Instead, I am going in, even to the heart of this mischancy place; and you must go with me.'

But the lad shook his lovely evil head. 'No: for, now that the Sylan is about to become human, they tell me, at the heart of the Sylan's House is to be found pity and terror; and both of these must remain forever unknown to me.'

'Well, but why?' said Guivric, 'why need those two cathartics which Aristotle most highly recommends remain forever unknown to you in particular?'

'Ah,' replied the boy, 'that is a mystery. I only know it is decreed – and is decreed, for that matter, in the name of Eloim, Muthraton, Adonay, and Semiphoras – that my rod here as it was first raised up in Gomorrah should possess quite other virtues than the rods of Moses and of Jacob.'

'Oh, in Gomorrah! So it was in that wicked city of the plain

of Jordan, my spoiled child, that they first spared the rod! I
see. For is not that rod to be used – thus?'

And Guivric showed with discreet but obvious gesture what he
meant.

The lad fearlessly answered him.

Chapter XXXVII

Too Many Mouths

So Guivric quitted his appointed enemy. And at the next door sat a discomfortable looking dyspeptic, crowned and wearing an old shroud, and huddled up, as if by spasms of pain, upon a tombstone, very neatly engraved with the arms and the name and the parentage and the titles of Guivric of Perdigon. Only the date and the manner of Guivric's decease remained as yet vacant. And the crowned toiler put aside his chisel, and he grinned at Guivric rather pitiably.

'I really must be more careful,' observed this second warden groaning and fidgeting and shaking his fleshless head, but of necessity grinning all the while, because he had no lips. 'I am decreed, you see, to keep no measure in my diet; I must eat sheep as well as lambs; and afterward I find out only too plainly that there is not any medicine for death.'

Guivric, without a word of condolence, took out of his pocket a handful of coins, and he selected from among the thalers and pistoles a newly minted mark. This coin he tendered to the second warden, and the tomb-maker accepted lovingly this shining mark. Then Guivric walked widdershins in a circle about this warden also: and when the king of terrors had been thus circumvented, Guivric went forward into the next room. A sweet and piercing and heavy odor now went with Guivric, and clung to him, and it was like the odor of embalming spices.

This room was hung with white and gold; and in this room a plump and naked man, wearing only a miter, was praying to nine gods. He arose and, after brushing off his reddened knees, he said to Guivric, 'It is needful that you should believe.'

'I wish to believe,' replied Guivric. 'Yet when I ask – Well, but you know what always happens.'

'Such, my dear errant son, is the accustomed punishment of

unhallowed curiosity. It should, equally, be looked for and overlooked. The important thing is to believe.'

Guivric smiled rather bleakly now, beneath his cap of owl feathers. He said, like one who repeats a familiar ritual, 'What should I believe?'

Upon the arms and upon the chest and upon the belly, and everywhere upon the naked body of the mitered man, opened red and precise-looking mouths, and each mouth answered Guivric's question differently, and in the while that they all spoke together no one of these answers was clear. The utmost which Guivric could distinguish in the confusion was the piping babblement about Manuel the Redeemer. Then the mouths ended their speaking, and closed, and became invisible. The mitered man now seemed like any other benevolent gentleman in the middle years of a well-fed existence, and he was no longer horrible.

'You see,' said Guivric, with a shrug. 'You see what always happens. I ask, and I am answered. Afterward I am impressed by the unusual phenomena, and I am slightly nauseated: but I, none the less, do not know which one of your countless mouths I should put faith in, and so bribe it to smile at me and prophesy good things.'

'That does not matter at all, my son. You have but to believe in whatsoever divine revealment you prefer as to what especial Redeemer will come tomorrow, and then you will live strongly and happily, you will go no longer as a phantom in the Sylan's House.'

'Heyday!' said Guivric, 'but it is you who are the phantom and not I!'

The other for a moment was silent. Then he too shrugged. 'With secular opinions as to such unimportant and wholly personal matters no belief is concerned.'

'I,' Guivric pointed out, 'do not think this an unimportant matter. At all events, each one of your mouths speaks to me with the same authority and resonance: and in consequence, I can hear none of them.'

'Well, well!' said the plump mitered man, resignedly, 'that sometimes happens, they tell me, when the Sylan is at odds with anybody. But, for one, I keep away from the Sylan, now that the Sylan is about to become human, because I suspect that at the heart of the Sylan's House abides that which is too pitiable and too terrible for any of my mouths to aid.'

'I do not know about your aiding such things or any other things,' replied Guivric. 'But I do know that, even though you dare not accompany me, I intend to match my thaumaturgies against the Sylan's magic; and that we shall very shortly see what comes of it.'

Chapter XXXVIII

The Appointed Lover

Now at the next door sat a fierce and jealous destroyer, with a waned glory about his venerable Semitic head. The upper half of him was like amber, his lower parts shone as if with a fading fire. He seemed forlorn and unspeakably outworn. He looked without love at Guivric, saying 'AHIH ASHR AHIH.'

'No deity could put it fairer than that, sir,' replied Guivric. 'I respect the circumstances. Nevertheless, I have made a note of your number, and it is five hundred and forty-three.'

Then about this warden also Guivric walked widdershins, in a complete circle.

'Issachar is a large-limbed ass,' said Guivric, soberly. 'He has become a servant under taskwork. Yet his is the circumambulation.'

Whereafter Guivric still went onward, into the next room: and Guivric's feet now glittered each with a pallid halo, for in that instant he had trodden very near to God, and glory clung to them.

And in this room, which was hung with green and rose-color, white pigeons were walking about and eating barley. In the midst of the room a woman was burning violets and white rose- petals and olive wood in a new earthen dish. She arose from this employment, smiling. And her loveliness was not a matter of mere color and shaping, such as may be found elsewhere in material things: rather, was this loveliness a light which lived and was kindly. If there was a fault in this woman it was not apparent to the eyes of Guivric; nor would, whatever his eyes had reported, his heart have admitted the existence of any fault.

Now this dear woman too began, 'It is needful – '

'I think it is not at all needful, madame, to explain what human faculty you would exhort me to exercise.'

Guivric said this with a gallant frivolity: and yet he was trembling.

And after a while of looking at him somewhat sadly, the woman asked, 'Do you not, then, remember me?'

'It is a strange thing, madame,' he answered, 'it is a very strange thing that I should so poignantly remember you whom I have not ever seen before today. For I am shaken by old and terrible memories, I am troubled by the greatness of ancient losses not ever to be atoned for, in the exact moment that I cannot, for the life of me, say what these memories and these losses are.'

'You have loved me – not once, but many times, my appointed lover.'

'I have loved a number of women, madame – although I have of course avoided giving rise to any regrettable scandal. And it has been very pleasant to love women without annoying the prejudices of their recognised and legitimate proprietors. It enables one to combine physical with mental exercise. But this is not pleasant. To the contrary I am frightened. I am become as a straw in a wide and rapid river: I am indulging in no pastime: that which is stronger than I can imagine is hurrying me toward that of which I am ignorant.'

'I know,' she answered. 'Time upon time it has been so with us. But something has gone wrong – '

'What has happened, madame, is that the Sylan is at odds with me; and covets, so my dactyliomancy informed me, some one thing or it may be two things which I possess.'

"The Sylan is about to become human. That is why your saga has been perverted, and that is the reason of your having been ensnared as a phantom into the Sylan's House – '

'Eh, then, and do you also, madame, dismiss me as a phantom!'

'Why, but of course no person's body may enter into this mischancy place! The body which I have today, my appointed lover, is that of a very old woman in Cataia, nodding among my body's many children and grandchildren, and dreaming of the love this life has denied to me. It is a blotched and shriveled body, colored like a rotting apple: and the bodies which we now have may not ever encounter. So all our living wears thin, and the lives that we now have must both be wasted tepidly, as a lukewarm water is poured out: and there is now no help for it, now that the Sylan is at odds with you.'

'I go to match my thaumaturgies against his magic,' said Guivric stoutly.

'You go, my dearest, to face that thing which is most pitiable and terrible of all things that be! You go to face your own destruction!'

'Nevertheless,' said Guivric. 'I go.'

Yet still he looked at this woman. And Guivric's thin hard lips moved restively. He sighed. He turned away and went on silently. His face could not be seen under his cap of owl feathers, but his broad shoulders sagged a little.

Chapter XXXIX

One Warden Left Uncircumvented

Beside the next door lay a huge white stallion. And as Guivric approached this door, it opened. Through the brown curtains came that ambiguous young man called Horvendile, with whom Guivric, off and on, had held considerable traffic during a forty years' practice of thaumaturgies.

The stallion now arose, before Guivric could walk widdershins about him, and the stallion went statelily away. And Horvendile gazed after the superb beast, rather wistfully.

'He, too,' said Horvendile, 'goes as a phantom here. Is it not a pity, Guivric, that this Kalki will not come in our day, and that we shall not ever behold his complete glory? I cry a lament for that Kalki who will some day bring back to their appointed places high faith and very ardent loves and hatreds; and who will see to it that human passions are never in a poor way to find expression with adequate speech and action. Ohé, I cry a loud lament for Kalki! The little silver effigies which his postulants fashion and adore are well enough: but Kalki is a horse of another color.'

'I did not come into this accursed place to talk about horses and nightmares,' replied Guivric, 'but to attend to the righting of the wrongs contrived by one Glaum-Without-Bones, who is at odds with me, and who has perverted my saga.'

Now Horvendile reflected for an instant. He said, 'You have then, after so many years, come of your own will into the East, just as I prophesied, to face the most pitiable and terrible of all things?'

Guivric answered, guardedly, 'I cannot permit my saga to be perverted.'

Horvendile said then: 'Nevertheless, I consider the saga of no lord of the Silver Stallion to be worth squabbling over. Your sagas in the end must all be perverted and engulfed by the great legend about Manuel. No matter how you may strive against that legend, it will conquer: no matter what you may do and suffer, my doomed Guivric, your saga will be recast until it conforms in everything to the legend begotten by the terrified imaginings of a lost child. For men dare not face the universe with no better backing than their own resources; all men that live, and that go perforce about this world like blundering lost children whose rescuer is not yet in sight, have a vital need to believe in this sustaining legend about the Redeemer: and the wickedness and the foolishness of no man can avail against the foolishness and the fond optimism of mankind.'

'These aphorisms,' Guivric conceded, 'may be judicious, they may be valuable, they may even have some kernel somewhere of rational meaning. But, in any case, they do not justify my living's having been upset and generally meddled with by a lecherous and immodest Sylan who goes about wearing not even a skeleton.'

Horvendile replied: 'I can see no flaw in your way of living. You are the chief of Emmerick's barons now that Anavalt is gnawed bones in Elfhame: you have wealth and rather more than as much power as Emmerick himself, now that your son is Emmerick's brother-in-law, and poor Emmerick is married to a widow. You are a well-thought-of thaumaturgist, and you are, indeed, excelled in your art by nobody since Miramon Lluagor's death. And you have also, they tell me, a high name for wisdom and for learning now that Kerin has gone down under the earth. What more can anybody ask.'

'I ask for much more than for this sort of cautious and secondary excellence.' Guivric seemed strangely desperate. He spoke now, with a voice which was not in anything prim and wary, saying, 'I ask for the man whom I can hate, for the priest whom I can believe, and for the woman whom I can love!'

But Horvendile shook his red curls, and he smiled a little cruelly. 'Successful persons, my poor careful Guivric, cannot afford to have any of these luxuries. And one misses them. I know. The Sylan too is, in his crude naïve way, a successful person. He is now almost human. He cherishes phantoms, therefore, and I suspect these phantoms have been troubling you with their nonsense, since it is well known that all illusions haunt the corridors of this mischancy place into which phantoms alone may enter.'

'Yet I have entered it,' Guivric pointed out.

'Yes,' Horvendile said, non-committally.

'And I now enter,' Guivric stated, 'to the heart of it, to match my thaumaturgies against the Sylan's magic.'

Chapter XL

Economics of Glaum-Without-Bones

Then Guivric passed through this door likewise; and so, with glowing feet and with an odor of funeral spices, Guivric came into the room in which was the Sylan. Glaum-Without-Bones looked up from his writing, tranquilly. Glaum said nothing: he merely smiled. All was quiet.

Guivric noticed a strange thing, and it was that this room was hung with brown and was furnished with books and pictures which had a familiar seeming. And then he saw that this room was in everything like the brown room at Asch in which now for so many years he had conducted his studies and his thaumaturgies; and that in this mischancy place, for all his arduous traveling beyond the Country of Widows and the fearful Isle of the Ten Carpenters and the high Wall of the Sassanid, here you still saw, through well-known windows, the familiar country about Asch and the gleaming of the Duardenez river, and beyond this the long plain of Amneran and the tall Forest of Acaire. And Guivric saw that this Glaum-Without-Bones, who sat there smiling up at Guivric, from under a cap of owl feathers, had in everything the appearance of the aging man who had so long sat in this room; and that Glaum-Without-Bones did not differ in anything from Guivric the Sage.

Guivric spoke first. He said:

'This is a strong magic. This is a sententious magic. They had warned me that I would here face my own destruction, that I would here face the most pitiable and terrible of all things: and I face here that which I have made of life, and life of me. I shudder; I am conscious of every appropriate sentiment. Nevertheless, sir, I must venture the suggestion that mere, explicit allegory as a form of art is somewhat obsolete.'

Glaum-Without-Bones replied: 'What have I to do with forms of art? My need was of a form of flesh and blood. I had need of a human body and of human ties and of a human saga of the Norn's most ruthless weaving. We Sylans have our powers and our privileges, but we are not the children of any god; and so, when we have lived out our permitted centuries, we must perish utterly unless we can contrive to become human. Therefore I had sore need of all human discomforts, so that a soul might sprout in me under oppression and chastening, and might, upon fair behavior, be preserved in eternal bliss, and not ever perish as we Sylans perish.'

'Everybody has heard of these familiar facts about you Sylans,' returned Guivric, impatiently, 'and it is your stealing, in this shabby fashion, of my own particular human ties that I consider unheard-of – '

'Yes, yes,' said Glaum, with some complacence, 'that was done through a rare magic, and through a strong magic, and through a magic against which there is no remedy.'

'That we shall see about! For what has happened to me is not fair – '

'Of course it is not,' Glaum assented. 'The doom which is now upon you is no fairer than the doom which was upon me yesterday, to perish utterly like a weed or an old tomcat.'

' – And so I have come hither to match my resistless thaumaturgies against your piddling magic, and to compel you to restore to me your pilferings – '

'I shall restore to you,' Glaum stated, 'nothing. And I have taken all. Your saga is now my saga, your castles are my castles, your son is my son, and your body is my body. Inside that body I intend to live self-mortifyingly and virtuously, for some ten years or so; and then that body will die: but by that time a soul will have sprouted in me, an immortal soul which, you may be certain, I shall keep stainless, because I at least know how to appreciate such a remunerative bit of property. Thus, when your tomb becomes my tomb, that soul will of course ascend to eternal bliss.'

'But what,' said Guivric, scornfully, 'what if I do not consent to be robbed of the salvation assured to me by sixty years of careful and respectable living? And what if I compel you – ?'

'I think that, in your sorry case, you should not speak of

compelling anybody to do anything. Nor is it altogether my doing that your house is now the Sylan's House. Self-centered and self-righteous man, you had no longer any strength nor real desires, but only many little habits. Nothing at all solid remained really yours, not even when I first set about my magicking. Oho, and then you were an easy prey! and the human ties you held so lightly slipped very lightly away from you who had so long been living without any love or hatred or belief. For throughout that overcomfortable while the strength and the desire had been oozing out of you, and all your living wore thin. I had only to complete the emaciation. And in consequence' – Glaum gestured, rather gracefully, with Guivric's long thin hands – 'in consequence, you go as a phantom.'

Guivric saw this was regrettably true. He saw it was as a slight grayish mist, through which he was looking down unhindered at the familiar rug behind him, that he now wavered and undulated in the midst of this room in which he had for so many years pursued his studies without a hint of such levity. Yet nothing was changed. Guivric of Perdigon still sat there, behind the oak table with copper corners. Guivric of Perdigon kept his accustomed place, palpable and prim and wary, as vigorous as could be hoped for at his age, and honored and well-to-do, and, in fine, with nothing left to ask for, as men estimate prosperity.

And the living of this Guivric was reasonably assured of going on like that, for year after year, quite comfortably, and with people everywhere applauding, and with nothing anywhere alluring you toward any rash excesses in the way of emotion. It was from this established and looked-up-to sort of living that a nefarious Sylan was planning to oust Guivric the Sage; and to leave Guivric a mere phantom, a thing as transitory and as disreputable – and of course, in a manner of speaking, as free too, and as lusty and as ageless – as the Sylan's self had been only yesterday. . . . For those abominable thieves and ravishers of maidens did not grow old and vigorless and tired: instead, when the appointed hour had struck, they vanished. . . .

'Well, well!' said Guivric, and he now flickered into a sitting posture, more companionably. 'This sort of eviction from every human tie is unexpected and high-handed and deplorable and so on. But we ought, even when all else is being lost, to retain composure.'

The Sylan let him talk. . . .

And Guivric went on: 'So, you are indissuadably resolved, at the cost of any possible conflict between my thaumaturgies and your magic, to leave me just a disembodied intelligence! Do you know, Messire Glaum, I cannot quite regard it as a compliment, that you refuse to take over my intelligence! Yet you, no doubt, prefer your own intelligence —'

The Sylan let him talk. . . .

But Guivric had paused. For the Sylan's intelligence had, after all, enabled Glaum to acquire — through howsoever irregular methods — the utmost that a reasonable mind could look for in the way of success and comfort and of future famousness long after Glaum-Without-Bones had ascended to the eternal bliss assured by a careful and respectable past. The Sylan's intelligence had gained for him the very best that any man could hope for. There was thus no firm ground, after all, upon which any human being could disrespect the Sylan's intelligence. . . . It was only that these Sylans, always so regrettably lewd and spry, did not ever grow old and tired and vigorless: they did not ever, except of their own volition, become disgustingly smug-looking old prigs: instead, when the appointed hour had struck, they vanished.

' — For your intelligence appears to me a very terrible sort of intelligence,' Guivric continued, 'and I have no doubt that your magic is upon a plane with it. My little thaumaturgies could have no chance whatever against such magic and such intelligence. Oh, dear me, no! So I concede my helplessness, Messire Glaum, without mounting the high and skittish horse of virtuous indignation. I avoid the spectacle of an unseemly wrangle between fellow artists: and, in asking you to restore to me the customary rewards of a thrifty and virtuous and in every way prosperous existence, I can but appeal to your mercy.'

'I,' said the Sylan, 'have none.'

'So I had hoped' — here Guivric coughed. 'Anguish, sheer anguish, sir, deprives me of proper control of my tongue. For I had of course meant to say,' Guivric continued, upon a more tragic note — 'so I had hoped in vain! Now every hope is gone.

Henceforward you are human, and I am only an unhonored vague Sylan! Well, it is all very terrible; but nothing can be done about it, I suppose.'

'Nothing whatever can be done about it – unless you prefer to court something worse with those thaumaturgies of yours?'

Guivric was pained. 'But, between fellow artists!' he stared. 'Oh, no, dear Glaum, that sort of open ostentatious rivalry, for merely material gains, seems always rather regrettably vulgar.'

'Why, then, if you will pardon me,' the Sylan submitted, in Guivric's most civil manner when dealing with unimportant persons, 'I shall ask to be excused from prolonging our highly enjoyable chat. Some other time, perhaps – But I really am quite busy this morning: and, besides, our wife will be coming in here any minute, to call me to dinner.'

'I shall not intrude.' Vaporously arising, Guivric now smiled, with a new flavor of sympathy. 'A rather terrible woman, that, you will find! And, Lord, how a young Guivric did adore her once! Nowadays she is one of the innumerous reasons which lead me to question if you have been quite happily inspired, even with the delights of heaven impendent. You see, she is certainly going to heaven. And Michael too – do you know, I think you will find Michael, also, something of a bore? He expects so much of his father, and when those expectations seem imperiled he does look at you so exactly like a hurt, high-minded cow! Now it is you who will have to live up to his notions, and to the notions of that fond, fretful, foolish woman, and it is you who will be bothered with an ever-present sense of something lost and betrayed. . . . But you will live up to their idiotic notions, none the less! And I do not doubt that, just as you say, the oppression and the chastening will be good for you.'

The Sylan answered, sternly, 'Poor shallow learned selfish fool! It is that love and pride, it is their faith and their jealousy to hide away your shortcomings, it is the things you feebly jeer at, which will create in me a soul!'

'No doubt – ' Then Guivric went on hastily, and in a tone of cordial encouragement. 'Oh, yes, my dear fellow, there is not a doubt of it! and I am sure you will find the birth-pangs well rewarded. Heaven, everybody tells me, is a most charming place. Meanwhile, if you do not mind, just for a minute, pray do not contort my face so unbecomingly until after I am quite gone! To see what right thinking and a respectably inflated impatience with frivolity can make of my face, and has so often made of my face,' reflected Guivric, as he luxuriously drifted out of the familiar window like a smoke, 'is even now a little humiliating. But, then, the most salutary lessons are invariably the most shocking.'

Chapter XLI

The Gratifying Sequel

Thus the true Guivric passed beyond the knowledge of men: and the false Guivric gathered up his papers and took off his cap of owl-feathers and prepared for dinner.

The wife and the son of Guivric from that time forth delighted in his affection and geniality: and it was observed, for another wonder, that Guivric of Perdigon had, with increasing age, graduated from a cool reserve about religious matters into very active beneficence and piety. The legend of Manuel had nowhere, now, a more fervent adherent and expounder, because Glaum nourished his sprouting soul with every sort of religious fertiliser. Nor was his loving-kindness confined to talking about itself, for the good works of Glaum were untiring and remarkably free-handed, since he had everything to gain by being liberal with Guivric's property.

The old gentleman thus became a marked favorite with Holy Holmendis: and indeed it was Glaum who at this time, when Guivric's ancient comrade Kerin of Nointel came back into Poictesme, chiefly assisted Holmendis in converting Kerin to the great legend of Manuel.

In fine, Glaum lived, without detection, in Guivric's body; and preserved it in unquestioned virtue, since a well-to-do nobleman is, after sixty, subject to very few temptations which cannot be gratified quietly without scandal. He died in the assurance of a blessed resurrection, which he no doubt attained.

As for the true Guivric, nothing more was ever quite definitely known of him. It was remarked, however, that for many years thereafter an amorous devil went invisibly about the hill country behind Perdigon. The girls of Valnères and Ogde reported that by three traits alone could the presence of this demon be detected: for one thing, he diffused a sweet and poignant odor, not unlike that of an embalmer's spiceries; and, for another, the soles of his

feet had been observed, after dusk, to be luminous. A third
infallible sign of his being anywhere near youthey, with blushes
and some giggling, declined to reveal.

Book Seven

What Saraïde Wanted

'None shall want her mate.'
ISAIAH, XXXIV, 16

Chapter XLII

Generalities at Ogde

Now the tale tells that it was in the winter after Guivric's encounter with the Sylan that Kerin of Nointel returned into Poictesme to become yet another convert to the great legend of Manuel; and tells also of how for the first time men learned why and in what fashion Kerin had gone out of Poictesme.

Therefore the tale harks back to very ancient days, in the May month which followed the passing of Manuel, and the tale speaks of a season wherein it appeared to Kerin of Nointel that he could understand his third wife no better than he had done the others. But for that perhaps unavoidable drawback to matrimony, he was then living comfortably enough with this Saraïde, whom many called a witch, in her ill-spoken-of eight-sided home beside the notorious dry Well of Ogde. This home was gray, with a thatched roof upon which grew abundant mosses and many small wild plants; a pair of storks nested on the gable; and elder-trees shaded all.

It was a very quiet and peaceful place, in which, so Kerin estimated, two persons might well have lived in untroubled serenity, now that the Fellowship of the Silver Stallion was disbanded, and a younger Kerin's glorious warfaring under Dom Manuel was done with forever.

Mild-mannered, blinking Kerin, for one, did not regret Dom Manuel's passing. The man had kept you fighting always, whether it was with the Easterlings or the Northmen, or with Othmar Black-Tooth or with old yellow Sclaug or with Manuel's father, blind Oriander. It was a life which left you no time whatever for the pursuit of any culture. Kerin liked fighting, within moderation, with persons of admitted repute. But Kerin, after four years of riding into all quarters of the earth at the behest of this never-resting Manuel, was heartily tired of killing strangers in whom Kerin was in no way interested.

So, upon the whole, it was a relief to be rid of Manuel and to be able once more to marry, and to settle down at Ogde in the eight-sided house under the elder-trees. Yet, even in this lovely quietude, the tale repeats, the third wife of Kerin seemed every night to bother herself, and in consequence her husband, about a great many incomprehensible matters.

Now of the origin of Saraïde nothing can here be told with profit and decorum: here it is enough to say that an ambiguous parentage had provided this Saraïde with a talisman by which you might know the truth when truth was found. And one of the many things about Kerin's wife which Kerin could not quite understand, was her constant complaining that she had not found out assuredly the truth about anything, and, in particular, the truth as to Saraïde.

'I exist,' she would observe to her husband, 'and I am in the main as other women. Therefore, this Saraïde is very certainly a natural phenomenon. And in nature everything appears to be intended for this, that or the other purpose. Indeed, after howsoever hasty consideration of the young woman known as Saraïde, one inevitably deduces that so much of loveliness and wit and aspiration, of color and perfume and tenderness, was not put together haphazardly; and that the compound was painstakingly designed to serve some purpose or another purpose. It is about that purpose I want knowledge.'

And Kerin would reply, 'As you like, my dear.'

So this young Saraïde, whom many called a witch, had sought, night after night, for the desired knowledge, in widely various surroundings, from the clergy, from men of business, from poets, and from fiends; and had wakened in her talisman every color save only that golden shining which would proclaim her capture of the truth. This clear soft yellow ray, as she explained to Kerin, would have to be evoked, if ever, in the night season, because by day its radiance might pass unnoticed and her perception of the truth be lost.

Kerin could understand the common-sense of this, at any rate. And so young Saraïde was unfailingly heartened in all such nocturnal experiments by the encouragement of her fond husband.

'And do not be discouraged, wife,' he would exhort her, as he was now exhorting, upon this fine spring evening, 'for women and their belongings are, beyond doubt, of some use or another, which by and by will be discovered. Meanwhile, my darling, what were you saying there is for supper? For that at least is a matter of real importance – '

But Saraïde said only, in that quick, inconsequential childish way of hers. 'O Kerin of my heart, I do so want to know the truth about this, and about all other matters!'

'Come, come, Saraïde! let us not despair about the truth, either; for they tell me that truth lies somewhere at the bottom of a well, and at virtually the door of our home is a most notable if long dried well. Our location is thus quite favourable, if we but keep patience. And sooner or later the truth comes to light, they tell me, also – out of, it may be, the darkness of this same abandoned Well of Ogde – because truth is mighty and will prevail.'

'No doubt,' said Saraïde: 'but throughout all the long while between now and then, my Kerin, you will be voicing just such sentiments!'

'– For truth is stranger than fiction. Yes, and as Lactantius tells us, truth will sometimes come even out of the devil's mouth.'

Saraïde fidgeted. And what now came out of her own angelic mouth was a yawn.

'Truth is not easily found,' her Kerin continued. 'The truth is hard to come to: roses and truth have thorns about them.'

'Perhaps,' said Saraïde. 'But against banalties a married woman has no protection whatever!'

'Yet truth,' now Kerin went on with his kindly encouragement, 'may languish, but can never perish. Isidore of Seville records the fine saying that, though malice may darken truth, it cannot put it out.'

'Husband of mine,' said Saraïde, 'sometimes I find your wisdom such that I wonder how I ever came to marry you!'

But Kerin waved aside her tribute modestly. 'It is merely that I, too, admire the truth. For truth is the best buckler. Truth never grows old. Truth, in the words of Tertullian, seeks no corners. Truth makes the devil blush.'

'Good Lord!' said Saraïde. And for no reason at all she stamped her foot.

' – So everybody, in whatsoever surroundings, ought to be as truthful as I am now, my pet, in observing that this hour is considerably past our usual hour for supper, and I have had rather a hard day of it – '

But Saraïde had gone from him, as if in meditation, toward the curbing about the great bottomless Well of Ogde. 'Among these general observations, about devils and bucklers and supper time, I find only one which may perhaps be helpful. Truth lies, you tell me, at the bottom of a well just such as this well.'

'That is the contention alike of Cleanthes and of Democritos the derider.'

'May the truth not lie indeed, then, just as you suggested, at the bottom of this identical well? For the Zhar-Ptitza alone knows the truth about all things, and I recall an old legend that the bird who has the true wisdom used to nest in this part of Poictesme.'

Kerin looked over the stone ledge about the great and bottomless Well of Ogde, peering downwards as far as might be. 'I consider it improbable, dear wife, that the Zhar-Ptitza, who is everywhere known to be the most wise and most ancient of birds and of all living creatures, would select such a cheerless looking hole to live in. Still, you never can tell: the wise affect profundity; and this well is known to be deep beyond the knowledge of man. Now nature, as Cicero informs us, *in profundo veritatem penitus abstruserit* – '

'Good Lord!' said Saraïde again, but with more emphasis. 'Do you slip down there, then, like a dear fellow, and find the truth for me.'

Saying this, she clapped both hands to his backside, and she pushed her husband into the great and bottomless Well of Ogde.

Chapter XLIII

Prayer and the Lizard Maids

The unexpectedness of it all, alike of Saraïde's assault and of the astonishing discovery that you could fall for hundreds after hundreds of feet, full upon your head, without getting even a bruise, a little bewildered Kerin when he first sat up at the bottom of the dry well. He shouted cheerily, 'Wife, wife, I am not hurt a bit!' because the fact seemed so remarkably fortunate and so unaccountable.

But at once large stones began to fall everywhere about him, as though Saraïde upon hearing his voice had begun desperately to heave these stones into the well. Kerin thought this an inordinate manner of spurring him onward in the quest of knowledge and truth, because the habitual impetuosity of Saraïde, when thus expressed with cobblestones, would infallibly have been his death had he not sought shelter in the opening he very luckily found to the southwest side. There was really no understanding these women who married you, Kerin reflected, as after crawling for a while upon hands and feet, he came to a yet larger opening, in which he could stand erect.

But this passage led Kerin presently to an underground lake, which filled all that part of the cavern, so that he could venture no farther. Instead, he sat down upon the borders of these gloomy and endless looking waters. He could see these waters because of the many ignes fatui, such as are called corpse candles, which flickered and danced above the dark lake's surface everywhere.

Kerin in such dismal circumstances began to pray. He loyally gave precedence to his own faith, and said, first, all the prayers of his church that he could remember. He addressed such saints as seemed appropriate, and when, after the liveliest representation of Kerin's plight, sixteen of them had failed in any visible way to intervene, then Kerin tried the Angels, Seraphim, Cherubim, Thrones, Dominions, Virtues, Powers, Principalities and Archangels.

Yet later, when no response whatever was vouchsafed by any member of this celestial hierarchy, Kerin inferred that he had no doubt, in falling so far, descended into heretical regions and into the nefarious control of unchristian deities. So he now prayed to all the accursed gods of the heathen that he could remember as being most potent in dark places. He prayed to Aïdoneus the Laughterless, the Much-Receiving, the People-Collecting, the Invincible and the Hateful; to the implacable Kerês, those most dreadful cave-dwellers who are nourished by the blood of slain warriors; to the gloom-roaming Erinnyes, to the Gray-Maids, to the Snatchers, and, most fervently, to Korê, that hidden and very lovely sable-vested Virgin to whom belonged, men said, all the dim underworld.

But nothing happened.

Then Kerin tried new targets for his praying. He addressed himself to Susanoō, that emperor of darkness who was used to beget children by chewing up a sword and spitting out the pieces; to Ekchuah, the Old Black One, who at least chewed nothing with his one tooth; to the red Maruts, patched together from the bits of a shattered divine embryo; to Onniont, the great, horned, brown and yellow serpent, whose lair might well be hereabouts; to Tethra, yet another master of underground places; to Apep also, and to Set, and to Uhat, the Chief of Scorpions; to Camazotz, the Ruler of Bats; to Fenris, the wolf who waited somewhere in a cave very like this cave, against the oncoming time when Fenris would overthrow and devour God the All-Mighty Father; and to Sraosha, who had charge of all worlds during the night season.

And still nothing happened: and Kerin could see only endless looking waters and, above them, those monotonously dancing corpse candles.

Kerin nevertheless well knew, as a loyal son of the Church, the efficacy of prayer; and he now began, in consequence, to pray to the corpse candles, because these might, he reflected, rank as deities in this peculiarly depressing place. And his comfort was considerable when, after an ave or two, some of these drifting lights came flitting toward him; but his surprise was greater when he saw that each of the ignes fatui was a living creature like a tiny phosphorescent maiden in everything except that each had the head of a lizard.

'What is your nature?' Kerin asked, 'and what are you doing in this cold dark place?'

'Should we answer either of those questions,' one of the small monsters said, in a shrill little voice, as though a cricket were talking, 'it would be the worse for you.'

'Then, by all means, do not answer! Instead, do you tell me if knowledge and truth are to be found hereabouts, for it is of them that I go in search.'

'How should we know? It was not in pursuit of these luxuries that we came hither, very unwillingly.'

'Then, how does one get out of this place?'

Now they all twittered together, and they flittered around Kerin with small squeakings. 'One does not get out of this place.'

Kerin did not cry pettishly, as Saraïde would have done, 'Good Lord!' Instead, he said, 'Dear me!'

'Nor have we any wish to leave this place,' said the small lizard-women. 'These waters hold us here with the dark loveliness of doom; we have fallen into an abiding hatred of these waters; we may not leave them because of our fear. It is not possible for any man to imagine the cruelty of these waters. Therefore we dance above them; and all the while that we dance we think about warmth and food instead of about these waters.'

'And have you no food here nor any warmth, not even brim stone? For I remember that, up yonder in Poictesme, our priests were used to threaten – '

'We do not bother about priests any longer. But a sort of god provides our appointed food.'

'Come, come now, that is much better. For, as I was just saying to my wife, supper is a matter of vital importance, after a hard day of it – But who is this sort of god?'

'We do not know. We only know that he has nineteen names.'

'My very dear little ladies,' said Kerin, 'your information appears so limited, and your brightness so entirely physical, that I now hesitate to ask if you know for what reason somebody is sounding that faroff gong which I can hear?'

'That gong means, sir, that our appointed food is ready.'

'Alas, my friends, but it is quite unbearable,' declared Kerin, 'that food should be upon that side of the dark water, and I, who have had rather a hard day of it, should be upon this side!'

'No, no!' they reassured him, 'it is not unbearable, for we do not mind in the least.'

Then the squeaking little creatures all went away from Kerin, flitting and skimming and twinkling over broad waters which seemed repellently cold and very dreadfully deep. Nevertheless, Kerin, in his desperation – now that no god answered his prayer, and even the ignes fatui had deserted him, and only a great hungering remained with Kerin in the darkness – Kerin now arose and went as a diver speeds into those most unfriendly looking waters.

The result was surprising and rather painful: for as Kerin thus discovered, these waters were not more than two feet in depth. He stood up, a bit sheepishly, dripping wet, and rubbing his head. Then Kerin waded onward in a broad shallow puddle about which there was no conceivable need to bother any god.

Kerin thus came without any hindrance to dry land, and to a place where the shining concourse of lizard-women had already begun to nibble and tug and gulp. But Kerin, after having perceived the nature of their appointed food, and after having shivered, walked on beyond this place, toward the light he detected a little above him.

'For supper,' he observed, 'is a matter of vital importance; and it really is necessary to draw the line somewhere.'

Chapter XLIV

Fine Cordiality of Sclaug

Now Kerin seemed in the dark to be mounting a flight of nineteen stairs. He came thus into a vast gray corridor, inset upon the left side with nineteen alcoves: each alcove was full of books, and beside each alcove stood a lighted, rather large candle as thick about as a stallion's body. And Kerin's surprise was great to find, near the first alcove, that very Sclaug with whom Kerin pleasurably remembered having had so much chivalrous trouble, and such fine combats, before, some years ago, this Sclaug had been killed and painstakingly burned.

Nevertheless, here was the old yellow gentleman intact and prowling about restively on all fours, in just the wolflike fashion he had formerly affected. But after one brief snarl of surprise he stood erect; and, rubbing together the long thin hands which were webbed between the fingers like the feet of a frog, Sclaug asked whatever could have brought Kerin so far down in the world.

For Kerin this instant was a bit awkward, since he knew not quite what etiquette ought to govern re-encounters with persons whom you have killed. Yet Kerin was always as ready as anybody to let bygones be cast off. So Kerin frankly told his tale.

Then Sclaug embraced Kerin, and bade him welcome, and Sclaug laughed with the thin, easy, neighing laughter of the aged.

'As for what occurred at Lorcha, dear Kerin, do not think of it any more than I do. It was in some features unpleasant at the time: but, after all, you burned my body without first driving a stake through my rebellious and invective heart, and so since then I have not lacked amusements. And as for this knowledge and truth of which you go in search, here is all knowledge, in the books that I keep watch over in this Naraka – during the intervals between my little amusements – for a sort of god.'

Kerin scratched among the wiry looking black curls of Kerin's hair, and he again glanced up and down the corridor. 'There are certainly a great many of them. But Saraïde desired, I think, all knowledge, so near as I could understand her.'

'Let us take things in the order of their difficulty,' replied Sclaug. 'Do you acquire all knowledge first, and hope for understanding later.'

The courteous old gentleman then provided Kerin with white wine and with food very gratefully unlike that of the ignes fatui, and Sclaug placed before Kerin one of the books.

'Let us eat first,' said Kerin, 'for supper, in any event, is a matter of vital importance, where knowledge and truth may turn out to be only a womanish whim.'

He ate. Then Kerin began comfortably to read, after, as he informed Sclaug, rather a hard day of it.

Now the book which Kerin had was the book written by the patriarch Abraham in the seventy-first year of his age: and by and by Kerin looked up from it, and said, 'Already I have learned from this book one thing which is wholly true.'

'You progress speedily!' answered Sclaug. 'That is very nice.'

'Well,' Kerin admitted, 'such is one way of describing the matter. But no doubt other things are equally true: and optimism, anyhow, costs nothing.'

Chapter XLV

The Gander Also
Generalizes

So began a snug life for Kerin. The nineteen candles remained always as he had first seen them, tranquilly lighting the vast windless corridor, burning, but not ever burning down, nor guttering, nor even needing to be snuffed: and Kerin worked his way from one candle to another, as Kerin read each book in every alcove. When Kerin was tired he slept: all the while that he waked he gave to acquiring knowledge: he had no method nor any necessity of distinguishing between his daily and his nocturnal studies.

Sclaug went out and came back intermittently, bringing food for Kerin. Sclaug returned as a rule with blood upon his lips and chin. When Sclaug was away, Kerin had to make the best – a poor best – of the company of the garrulous large gander which lived in the brown cage.

Then, also, unusual creatures, many of them not unlike men and women, would come sometimes, during these absences of Sclaug – whom, for some reason or another, they seemed to dislike – and they invoked the gander, and paid his price, and ceremonies would ensue. Ever-busy Kerin could not, of course, spare from his reading much time to notice these ornithomantic and probably pagan rites. Yet he endured such interruptions philosophically; because, at least, he reflected, they put an end for that while to the gander's perilously sweet and most distracting singing.

And several years thus passed; and Kerin had no worries in any manner to interrupt him except the gander. That inconsiderate bird insisted upon singing, with a foolish, damnable sort of charm; and so, was continually checking Kerin's pursuit of knowledge, with anserine rhapsodies about beauty and mystery and holiness and heroism and immortality, and about a variety of other unscientific matters.

'For life is very marvellous,' this gander was prone to remark, 'and to the wonders of earth there is no end appointed.'

'Well, I would not say that, precisely,' Kerin would reply, good-temperedly looking up for the while from his book, 'because geology has made great progress of late. And so, Messire Gander, I would not say quite that. Rather, I would say that Earth is a planet infested with the fauna best suited to survive in this particular stage of the planet's existence. In any case, I finished long ago with earth, and with all ordinary terrestrial phenomena, such as earthquakes, and the formation of continents, and elevation of islands, and with stars and meteorics and with cosmography in general.'

' – And of all creatures man is the most miraculous – '

'The study of anthropology is of course important. So I have learned too about man, his birth and organisation, his invention and practice of the arts, his polities at large, and about the sidereal influences which control the horoscope and actions of each person as an individual.'

' – A child of god, a brother to the beasts – !'

'Well, now, I question too the scientific value of the zoömorphism: yet the facts about beasts, I admit, are interesting. For example, there are two kinds of camels; the age of the stag can be told by inspection of his horns; the period of gestation among sheep is one hundred and fifty days; and in the tail of the wolf is a small lock of hair which is a supreme love charm.'

'You catalogue, poor Kerin,' said the gander; 'you collect your bits of knowledge as a magpie gathers shining pebbles; you toil through one book to another book as methodically as a worm gnaws out the same advance: but you learn nothing, in the wasted while that your youth goes.'

'To the contrary, I am at this very moment learning,' replied Kerin, 'I am learning about the different kinds of stone and marble, including lime and sand and gypsum. I am learning that the artists who excelled in sculpture were Phidias, Scopas and Praxiteles. The last-named, I have just learned also, left a son called Cephisodotos, who inherited much of his father's talent, and made a notably fine Group of Wrestlers.'

'You and your wrestlers,' said the gander, 'are profoundly absurd! But time is the king of wrestlers; and he already prepares to try a fall with you.'

'Now, indeed, those Wrestlers were not absurd,' replied Kerin. 'And the proof of it is that they were for a long while the particular glory of Pergamos.'

At that the gander seemed to give him up, saying, after a little hissing: 'Very well, then, do you catalogue your facts about Pergamos and stag-horns and planets! But I shall sing.'

Kerin now for a while regarded his fellow prisoner with a trace of mild disapproval. And Kerin said:

'Yet I catalogue verities which are well proven and assured. But you, who live in a brown cage that is buried deep in this gray and lonely corridor, you can have no first-hand information as to beauty and mystery and holiness and heroism and immortality, you encourage people in a business of which you are ignorant, and you sing about ardors and raptures and, above all, about a future of which you can know nothing.'

'That may very well be just why I sing of these things so movingly. And in any event, I do not seek to copy nature. I, on the contrary, create to divert me such faith and dreams as living among men would tend to destroy. But as it is, my worshipers depart from me drunk with my very potent music; they tread high-heartedly, in this gray corridor, and they are devoid of fear and parvanimity; for the effect of my singing, like that of all great singing, is to fill my hearers with a sentiment of their importance as moral beings and of the greatness of their destinies.'

'Oh, but,' said Kerin, 'but I finished long ago with the various schools of morals, and I am now, as I told you, well forward in petrology. Nor shall I desist from learning until I have come by all knowledge and all truth which can content my Saraïde. And she, Messire Gander, is a remarkably clearsighted young woman, to whom the romantic illusions which you provide could be of no least importance.'

'Nothing,' returned the gander, 'nothing in the universe, is of importance, or is authentic to any serious sense, except the illusions of romance. For man alone of animals plays the ape to his dreams. These axioms – poor, deaf and blinded spendthrift! – are none the less valuable for being quoted.'

'Nor are they, I suspect,' replied Kerin, 'any the less generally quoted for being bosh.'

With that he returned to his books; and the gander resumed its singing.

And many more years thus passed: overhead, the legend of Manuel had come into being and was flourishing, and before its increase the brawling bleak rough joyous times which Kerin had known, were, howsoever slowly, passing away from Poictesme, not ever to return. Overhead, Count Emmerick was ruling – inefficiently enough, but at least with a marked bent toward the justice and mercy and kindliness imposed upon him by the legend – where Dom Manuel had ruled according to his own will alone. Overhead, Dame Niafer and Holmendis were building everywhere their shrines and convents and hospitals; and were now beginning, a little by a little, to persecute, with the Saint's rather ruthless miracle-working, the fairies and the demons and all other unorthodox spirits aboriginal to this land; and were beginning, too, to extirpate the human heretics who here and there had showed such a lack of patriotism and of religious faith as to question the legend of Manuel and the transcending future of Poictesme.

The need of doing this was a grief to Niafer and Holmendis, as well as a troubling tax upon their hours of leisure: but, nevertheless, as clear-headed philanthropists, they here faced honestly the requirements of honest faith in any as yet revealed religion – by which all unbelievers must be regarded as lost in any event, and cannot be permitted to continue in life except as a source of yet other immortal souls' pollution and ruin.

Meanwhile the gander also exalted the illusions of romance: and Kerin read. His eyes journeyed over millions upon millions of pages in the while that Kerin sat snug: and except for the gander's perilously sweet and most distracting singing, Kerin had no worries in any manner to interrupt him, and no bothers whatever, save only the increasing infirmities of his age.

Chapter XLVI

Kerin Rises in the World

Then old Sclaug said to Kerin, who now seemed so much older than Sclaug seemed: 'It is time for you and me to cry quits with studying: for you have worked your way as a worm goes through every alcove in this place, you have read every book that was ever written; and I have seen that vigor which destroyed me destroyed. I go into another Nakara: and you must now return, omniscient Kerin, into the world of men.'

'That is well,' said Kerin, 'because, after all, I have been away from home a long while. Yes, that is well enough, although I shall regret to leave the books of that god of whom you told me – and whom, by the way, I have not yet seen.'

'I said, of a sort of god. He is not worshiped, I must tell you, by the very learned nor by the dull. However!' Sclaug said, after a tiny silence, 'however, I was wondering if you have found in these books the knowledge you were looking for?'

'I suppose so,' Kerin answered, 'because I have acquired all knowledge.'

'And have you found out also the truth?'

'Oh yes!' said Kerin, speaking now without hesitancy.

Kerin took down from its place the very first book which Sclaug had given him to read, when Kerin was yet young, the book which had been written – upon leaves of tree bark, with the assistance of a divine collaborator – by the patriarch Abraham when a horror of darkness fell upon him in the plain of Mamrê. This book explained the wisdom of the temple, the various master-words of chance, the seven ways of thwarting destiny, and one thing which is wholly true. And Kerin half opened this book, at the picture of an old naked eunuch who with a scythe was hacking off the feet of a naked youth gashed everywhere with many small wounds; then turned to a picture of a serpent crucified; and, shrugging, put by the book.

' – For it appears,' said Kerin, 'that, after all, only one thing is wholly true. I have found nowhere any other truth: and this one truth, revealed to us here, is a truth which nobody will blame the patriarch for omitting from his more widely circulated works. Nevertheless, I have copied out every word of it, upon this bit of paper, to show to and make glad the dear bright eyes of my young wife.'

But Sclaug replied, without looking at the proffered paper, 'The truth does not matter to the dead, who have done with all endeavor, and who can change nothing.'

Then he told Kerin goodbye; and Kerin opened the door out of which Sclaug was used to go in search of Sclaug's little amusements. When Kerin had passed through this door he drew it to behind him: and in that instant the door vanished, and Kerin stood alone in a dim winter-wasted field, fingering no longer a copper door-knob but only the chill air.

Leafless elder-trees rose about him, not twenty paces before Kerin was the Well of Ogde: and beyond its dilapidated curbing, a good half of which somebody had heaved down into the well, he saw, through wintry twilight, the gray eight-sided house in which he had been used to live with the young Saraïde whom many called a witch.

Chapter XLVII

Economics of Saraïde

Kerin went forward, beneath naked elder boughs, toward his dear home, and he saw coming out of the door of the gray house the appearance of a man who vaguely passed to the right hand of Kerin in the twilight. But a woman's figure waited at the door; and Kerin, still going onward, came thus, in the November twilight, again to Saraïde.

'Who is that man?' said Kerin, first of all. 'And what is he doing here?'

'Does that matter?' Saraïde answered him, without any outcry or other sign of surprise.

'Yes, I think it matters that a naked man with a red shining about his body should be seen leaving here at this hour, in the dead of winter, for it is a thing to provoke great scandal.'

'But nobody has seen him, Kerin, except my husband. And certainly my own husband would not stir up any scandal about me.'

Kerin scratched his white head. 'Yes, that,' said Kerin, 'that seems reasonable, according to the best of my knowledge. And the word "knowledge" reminds me, Saraïde, that you sent me in search of knowledge as to why life is given to human beings, so that you might in the light of this knowledge appropriately dispose of your youth. Well, I have solved your problem, and the answer is, Nobody knows. For I have acquired all knowledge. All that any man has ever known, I am now familiar with, from the medicinal properties of the bark aabec to the habits of the dragonfly called zyxomma: but no man, I find, has ever known for what ends he may either help or hinder in any of his flounderings about earth and water.'

'I remember,' Saraïde said now, as if in a faint wonder. 'I wanted, once, when I was young and when the eye of no man went over me without lingering, then I wanted to know the truth about everything. Yet the truth does not really matter to the young, who are happy; and who in any case have not the shrewdness nor the power to change anything: and it all seems strange and unimportant now. For you have been a long time gone, my Kerin, and I have lived through many years, with many and many a companion, in the great while that you have been down yonder getting so much knowledge from the bird who has the true wisdom.'

'Of whatever bird can you be talking?' said Kerin, puzzled. 'Oh, yes, now I also remember! But, no, there is nothing in that old story, my darling, and there is no Zhar-Ptitza in the Well of Ogde. Instead, there is a particularly fine historical and scientific library: and from it I have acquired all knowledge, and have thus happily solved your problem. Nor is that the end of the tale: for you wanted not merely knowledge but truth also, and in consequence I have found out for you the one thing which – according to Abraham's divine collaborator, in a moment of remarkable and, I suppose, praiseworthy candor – is wholly true. And that truth I have neatly copied out for you upon this bit of paper – '

But there was really no understanding these women who despatched you upon hazardous and quite lengthy quests. For Saraïde had interrupted him without the least sign of such delight and satisfaction, or even of pride in her husband's exploits, as would have seemed only natural. And Saraïde said:

'The truth does not matter to the aged. Of what good is the truth to you or to me either, now that all the years of our youth are gone, and nothing in our living can be changed?'

'Well, well!' observed Kerin, comfortably, and passing over her defects in appreciation, 'so the most of our lifetime has slipped by since I slipped over that well-curbing! But how time flies, to be sure! Did you say anything, my dear?'

'I groaned,' replied Saraïde, 'to have you back again with your frayed tags of speech and the desolation of your platitudes: but that does not matter either.'

'No, of course not: for all is well, as they say, that ends well. So out with your talisman, and let us quicken the golden shining which will attest the truth I have fetched back to you!'

She answered rather moodily: 'I have not that talisman any longer. A man wanted it. And I gave it to him.'

'Since generosity is a virtue, I have no doubt that you did well. But to what man, Saraïde, did you give the jewel that in youth you thought was priceless?'

'Does that matter, now? and, indeed, how should I remember? There have been so many men, my Kerin, in the tumultuous and merry years that are gone by forever. And all of them – ' Here Saraïde breathed deeply. 'Oh, but I loved them, my Kerin!'

'It is our Christian duty to love our neighbors. So I do not doubt that, here again, you have done well. Still, one discriminates, one is guided, even in philanthropy, by instinctive preferences. And therefore I am wondering for what especial reason, Saraïde, did you love these particular persons?'

'They were so beautiful,' she said, 'so young, so confident in what was to be, and so pitiable! And now some of them are gone away into the far-off parts of earth, and some of them are gone down under the earth in their black narrow coffins, and the husks of those that remain hereabouts are strange and staid and withered and do not matter any longer. Life is a pageant that passes very quickly, going hastily from one darkness to another darkness with only ignes fatui to guide; and there is no sense in it. I learned that, Kerin, without moiling over books. But life is a fine ardent spectacle; and I have loved the actors in it: and I have loved their youth and their high-heartedness, and their ungrounded faiths, and their queer dreams, my Kerin, about their own importance and about the greatness of the destiny that awaited them – while you were piddling after, of all things, the truth!'

'Still, if you will remember, my darling, it was you yourself who said, as you no doubt recall, just as you shoved me – '

'Well! I say now that I have loved too utterly these irrational fine things to have the heart, even now, to disbelieve in them, entirely: and I am content.'

'Yes, yes, my dear, we two may both well be content. For we at last can settle down and live serenely in this place, without undue indulgence in philanthropy; and we two alone will know the one truth which is wholly true.'

'Good Lord!' said Saraïde, and added, incoherently, 'But you were always like that!'

Chapter XLVIII

The Golden Shining

They went then, silently, from the twilight into the darkness of the house which had been their shared home in youth, and in which now there was no youth and no sound and no assured light anywhere. Yet a glow of pallidly veiled embers, not quite extinct where all else seemed dead, showed where the hearth would be. And Saraïde said:

'It is droll that we have not yet seen each other's faces! Give me your foolish paper, Kerin of my heart, that I may put it to some use and light this lamp.'

Kerin, a bit disconsolately, obeyed: and Saraïde touched the low red embers with the paper which told about the one thing which is wholly true. The paper blazed. Kerin saw thus speedily wasted the fruit of Kerin's long endeavor. Saraïde had lighted her lamp. The lamp cast everywhither now a golden shining: and in its clear soft yellow radiancy, Saraïde was putting fresh wood upon the fire, and making tidy her hearth.

After that necessary bit of housework she turned to her husband, and they looked at each other for the first time since both were young. Kerin saw a bent, dapper, not unkindly witch-woman peering up at him, with shrewd eyes, over the handle of her broom. But through the burning of that paper, as Kerin saw also, their small eight-sided home had become snug and warm and cozy looking, it even had an air of durability: and Kerin laughed, with the thin, easy, neighing laughter of the aged.

For, after all, he reflected, it could benefit nobody ever to recognise – either in youth or in gray age or after death – that time, like an old envious eunuch, must endlessly deface and maim, and make an end of, whatever anywhere was young and strong and beautiful or even cozy; and that such was the one truth which had ever been revealed to any man, assuredly. Saraïde, for that matter, seemed to have found out for herself, somewhere in philanthropic fields, the one thing which was wholly true; and she seemed, also, to prefer to ignore it, in favor of life's unimportant, superficial, familiar tasks. . . . Well, and Saraïde, as usual, was in the right! It was the summit of actual wisdom to treat the one thing which was wholly true as if it were not true at all. For the truth was discomposing, and without remedy, and was too chillingly strange ever to be really faced: meanwhile, in the familiar and the superficial, and in temperate bodily pleasures, one found a certain cheerfulness. . . .

He temperately kissed his wife, and he temperately inquired, 'My darling, what is there for supper?'

Chapter XLIX

They of Nointel

Thus, then, it was that, in the November following Guivric's encounter with the Sylan, Kerin of Nointel came back into Poictesme, to become yet another convert to the great legend of Manuel.

Kerin was converted almost instantaneously. For when the news of Kerin's return was public, Holmendis soon came that way, performing very devastating miracles en route among the various evil and ambiguous spirits which yet lurked in the rural districts of Poictesme. The Saint was now without any mercy imprisoning all such detected immortals right and left, in tree-trunks and dry wells and consecrated bottles, and condemning them in such exiguous sad quarters to await the holy Morrow of Judgement. With Holmendis as his coadjutor in these praise-worthy labors, traveled the appearance of Guivric the Sage.

And when St Holmendis and Glaum-Without-Bones (in Guivric's stolen body) had talked to Kerin of Nointel about the great cult of Manuel the Redeemer which had sprung up during Kerin's pursuit of knowledge underground, and had showed him the holy sepulchre at Storisende and Manuel's bright jewel-encrusted effigy, and had told about Manuel's ascent into heaven, then old Kerin only blinked, with mild, considerate, tired eyes.

'It is very likely,' Kerin said, 'since it was Manuel who gave to us of Poictesme our law that all things must go by tens forever.'

'Now, what,' said Glaum, in open but wholly amiable sur-prise, 'has that to do with it?'

'I have learned that a number of other persons have entered alive into heaven. I allude of course to Enoch, whose smell the cherubim found so objectionable that they recoiled from him a distance of five thousand, three hundred and eighty miles. I allude also to Elijah; to Eliezer, the servant of Abraham; to

Hiram, King of Tyre; to Ebed Melek the Ethiop; to Jabez, the
son of Prince Jehuda; to Bathia, the daughter of a Pharaoh; to
Sarah, the daughter of Asher; and to Yoshua, the son of Levi,
who did not go in by the gateway, but climbed over the wall.
And I consider it quite likely that Dom Manuel would elect to
make of this company, as he did of everything else, a tenth.'

Thereafter Holmendis said, rather dubiously, 'Well – !' And
Holmendis talked again of Manuel. . . .

'That too seems likely enough,' Kerin agreed. 'I have learned
that these messengers from the gods to our race upon earth are
sent with commendable regularity every six hundred years. The
Enoch of whom I was speaking but a moment since was the first
of them, in the six-hundredth year after Adam. Then, as the
happy upshot of a love-affair between a Mongolian empress and
a rainbow, came into this world Fo-hi, six hundred years after
Enoch's living; and six hundred years after the days of Fo-hi was
Brighou sent to the Hindoos. At the same interval of time or
thereabouts have since come Zoroaster to the Persians, and
Thoth the Thrice Powerful to the Egyptians, and Moses to the
Jews, and Lao Tse to the men of China, and Paul of Tarsus to
the Gentiles, and Mohammed to the men of Islam. Mohammed
flourished just six hundred years before our Manuel. Yes,
Messire Holmendis, it seems likely enough that, here too,
Manuel would elect to make a tenth.'

The pious gentle old Glaum-Without-Bones began to speak
with joy and loving reverence about the glories of Manuel's
second coming. . . .

'No doubt, dear Guivric: for I have learned that all the great
captains are coming again,' said Kerin, almost wearily. 'There is
Arthur, there is Ogier, there is Charlemagne, there is Barbar-
ossa, there is Finn, the son of Cumhal – there is in every land, in
fine, a fore-knowledge of that hero who will return at his appointed time and bring with him all glory and prosperity. Prince
Siddartha also is to return, and Saoshyant, and Alexander of
Macedon, and Satan too, for that matter, is expected to return,
for his last fling, a little before the holy Morrow of Judgement.
Therefore I consider it not unlikely that, here again, Dom
Manuel may elect to make a tenth.'

In short, the old fellow took Poictesme's epiphany almost too calmly. . . . Glaum was satisfied, on the ground that a conversion was a conversion, and an outing for all the angels in heaven. But it was apparent that Holy Holmendis did not quite like the posture of affairs. . . . You could not, of course, detect in this incurious receptiveness any skepticism; nor could a person who went ten times too far in the way of faith be, very rationally, termed an unbeliever. It was, rather, as if Kerin viewed the truth without joy: it was as if Kerin had, somehow, become over-familiar with the sublime truths about Manuel the Redeemer some while before he heard them; and so, was hearing them, now at long last, without the appropriate upliftedness and flow of spirits. Kerin merely accepted these tremendous truths; and seemed upon the whole to be more interested in life's unimportant, superficial, familiar tasks, and in his food.

Holmendis must have felt that the desiderata here were intangible. In any event, he shook his aureoled head; and, speaking in the tongue of his native Philistia, he said something to Glaum-Without-Bones – which Glaum could not at all understand – about 'the intelligentsia, so-called.' But Holmendis did not resort to any dreadful miracle by which old Kerin might have been appalled into a more proper excitement and joyousness. . . .

Yet it was a very unbounded joy, and a joy indeed at which all beholders wondered, to Kerin of Nointel, when he saw and embraced the fine son, named Fauxpas, who had been born to Saraïde during the fifth year of Kerin's studies underground. For Kerin's studies had informed him that such remarkably prolonged gestations are the infallible heralds of one or another form of greatness – a fact evinced by the birth of Phœbos Apollo and of Osiris and of several other gods and of all elephants – and Kerin deduced that his son would in some way or another rise to worldly pre-eminence.

And that inference proved to be reasonably true, since it was this Fauxpas de Nointel who, when but a lad of twenty, led Count Emmerick's troops for him in the evil days of Maugis d'Aigremont's rebellion, and who held Poictesme for Manuel's son until aid came from the Comte de la Forêt. For twelve years at least this son of Kerin was thus pre-eminent among most of his associates, and twelve years is a reasonable slice out of any man's life. And the eldest son of Fauxpas de Nointel was that Ralph who married Madame Adelaide, the daughter of the Comte de la Forêt, and the granddaughter of Dom Manuel, and who builded at Nointel the great castle with seven towers which still endures.

Book Eight

The Candid Footprint

'They have reproached the footsteps of thine anointed.'
PSALMS, lxxxix, 51

Chapter L

Indiscretion of a Bailiff

Now the tale tells that upon the day of the birth of the first son begotten by Count Emmerick, in lawful marriage and with the aid of his own wife Radegonde, there was such a drinking of healths and toasts as never before was known at Storisende. The tale speaks of a most notable banquet, at which twelve dishes were served to every two persons, with a great plenty of the best wine and beer. In the minstrels' gallery were fiddlers, trumpeters and drummers, those who tossed tambourines, and those who played upon the flute. Ten poets discoursed meanwhile on the feats of Dom Manuel, and presented in even livelier colors the impendent achievements of the Redeemer's second coming into Poictesme with a ferocious heavenly cortège. And meanwhile also the company drank, and the intoxication of verse was abetted with red wine and white.

Since the poems were rather long, all this resulted in an entertainment from which the High Bailiff of Upper Ardra went homeward hiccoughing and even more than usually benevolent, and without any consciousness of that one single misstep – induced by the allied virtues of patriotism and of alcohol – which had imperiled his continued stay upon earth.

For Ninzian of Yair and Upper Ardra had not wholly broken with the heroic cenatory ways of the years wherein Dom Manuel ruled over Poictesme. This seemed the more regrettable because Ninzian, always a pious and philanthropic person, had otherwise become with age appropriately staid. He in theory approved of every one of the reforms enacted everywhere by the Countess Niafer, and confirmed by the Countess Radegonde; and, in practice, Ninzian was of course a staunch supporter of his revered and intimate associate, St Holmendis, in all the salutary crusades against elves and satyrs and trolls and other uncanonical survivals from unorthodox mythologies, and against the free-thinking of persons who questioned the legend of Manuel, and in the holy man's hunting down of such demons and stringing up of such heretics, and in all other devout labors. But there, nevertheless, was no disputing that the benevolent and florid bailiff of Upper Ardra had kept a taint of the robustious social customs of Dom Manuel's worldly heyday.

It followed that Ninzian evaded none of the toasts at Count Emmerick's banquet and left no friend unpledged. Instead, sleek Ninzian drank the wines of Orléans, of Anjou and of Burgundy; of Auxerre and Beaune, and of St Jean and St Porçain. He drank Malvoisin, and Montrose, and Vernage, and Runey. He drank the wines of Greece, both Patras and Farnese; he drank spiced beers; he drank muscatel; and he drank hypocras. He did not ignore the cider nor the pear cider; to the sweet white sparkling wine of Volnay he confessed, and he exhibited, an especial predilection; and he drank copiously, also, of the Alsatian sherry and of the Hungarian tokay.

Thereafter Ninzian went homeward with a pleasurable at-randomness, for which – in a so liberal contributor to every pious cause and persecution – appropriate allowances were made by St Holmendis and everybody else except one person only. Ninzian was married.

Chapter LI

The Queer Bird

The next evening Ninzian and his wife were walking in the garden. They were a handsome couple, and the high-hearted love that had been between them in their youth was a tale which many poets had embroidered. It was an affection, too, which had survived its consummation with so slight impairment that Ninzian during the long while since he had promised eternal fidelity was not known to have begotten but one by-blow. Even that, as he was careful to explain, was by way of charity: for well-thought-of, rich old Pettipas, the pawnbroker at Beauvillage, had lived childlessly with his buxom young second wife for nearly three years before Ninzian, in odd moments, provided this deserving couple with a young heiress.

But in the main Ninzian preferred his own lean and pietistic wife above all other women, even so long after he had won her in the heyday of their adventurous youth. Now they who were in the evening of life were lighted by a golden sunset as they went upon a flagged walkway, made of white and blue stones; and to either side were the small glossy leaves and the crimson flowering of well-tended rose-bushes. They waited thus for Holy Holmendis, their fellow laborer in multifarious forms of church work and social betterment, for the Saint had promised to have supper with them. And Balthis (for that was the name of Ninzian's wife) said, 'Look, my dear, and tell me what is that?'

Ninzian inspected the flower-bed by the side of the walkway, and he replied, 'My darling, it appears to be the track of a bird.'

'But surely there is in Poictesme no fowl with a foot so huge!'

'No. But many migratory monsters pass by in the night, on their way north, at this time of year: and, clearly, one of some rare species has paused here to rest. However, as I was telling you, my pet, we have now in hand – '

'Why, but think of it, Ninzian! The print is as big as a man's foot!'

'Come, precious, you exaggerate! It is the track of a largish bird – an eagle, or perhaps a roc, or, it may be, the Zhar-Ptitza passed here – but it is nothing remarkable. Besides, as I was telling you, we have already in hand, for the edifying of the faithful, a bit of Mary Magdalene's haircloth, the left ring-finger of John the Baptist, a suit of Dom Manuel's underclothes, and one of the smaller stones with which St Stephen was martyred – '

But Balthis, he saw now, was determined not to go on in talk about the church which Ninzian had builded in honor of Manuel the Redeemer, and which Ninzian was stocking with very holy relics. Instead, she asserted with deliberation: 'Ninzian, I think it is fully as big as a man's foot.'

'Well, be it as you like, my pet!'

'But I will not be put off in that way! Do you tread beside it in the flower-bed there, and, by comparing the print of your foot with the bird track, we shall easily see which is the larger.'

Ninzian was not so ruddy as he had been. Yet he said with dignity, and lightly enough, he hoped:

'Balthis, you are unreasonable. I do not intend to get my sandals all over mud to settle any such foolish point. The track is just the size of a man's foot, or it is much larger than a man's foot, or it is smaller than a man's foot – it is, in fine, of any size which you prefer. And we will let that be the end of it.'

'So, Ninzian, you will not tread in that new-digged earth?' said Balthis, queerly.

'Of course I will not ruin my second-best sandals for any such foolish reason!'

'You trod there yesterday in your very best sandals, Ninzian, for the reason that you were tipsy. I saw the print you made there, in broad daylight, Ninzian, when you had just come from drinking with a blessed saint himself, and were reeling all over the neat ways of my garden. Ninzian, it is a fearful thing to know that when your husband walks in mud he leaves tracks like a bird.'

Now Ninzian was truly penitent for yesterday's over-indulgence. And Ninzian said:

'So, you have discovered this foible of mine, after all my carefulness! That is a great pity.'

Balthis replied, with the cold non-committalness of wives, 'Pity or no, you will now have to tell me the truth about it.'

That took did, in point of fact, seem so appallingly unavoidable that Ninzian settled down to it, with such airiness as would have warned any wife in the world exactly how far to trust him.

'Well, my darling, you must know that when I first came into Poictesme, I came rather unwillingly. Our friend St Holmendis, I need not tell you, was, even in the time of Dom Manuel's incarnation in frail human flesh, setting such a very high moral tone hereabouts, and the holy man is so impetuous with his miracles when anybody differs with him on religious matters, that the prospect was not alluring. But it was necessary that my prince should have some representative here as in all other places. So I came, from – well, from down yonder – '

'I know you came from the South, Ninzian! Everybody knows that. But that appears to me no excuse whatever for walking like a bird.'

'As if, my dearest, it could give me any pleasure to walk like a bird, or like a whole convoy of birds! To the contrary, I have always found this small accomplishment in doubtful taste, it exposes one to continual comment. But very long ago those who had served my prince with especial distinction were all put upon this footing, in order that true demerit might be encouraged, and that fine sportsmanship might be preserved, and so that, also our adversaries in the great game might be detecting us.'

Now Balthis fixed on him wide, scornful, terrible eyes. After a breathless while she said:

'Ninzian, I understand. You are an evil spirit, and you came out of hell in the appearance of a man to work wickedness in Poictesme!'

And his Balthis, as he saw with a pang of wild regret, was horribly upset and grieved to know the thing which her husband had so long hid away from her; and Ninzian began to feel rather ashamed of not having trusted her with this secret, now it was discovered. At all events, he would try what being reasonable might do.

'Darling,' said he, with patient rationality, 'no sensible wife will

² ever pry into what her husband may have been or done before she married him. Her concern is merely with his misdemeanours after that ceremony; and, I think, you have had no heavy reason to complain. Nobody can for one moment assert that in Poictesme I have not led an appallingly upright and immaculate existence.'

She said, indignantly: 'You had fear of Holmendis! You came all this long way to do your devil work, and then had not the pluck to face him!'

Ninzian found this just near enough the truth to be irritating. So he spoke now with airy condescension.

'Precious, it is true the lean man can work miracles, but then, without desiring to appear boastful, I must tell you that I have mastery of a more venerable and blacker magic. Oh, I assure you, he could not have exorcised or excommunicated or tried any other of his sacerdotal trick-work upon me without sweating for it! Still, it seemed better to avoid such painful scenes: for when one has trouble with these saints the supporters of both sides are apt to intervene; the skies are blackened and the earth shakes, and whirlwinds and meteors and thunderbolts and seraphim upset things generally: and it all seems rather boisterous and old-fashioned. So it really did appear more sensible, and in better taste, to respect, at all events during his lifetime, the well-meaning creature's religious convictions – in which you share, I know, my pet – and, well!' said Ninzian, with a shrug, 'to temporise! to keep matters comfortable all around, you understand, my darling, by evincing a suitable interest in church work and in whatever else appeared expected of the reputable in my surroundings.'

But Balthis was not to be soothed. 'Ninzian, this is a terrible thing for me to be learning! There was never a husband who better knew his place, and the only baby you ever upset me with is at the pawnbroker's, and Holy Church has not ever had a more loyal servitor – '

'No,' Ninzian said, quietly.

' – But you have been a hideous demon in deep hell, and the man that I have loved is a false seeming, and the moment St Holmendis ascends to bliss you mean to go on with your foul iniquities. That is foolish of you, because of course I would never permit it. But, even so – ! Oh, Ninzian, my faith and my happiness are buried now in the one grave, now that all ends between us!'

Ninzian asked, still very quietly: 'And do you think I will leave you, my Balthis, because of some disarranged fresh earth? Could any handful of dirt have parted us when because of my great love for you I fought the seven knights at Évre – '

'What chance had the poor fellows against a devil!'

'It is the principle of the thing, my darling – as well as the mathematics. Also, as I was going on to observe, you would never have been flinging mud in my face when for your sake I overthrew Duke Oribert and his deplorable custom of the cat and the serpent, and cast the Spotted Dun of Lorcha down from a high hill.'

She answered without pity: 'You will be lucky to get out of this mud with a whole skin. For it is on this evening of the month that St Holmendis hears my confession, and I must confess everything, and you know as well as I do of his devastating miracles.'

Ninzian, having thus failed in his appeal to the better qualities of his wife, forthwith returned to soliciting her powers of reason.

'Balthis, my sweet, now, after all, what complaint have you against me? You cannot help feeling that the no doubt ill-advised rebellion in which I was concerned in youth, unarithmeticable æons before this Earth was thought of, took place quite long enough ago to be forgotten. Besides, you know by experience that I am only too easily guided by others, that I have never learned, as you so eloquently phrase it, to have any backbone. And I do not really see, either, how you can want to punish me today for iniquities which, you grant, I have not ever committed, but – so you assume, without any warrant known to me – have just vaguely thought of committing by and by, and it may be, not for years to come – my adorable pouting darling – because this stringy Holmendis seems tough as whit-leather – '

Ninzian's stammered talking died away. He saw there was no moving her.

'No Ninzian, I simply cannot stand having a husband who walks like a bird, and is liable to be detected the next time it rains. It would be on my mind day and night, and people would say all sorts of things. No, Ninzian, it is quite out of the question. I will get your things together at once, and you can go to hell or over to that giggling ill-bred friend of yours at the pawnbroker's nasty shop, just as you elect: and I leave it to your conscience if, after the way I have worked and slaved for you, you had the right to play this wrong and treachery upon me.'

And Balthis said also: 'For it is a great wrong and treachery which you have played upon me, Ninzian of Yair, getting from me such love as men will not find the equal of in any of the noble places of this world until the end of life and time. This is a deep wound that you have given me. Upon your lips were wisdom and pleasant talking, there was kindliness in the gray eyes of Ninzian of Yair, your hands were strong at sword-play, and you were the most generous of companions all through the daytime and in the nighttime too. These things I delighted in, these things I regarded: I did not think of the low mire, I could not see what horrible markings your passing by had left to this side and to that side.'

Then Balthis said: 'Let every woman weep with me, for I now know that to every woman's loving is this end appointed. There is no woman that gives all to any man, but that woman is wasting her substance at bed and board with a greedy stranger, and there is no wife who escapes the bitter hour in which that knowledge smites her. So now let us touch hands, and now let our lips too part friendlily, because our bodies have so long been friends, the while that we knew nothing of each other, Ninzian of Yair, on account of the great wrong and treachery which you have played upon me.'

Thus speaking, Balthis kissed him. Then she went into the house that was no longer Ninzian's home.

Chapter LII

Remorse of a Poor Devil

Ninzian sat on a stone bench which was carved at each end with a crouching sphinx, and he waited there while the sunlight died away behind the poplars. The moment could not but seem to anybody pregnant with all danger. Holmendis was coming, and Holmendis would very soon be hearing the confession of Balthis, and these saints were over-often the prey of an excitability which damaged their cause.

These saints had many bad qualities, as Ninzian freely admitted; and in the main he approved of saints: but he did wish that holiness could be more urbane in its exercises and more long-sighted.

That impetuous Holmendis was quite as apt as not to resort out of hand to unbridled miracle-working, and with the fires of Heaven to annihilate his leading fellow laborer in every exercise of altruistic intermeddling – without pausing, rationally, to reflect what an annihilation the resultant scandal would be to Holmendis' own party of reform and uplift. Holmendis would no doubt be sorry afterward: but he would get no sympathy from Ninzian.

And, meanwhile, Ninzian loved his wife so greatly that prolonged existence without her did not tempt him. His wife, whoever she might be, had always seemed peculiarly dear to Ninzian. And now, as he looked back upon the exceeding love which he had borne his wife, in Nineveh and Thebes and Tyre and Babylon and Rome and Byzantium, and in all other cities that bred fine women, and as he weighed the evanescence of this love which was evading him after these few thousand years, it seemed to Ninzian a pitiable thing that his season of earthly contentment should thus be cut off in its flower and withered untimelily.

And his conscience troubled him, too. For the fiend had not been entirely candid with his Balthis, and Poictesme was not by any means the stage of the complaisant easy-going fellow's primal failure. So he now forlornly thought of how utterly he had failed in his mission upon Earth, ever since he first came to Mount Kaf to work evil among men, in the time of King Tchagi, a great while before the Deluge; and he considered with dismay the appalling catalogue of virtuous actions into which these women had betrayed him.

For always the cause of Ninzian's downfall had been the same: he would get to talking indiscretion to some lovely girl or another, just through his desire to be agreeable to everybody, and his devilish eloquence would so get the better of her that the girl would invariably marry him and ruthlessly set about making her husband a well-thought-of citizen. Nor did it avail him to argue. Women nowhere appeared to have any sympathy with Ninzian's appointed labor upon Earth: they seemed to have an instinctive bent toward Heaven and the public profession of every virtue. Just as in the case of that poor Miramon Lluagor, Ninzian reflected, Ninzian's wife also did not care two straws about her husband's career and the proper development of his talents.

Then Ninzian on a sudden recollected the cause of the disturbance which had been put upon his living. He drew his dagger, and, squatting on the paved walkway, he scratched out that incriminating footprint.

He was none too soon.

Chapter LIII

Continuation of Appalling Pieties

He was none too soon, because Ninzian rose from this erasement just in time to bump into no other than the energetic tough flesh of Holy Holmendis, who in the cool of the evening was coming up the walkway; and indeed, in rising, Ninzian jostled against the Saint rather roughly. So Ninzian apologised for his clumsiness, and explained that he was going fishing the next day, and was digging for worms: and Ninzian was in a bad taking, for he could not know how much this peppery and over-excitable Saint from out of Philistia had seen or suspected or might be up to the very next moment with one or another bull-headed miracle.

But Holy Holmendis said friendlily that no bones were broken, and he went on, with the soul-chilling joviality of the clergy, to make some depressing joke about fishers of men. 'And that is why I am here,' said the Saint, 'for this evening Dame Balthis is to confess to me whatever matters may be on her conscience.'

'Yes, yes,' said Ninzian, fondly, 'but we both know, my dear and honored friend, that Balthis has a particularly tender conscience, a conscience which is as sensitive to the missteps of others as a sore toe.'

'That is how everybody's conscience ought to be,' returned the Saint: and he went on to speak of the virtuous woman who is a crown to her husband. And he made a contrast between the fine high worth of Balthis and the shamelessness of that bad beggar-woman upon whom, just outside the gate, the Saint had put apoplexy and divine fire for speaking overlightly of the second coming of Manuel.

Ninzian fidgeted. He of course said sympathisingly that he would send some servants to remove the blasted carcass, and that it ought to be a lesson, and that there was no telling what the world was coming to unless right-thinking persons took strong steps through the proper channels. Nevertheless, he did not like the hard, pinched little mouth and glittering, very pale blue eyes of this gaunt Saint; and the nimbus about the thick white hair of Holy Holmendis was beginning to shine brighter and brighter as the dusk of evening thickened. Ninzian found it uncomfortable to be alone with this worker of miracles; piety is in all things so unpredictable: and Ninzian was unfeignedly glad when Balthis came out of the loved house that was no longer Ninzian's home, and when Balthis held open the door for Holmendis to enter where Ninzian might not come any more.

Yet, so tenacious is the charitableness of women, that even now, as Holmendis went in, Dame Balthis tried to speak, for the last time, sensibly and kindly with her husband.

'Pig with the head of a mule,' she said, in a lowered tone, 'do you stop looking at me like a sick calf, and go away! For I must confess in what a state of sin I have been living, as a devil's wife, and I have little faith in your black magic, and you know as well as I do that there is no telling what blasted tree-trunk or consecrated bottle or something of that sort he may seal you up in until the holy Morrow of Judgement, precisely as he has done all those other evil spirits.'

Ninzian replied, 'I shall not ever leave you of my free will.'

'But, Ninzian, it is as if I were putting you into the bottle, myself! For if I do not tell that spiteful old bag of bones' – she crossed herself – 'I mean, that beloved and blessed Saint, why, he would never have the sense, or rather, I intended to say that his faith in his fellow creatures is too great and admirable for him ever to suspect you, and so you see how it is!'

'Yes, my most cruel love,' said Ninzian, 'it is quite as if you yourself were thrusting me into a brazen bottle, for all that you know how dependent I am on open-air exercise, and as if you were setting to it the unbreakable seal of Sulieman-ben-Daoud with your own dear hands. But, nevertheless – !'

He took her hand and gallantly he kissed her finger-tips.

At that she boxed his jaws. 'You need not think to make a fool of me! no, not again, not after all these years! Oh, but I will show you!'

Then Balthis also went into the house where the gaunt Saint was making ready to hear her mensual confession.

Chapter LIV

Magic That Was Rusty

Poor-spirited, over-easy-going Ninzian sat upon the stone bench, an outcast now in his own garden; and he thought for a while about the pitiless miracles with which this Holmendis had harried the fairies and the elves and the salamanders and the trolls and the calcars and the succubæ and all the other amiable iniquities of Poictesme; and about the Saint's devastating crusades against moral laxity and freethinking and the curt conclusions which he had made with his ropes and his fires to the existence of mere heresy. It seemed uncomfortably likely that in dealing with a devil this violent and untactful Holmendis would go to even greater lengths, and would cast off all compunction, if somehow Ninzian could not get the better of him.

So Ninzian decided to stay upon the safe side of accident, by destroying the fellow out of hand, Ninzian took from his pocket the stone ematille, and he broke off a branch from a rose-bush. With the flowering rose branch Ninzian traced a largish circle about his sleek person, saying, 'I infernalise unto myself the circumference of nine feet about me.' Here the sign of Sargatanet was repeated by him thrice. Then Ninzian went on, 'From the east, Glavrab; from the west, Garron; from the north – '

He paused. He scratched his head. The boreal word of power was Cabinet or Cabochon or Capricorn or something of that kind, he knew: but what it was exactly was exactly what Ninzian had forgotten. He would have to try something else.

Ninzian therefore turned to the overthrowing of Holmendis by cold and by heat. Ninzian said:

'I invoke thee who are in the empty wind, terrible, invisible, all-potent contriver of destruction and bringer of desolation. I upraise before thee that rod from which proceeds the life abhorrent to thee, I invoke thee through thy veritable name, in virtue of which thou canst not refuse to hear – JOERBET-JOPAKER-BETH-JOBOLCHOSETH – '

But there he gave it up. That dreadful, jaw-cracking obscene appellation had, Ninzian recollected, eleven more sections: but in bewildered Ninzian's mind they were all jumbled and muddled and hopelessly confused.

After that a rather troubled High Bailiff rearranged his clothing; and he now tried to get in touch with Nebiros, the Field-Marshal and Inspector General of Hell. But again Ninzian was in his magic deplorably rusty.

'*Agla, Tagla, Malthon, Oarios* –' he rattled off, handily enough – and once more he bogged in an appalling stretch of unrememberably difficult words. Black magic was not an accomplishment in which you could stay expert without continual practice, and Ninzian had regrettably neglected all infernal arts for the last five centuries and over.

So in this desperate pinch he turned perforce to a simple abecedary conjuration such as mere wizards used; and the High Bailiff of Upper Ardra said, rather shame-facedly, 'Prince Lucifer, most dreadful master of all the Revolted Spirits, I entreat thee to favor me in the adjuration which I address to thy mighty minister, Lucifugé Rofocalé, being desirous to make a pact with him –'

And Ninzian got through this invocation at least, quite nicely, though he a trifle bungled the concluding words from the Grand Clavicle.

This conjuration, however, worked a bit too well. For instead of the hoped-for appearance of genial old Lucifugé Rofocalé endurably disinfected of his usual odor, now came to Ninzian, from among the sweet-smelling rose-bushes, the appearance of a proud gentleman in gold and sable; and a rather perturbed Ninzian bowed very low before his liege-lord, Lucifer, Prince over all the Fallen Angels.

Chapter LV

The Prince of Darkness

The Newcomer paused for an instant, as if he were reading what was in the troubled mind of Ninzian, and then he said: 'I see, Surkrag, whom mortals hereabouts call Ninzian! O unfaithful servant, now must you be punished for betraying the faith I put in you. Now is your requital coming swiftly from this ravening Saint, who will dispose of you without mercy. For your conjuring would disgrace a baby in diapers; you have forgotten long ago what little magic you ever knew; and when this Holmendis gets hold of you with one hand and exorcises you with the other, there will be hardly a cinder left.'

So did Ninzian know himself to stand friendlessly, between the wrath of evil and the malignity of holiness, both bent upon his ruin. He said, 'Have patience, my prince!'

But Lucifer answered sternly: 'My patience is outworn. No, Surkrag, there is no hope for you, and you become shameless in perfidy as steadily you go from good to better. Once you would have scorned the least deviation from the faith you owe me: but a little by a little you have made compromises with virtue, through your weak desire to live comfortably with your wives, and this continual indulgence of women's notions is draining from you the last drop of wickedness. Not fifty centuries ago you could have been shocked by a kindly thought. Twenty centuries back and you at least retained a proper feeling toward the Decalogue. Now you assist in all reforms and build churches without a blush. For is there nowadays, my deluded, lost Surkrag! in candor, is there any virtue howsoever exalted, is there a single revolting decency or any form of godliness, before which your gorge rises? No, my poor friend: you came hither to corrupt mankind, and instead they have made you little worse than human.'

The Angel of Darkness paused. He had spoken, as became such a famous gentleman, very temperately, without rage, but also without any concealing of his sorrow and disappointment. And Ninzian answered, contritely:

'My prince, I have not wholly kept faith, I know. But always the woman tempted me with the droll notion that our sports ought to open with a religious service, and so I have been now and then seduced into marriage. And my wife, no matter what eyes and hair and tint of flesh she might be wearing at the time, has always been bent upon having her husband looked up to by the neighbors; and in such circumstances a poor devil has no chance.'

'So that these women have been your ruin, and even now the latest of them is betraying your secret to that implacable Saint! Well, it is honest infernal justice, for since the time of Kaiumarth you have gained me not one follower in this place, and have lived openly in all manner of virtue when you should have been furthering my power upon Earth.'

Thus speaking, Lucifer took his seat upon the bench. Then Ninzian too sat down, and Ninzian leaned toward this other immortal, in the ever-thickening dusk; and Ninzian's plump face was sad.

'My prince, what does it matter? From the first I have let my fond wife have her will with me, because it pleased her, and did no real good. What do these human notions matter, even in so dear a form? A little while and Balthis will be dead. A little while and there will be no Yair nor Upper Ardra, and no shining holy sepulchre at Storisende, and all Poictesme will be forgotten. A little while and this Earth will be an ice-cold cinder. But you and I shall still be about our work, still playing for the universe, with stars and suns for counters. Does it really matter to you that, for the time this tiny trundling Earth exists and has women on it, I pause from playing at the great game, to entertain myself with these happy accidents of nature?'

Lucifer replied: 'It is not only your waste of time that troubles me. It is your shirking of every infernal duty, it is your cherubic lack of seriousness. Why, do you but think how many thousand women have passed through your fingers!'

'Yes, like a string of pearls, my prince,' said Ninzian fondly.

'Is that not childish sport for you that used to contend so mightily in the great game?'

But Ninzian now was plucking up heart, as the saying is, hand over fist. 'Recall the old days, my prince,' he urged, with the appropriate emotional quaver, 'when we two were only cherubs, with no bodies as yet sprouted from our little curly heads! Do you recall the merry romps and the kissing games we had as tiny angel-faces, sporting together so lovingly among the golden clouds of heaven, without any cares whatever, and with that collar of wings tickling so drolly one's ears! and do you let the memory move you, even to unmerited indulgence. I have contracted an odd fancy for this inconspicuous sphere of rock and mud, I like the women that walk glowingly about it. Oh, I concede my taste is disputable – '

'I dispute nothing, Surkrag. I merely point out that lechery is nowhere a generally received excuse for good works.'

'Well, but now and then,' said Ninzian, broadmindedly, 'the most conscientious may slip into beneficence. And, in any case, how does it matter what I do on Earth? Frankly, my prince, I think you take the place too seriously. For centuries I have watched those who serve you going about this planet in all manner of quaint guises, in curious masks which are impenetrable to anyone who does not know that your pre-eminent servitors tread with the footfall of a bird wherever they pass upon your errands – '

'Yes, but – ' said Lucifer.

' – For ages,' Ninzian continued, without heeding him, 'I have seen your emissaries devote much time and cunning to the tempting of men to commit wickedness: and to what end? Man rises from the dust: he struts and postures: he falls back into the dust. That is all. How can this midge work good or evil? His virtue passes as a thin scolding: the utmost reach of his iniquity is to indulge in the misdemeanor of supererogation, by destroying a man or two men, whom time would very soon destroy in any event. Meanwhile his sympathies incline – I know – by a hair-breadth or so, toward Heaven. Yes, but what does it matter? is it even a compliment to Heaven? Ah, prince, had I the say, I would leave men to perish in their unimportant starveling virtues, without raising all this bother over trifles.'

Ninzian could see that he had made a perceptible impression: yet, still, dark Lucifer was shaking his head. 'Surkrag, in abstract reason you may be right: but warfare is not conducted by reason, and to surrender anything to the Adversary, though it were no more than Earth and its inhabitants, would be a dangerous example.'

'Come, prince, do you think how many first-class constellations there are to strive for, made up of stars that are really desirable possessions! Turn that fine mind of yours to considerations worthy of it, sir! Consider Cassiopeia, and the Bull, and the dear little Triangle! and do you think about Orion, containing such sidereal masterpieces as Bellatrix and Betelgeuse and Rigel, and the most magnificent nebula known anywhere! Do you think also about that very interesting triple sun which is called Mizar, in the Great Bear, a veritable treasure for any connoisseur! and do you let me have this Earth to amuse me!'

Now Lucifer did not answer at once. The bats were out by this time, zigzagging about the garden: the air was touched with the scent of dew-drenched roses: and somewhere in the dusk a nightingale had tentatively raised its thrilling, long-drawn, plaintive voicing of desire. All everywhere about the two fiends was most soothing. And the Angel of Darkness laughed without a trace left in his manner of that earlier reserve.

'No, no, old wheedler! one cannot neglect the tiniest point, in the great game. Besides, I have my pride, I confess it, and to behold Earth given over entirely to good would vex me. Yet, after all, I can detect no unforgivable beneficence in your continuing to live virtuously here with your seraglio for such a while as the planet may last. These little holidays even freshen one for work. So, if you like, I will summon Amaimon or Baälzebub, or perhaps Succor-Benoth would enjoy the sport, and they will dispose of this two-penny Saint.'

But Ninzian seemed hesitant. 'My prince, I am afraid that some of those officious archangels would be coming too; and one thing might lead to another, and my wife would not at all like having any supernal battlings in her own garden, among her favorite rose-bushes. No, as I always say, it is much better to avoid these painful scenes.'

'Your wife!' said Lucifer, in high astonishment, 'and is it that thin faced pious wretch you are considering! Why, but your wife has repudiated you! She has caught just your trick of treacherousness and so she has betrayed you to that flint-hearted Saint!'

Ninzian in the dusk made bold to smile....

Chapter LVI

Economics of Ninzian

Ninzian in the dusk made bold to smile at this sort of bachelor talk. Lucifer really would be a bit more broadminded, a shade less notably naïve, if only the dear fellow had not stayed always so stubbornly prejudiced against marriage, merely because it was a sacrament. All that was required, alike to perfect him in some real knowledge of human nature and to secure everybody's well-being everywhere, Ninzian reflected, was for Lucifer just once to marry some capable woman. . . .

So Ninzian smiled. But Ninzian did not need to say anything, for at this moment Balthis came to the door, and – not being able in the twilight to see the Prince of Darkness – she called out that supper was getting stone-cold on the table, and that she really wished Ninzian would try to be a little more considerate, especially when they had company.

And Ninzian, rising, chuckled. 'My wife has been like that since Sidon was a village. Time and again she has found me out; and never yet has she let me off with a public exposure. Oh, if I could explain it, I would perhaps care less for her. In part, I think, it means that she loves me: in part, I fear – upon looking back – it means that no really conscientious person cares to entrust the proper punishment of her husband to anybody else. Of course, all that is merely theory. What is certain is that my wife's confession has been conducted tactfully, and that you and I are going in to talk solemn nonsense with St Holmendis.'

But Lucifer once more was shaking his head. He said, with firmness:

'No, Surkrag. No, I am not squeamish, but I have no use for saints.'

'Well, prince, I would not be over-hasty to agree with you. For Holmendis has some invaluable points. He is perfectly sincere, for one thing, and for another, he is energetic, and for a third, he

never pardons anyone who differs with him. Of course, he is all
for having men better than they were intended to be, and with his
tales about that second coming of Manuel he does frighten
people. . . . For they have been altering that legend, my prince,
considerably. Nowadays, it is not only glory and prosperity which
Manuel is to bring back with him. He is to return also, it seems,
with a large cargo of excruciate punishments for all persons who
differ in any way with the notions of Holmendis and Niafer.'

'Ah, the old story! It is really astonishing,' Lucifer commen-
ted, in frank wonder, 'how one finds everywhere this legend of the
Redeemer in just this form. It seems an instinct with the
creatures.'

'Well, but,' said Ninzian, tolerantly, 'it gives them something
to look forward to. It promises to gratify all their congenital
desires, including cruelty. And, above all, it prevents their going
mad, to believe that somebody somewhere is looking out for
them. In any event – as I was saying – this gaunt Holmendis does
frighten Poictesme into a great deal of public piety. Still, there are
always corners and bedrooms and other secluded places, in which
one strikes a balance, as it were; and abstinence and fear make
wonderful appetisers: so that, in the long run of affairs, I doubt if
you have anywhere upon Earth any more serviceable friends than
are these saints who will put up with nothing short of their own
especial sort of perfection.'

Lucifer was not convinced. 'It is proper of course that you
should attempt to exculpate your friend and associate during the
last twenty years. Nevertheless, all these extenuatory sayings,
about the viciousness of virtue, are the habitual banalties of
boyhood; and no beardless cynic, even when addicted to verse,
has ever yet been permanently injured by them.'

'But,' Ninzian returned, 'but here, I am not merely theorising.
I speak with rather high authority. For you will be remembering,
prince, that, by the rules of our game, when any mortal has gained
a hundred followers for you, Jahveh is penalised to put him upon
the same footing as the rest of us. And, well, sir! You may see here
in the mud, just where I jostled Holmendis from the walkway –'

Lucifer made luminous his finger-tips, and held them like five
candles to the Saint's footprint. The Angel of Darkness bowed
thereafter, with real respect, toward heaven.

'Our Adversary, to do Him justice, keeps an honest score. Come, Surkrag, now this is affecting! This very touchingly recalls that the great game is being played by the dear fellow with candor and fine sportsmanship. Meanwhile I must most certainly have supper with you; and the great game is far from over, since I yet make a fourth with the fanatic, the woman and the hypocrite.'

'Ah, prince,' said Ninzian, a little shocked, as they went into his sedate snug home, 'should you not say, more tactfully, with us three leaders of reform?'

Book Nine

Above Paradise

*'He was caught up into paradise;
and heard unspeakable words.'*
II CORINTHIANS, xii, 4

Chapter LVII

Maugis Makes Trouble

Now the tale speaks of the rebellion of Maugis, who was the son of Donander of Évre, the Thane of Aigremont. For Count Manuel's youngest child, Ettarre, born after her father's passing, was now come to the full flowering of her strange beauty: and it was at this time – with the result that two young gentlemen went out of their wits, four killed themselves, and seven married – that Ettarre was betrothed to Guiron des Rocques, of the famous house of Gâtinais. And it was at this time also that young Maugis d'Aigremont resorted to a more stirring solace than might be looked for in imbecility or death or a vicarious bedfellow. He seized and carried off Ettarre. His company of ten was pursued by Count Emmerick and Guiron with twenty followers; and after a skirmish in Vobion the girl was recaptured unharmed.

But Maugis escaped. And after that he went into open rebellion against Count Emmerick's authority, and occupied those fastnesses in the Taunenfels which Othmar Black-Tooth had once held for a long while against the assaults of Count Manuel himself.

History in fine appeared to honor banality by repeating itself, with the plain difference that gaunt Maugis was equally a great captain and a great lover and in every way more formidable than Othmar had been, whereas Emmerick, elsewhere than at a banquet, was not formidable at all. Moreover, Emmerick in these days lacked even any stronger kinsman to lean upon, for his brother-in-law Heitman Michael was now in Muscovy, Count Gui of Montors was dead, and Ayrart de Montors had removed to the court of King Theodoret. Emmerick had, thus, to lead his troops only that blustering but gifted young Fauxpas de Nointel or that utterly unreasonable Guiron, who expected, of all persons, the Count of Poictesme to lead these troops.

So Emmerick wavered; he made terms; he even winked at

Guiron's capture by the pirates of Caer Idryn, in order to be rid of this troublesome posturer who insisted upon dragging Emmerick into so much uncomfortable fighting: and Maugis, since these terms did not include his possession of Ettarre, soon broke them. Thus was the warring that now arose in Poictesme resumed: and, because of Maugis' great lust and daring, and Count Emmerick's supineness, and the ever-blundering obstinacy of loud Fauxpas de Nointel, this war dragged on for many wearying fevered years.

Then Emmerick's eldest sister, Madame Melicent, returned from oversea with her second husband, the Comte de la Forêt, a gentleman who remarkably lacked patience with brigands and with shilly-shallying. This Perion de la Forêt took charge of matters, with such resolution that out of hand Guiron was rescued from his captivity, Maugis was overpowered and killed, the Ettarre whom he had desired to his own hurt was married to Guiron, and Count Emmerick gave a banquet in honor of this event. Such was this Perion's impetuosity.

It is of these matters that the tale speaks in passing. For the tale now is of Donander of Évre, who was the father of Maugis, and who would not break faith with that Emmerick who, howsoever unworthily, sat in the place of that great master whom Donander had been privileged to serve even in this mortal life. For Donander was the only one of the lords of the Silver Stallion who accepted with joy and with unbounded faith the legend of Manuel, and who in all his living bore testimony to it.

This Donander of Évre had been the youngest of the fellowship, he was at this time but newly made a widower while yet in his forties, and whatsoever he lacked in brilliance of wit he atoned for with his hardiness in battle. Yet in this war he chose not to display his prowess, since the fighting was between the son of Dom Manuel and the son of Donander himself. He chose instead exile.

First, though, he went to Storisende; and, standing beside the holy sepulchre, he looked up for some while at the serene great effigy of Manuel, poised there in eternal watchfulness over Donander's native land, and bright with all the jewels of the world. Donander knelt and prayed in this sacred place, as he knew, for the last time. Then Donander, without any complaining, and without any grieving now for his wife's death, went out of

Poictesme, a landless man; and he piously took service under Prince Balein of Targamon (the same that twenty years ago had wooed Queen Morvyth, a little before the evil times of her long imprisonment and the cutting off of her head), because this always notably religious prince was now once more harrying the pagan Northmen.

Thus it was that Donander also at the last went out of Poictesme, not by his own election, to encounter the most strange of all the dooms which befell the lords of the Silver Stallion after the passing of Dom Manuel.

Chapter LVIII

Showing That Even Angels May Err

This doom began its workings in the long field below Rathgor, when Palnatoki rode forth and made his brag. 'I am the champion of the Ænseis. In the Northland there is nobody mightier than I; and if a mightier person live elsewhere, it is not yet proven. Who is there in this place will try a fall with me?'

Behind him the pagan army waited, innumerable, and terrible, and deplorably ill-mannered. These shouted now:

'We cry a holmgang. Who will fight with Red Palnatoki, that is overlord of the Swan's bath, and that slew the giants in Noenhir?'

Then from the opposed ranks came clanking, and shining in full armor, Donander of Évre. And he said:

'I, howsoever unworthy, messire, am the person who will withstand you. I also have fought before this morning. Under Count Manuel's banner of the Silver Stallion I have done what I might. That much I will again do here today, and upon every day between this day and the holy Morrow of Judgement.'

After that the Christian army shouted: 'There is none mightier than Donander! Also, he is very gratifyingly modest.'

But Palnatoki cried out scornfully: 'Your utmost will not avail this morning! Behind me musters all the might of the Ænseis, that are the most high of gods above Lærath, and their strength shall be shown here through me.'

'Behind the endeavors of every loyal son of the Church,' Donander said, 'are the blessed saints and the bright archangels.'

'Indeed, Donander, that may very well be the truth,' replied Red Palnatoki. 'The old gods and the gods of Rome have met today; and we are their swords.'

'Your gods confess their weakness, Messire Palnatoki, by picking the better weapon,' Donander answered him, courteously.

With these amenities discharged, they fought. Nowhere upon Earth could have been found a pair of more stalwart warriors: each had no equal anywhere existent between seas and mountains save in his adversary: so neatly were they matched indeed that, after a half-hour of incredible battling, it was natural enough they should kill each other simultaneously. And then the unfortunate error occurred, just as each naked soul escaped from the dying body.

For now out of the north came Kjalar, the fair guide of pagan warriors to eternal delights in the Hall of the Chosen; and from the zenith sped, like a shining plummet, Ithuriel to fetch the soul of the brave champion of Christendom to the felicities of the golden city walled about with jasper of the Lord God of Sabaoth. Both emissaries had been attending the combat until the arrival of their part therein; both, as seasoned virtuosi of warfare, had been delighted by this uncommonly fine fight: and in their pleased excitement they somehow made the error of retrieving each the other's appointed prey. It happened thus that the soul of Donander of Évre fared northward, asleep in the palm of Kjalar's hand, while Ithuriel conveyed the soul of Red Palnatoki to the heaven of Jahveh.

Chapter LIX

The Conversion of Palnatoki

Ithuriel's blunder, it is gratifying to record, did not in the outcome really matter. For Christendom just then was at heated odds over points of theology not very clearly understood in Jahveh's heaven, where in consequence no decisions were hazarded upon the merits of the controversy; and the daily invoices of Christian champions and martyrs of all sects were being admitted to blessedness as fast as they murdered one another.

Moreover, Red Palnatoki was, by the articles of his stern Nordic creed, a fatalist. When he discovered what had happened, and the strange salvation which had been put upon him, his religion therefore assured him that this too had been predestined by the wayward Norns, and he piously made no complaining. The eternal life which he had inherited, with no fighting in it for the present, and no stronger drink than milk, was not up to human expectation, but the tall sea-rover had long ago found out that few things are. Meanwhile he could, at any rate, look forward to that promised last great battle, when those praiseworthy captains Gog and Magog (with, as Palnatoki understood it, a considerable company of fine fighting-men) would attack the four-square city, and when Palnatoki would have again a chance really to enjoy himself in defending the camp of the saints.

And meanwhile too, he was interested in those girls. It seemed at best to anyone with his religious rearing quite unaccountable to find women in heaven, and this especial pair appeared to Palnatoki a remarkably quaint choice for exceptional favoritism. He could only deduce they had got in through some error similar to that which had procured his own admission, particularly as he saw no other women anywhere about.

And Palnatoki reflected that the enceinte lady, with eagle's wings and the crown of little stars, whom the presumably pet dragon followed everywhere with touching devotion, could not for as yet some months repay cultivating. But that very pretty brunette, with the golden cup and all those splendid clothes and with the placard on her forehead, who had just ridden by upon that seven-headed scarlet monster, rather took Palnatoki's fancy. That girl was not, you could see, a prude; she had come very near winking at him, if she, indeed, had not actually winked, in the moment she glanced back: so that the Great Whore of Babylon (which, as they told him, was this second lady's name) gave him, upon the whole, something else to look forward to.

Without any sulking under his halo, Palnatoki bent resolutely to his first harp-lesson; and, in place of protests, civilly voiced alleluias.

For, with two fine tomorrows to look forward to, Palnatoki was content enough. And in Jahveh's heaven, therefore, all went agreeably, and as smoothly as Red Palnatoki at just this point goes out of this story.

Chapter LX

In the Hall of the Chosen

When Donander of Évre awoke in the Northern paradise, he also was content enough. It was a strange and not what you would call a cozy place, this gold-roofed hall with its five hundred and forty mile-wide doors: and the monsters, in the likeness of a stag and of a she-goat, which straddled above the building, perpetually feeding upon the lower leaves of the great tree called Lærath, seemed to Donander pre-eminently outlandish creatures, animals under whose bellies no really considerate persons would have erected a residence. Yet, like Palnatoki, Donander of Évre was an old campaigner, who could be tolerably comfortable anywhere. Nor was to discover himself among pagans a novel experience, since in his mortal life Donander had ridden at adventure in most corners of the world, and rather more than half of his finest enemies and of his opponents in many delightful encounters had been infidels.

'Excepting always their unfortunate religious heresies,' he was used to concede, 'I have no fault to pick with heathen persons, whom in the daily and nocturnal affairs of life I have found quite as friendly and companionable as properly baptised ladies.'

In fine, he got on well enough with the flaxed-haired spirits of these Northern kings and skalds and jarls and vikingar. They stared, and some guffawed, when he fitted out a little shrine, in which Donander prayed decorously, every day at the correct hours, for the second coming of Manuel and for the welfare of Donander's soul upon the holy Morrow of Judgement. Yet, after all, these boreal ghosts conceded, in paradise if anywhere a man should be permitted utterly to follow his own tastes, even in imaginative eschatology. And when they talked their really pathetic nonsense about being the guests of Sidvrar the Weaver and Constrainer, and about living forever through his bounty thus happily in the Hall of the Chosen, it was Donander's turn to shrug. Even had there been no other discrepancies, everybody knew that heaven had, not five hundred and forty golden gates, but only twelve entrances, each carved from a single pearl and engraved with the name of a tribe of Israel.

'Besides,' Donander asked, 'who is this Weaver and Con strainer? Certainly, I never heard of him before.'

'He is the King and Father of the Ænseis,' they told him. 'He is overlord of that unimaginable folk who dwell in Ydalir; and who do not kill their deformed and weakling children, as we were used to do, but instead cast from the ivory ramparts of Ydalir all such degenerate offspring, to be the gods of races who are not blond and Nordic.'

Donander, as a loyal son of the Church, could only shake his head over such nonsense, and the innumerous other errors by which these heathens were being misled to everlasting ruin. Aloud, Donander repeated his final verdict as to the pretensions of this Sidvrar, by saying again, 'I never heard of him.'

Nevertheless, Donander went without real discontent among the pleasures of paradise, and he joined in all the local sports. In common with the other dead, he ate the flesh of the inexhaustible boar, and with them he drank of the strong mead which sustained them in perpetual tipsiness. And he sedately rode out with the others, every morning, into the meadows where these blessed pagan lords fought joyously among themselves until midday. At noon a peal of thunder would sound, the slain and wounded warriors were of a sudden revivified and cured of their hurts, and were re-united to whatsoever arms and heads and legs the contestants had lost in their gaming: and the company would return fraternally to the gold-roofed hall, where they ate and drank and made their brags until they slept.

'Yet perhaps our banquets might, messieurs,' Donander had suggested, after a century or so of these rough-and-ready pleasures, 'be not unadvantageously seasoned with the delights of feminine companionship, if only for dessert?'

'But it is one of our appointed blessings to have done with women and their silly ways,' cried out the vikingar, 'now that we have entered paradise.'

And Donander, who had always been notable for his affectionate nature, and who had served vigorously so many ladies par amours, seemed grieved to hear the uttering of a saying so unchivalrous. Still, he said nothing.

Much time passed thus: and the worlds were changed: but in the eyes of Donander of Évre, as in the eyes of all who feasted in the Hall of the Chosen, there was no knowledge nor any fear of time, because these blessed dead lived now in perpetual tipsiness. And, as befitted a loyal son of the Church, Donander, without any complaining, in the surroundings which Heaven out of Heaven's wisdom had selected for him, awaited the second coming of Manuel and the holy Morrow of Judgement.

Chapter LXI

Vanadis, Dear Lady of Reginlief

Then, from the highest part of this paradise, and from the unimaginable yew-vales of Ydalir which rose above the topmost branches of the tree called Lærath, descended blue-robed Vanadis, the Lady of Reginlief, dear to the Ænseis. She had disposed of five inefficient husbands, in impetuous mythological manners, but still a loneliness and a desire was upon her; and with the eternal optimism of widowhood she came to look for a sixth husband among these great-thewed heroes who jeered at women and their wiles.

But Donander of Évre was the person who for two reasons found instant favor in her eyes when she came upon Donander refreshing himself after the pleasant fatigues of that morning's combat, and about his daily bath in the shining waters of the river Gipul. So did the dead call that stream which flowed from the antlers of the monstrous stag who stood eternally nibbling and munching above the Hall of the Chosen.

'Here is an eminently suitable person,' Vanadis reflected. Aloud, she said, 'Hail, friend! and does a stout fine fellow of your length and of your thickness go languidly shunning work or seeking work?'

Stalwart Donander climbed out of the clear stream of Gipul. He came, smilingly and with a great exaltation, toward the first woman whom he had seen in seven hundred years. And, so constant is the nature of woman, that divine Vanadis regarded Donander in just the reflective wonder with which, more than seven hundred years ago, barbarian Utsumé had looked at Coth in the market-place of Porutsa.

Donander said, 'What is your meaning, madame?'

Vanadis replied, 'I have a desire which, a fine portent has informed me, agrees with your desire.'

Then Vanadis, with godlike candor, made wholly plain her meaning. And since Donander's nature was affectionate, he assented readily enough to the proposals of this somewhat ardent but remarkably handsome young woman, who went abroad thus unconventionally in a car drawn by two cats, and who, in her heathenish and figurative way, described herself as a goddess. He stipulated only that, so soon as he was dressed, they be respectably united according to whatever might be the marriage laws of her country and diocese.

The Ænseis were not used in such matters to stand upon ceremony. Nevertheless, they conferred together – Aduna and Ord and Hleifner and Rönn and Giermivul, and the other radiant sons of Sidvrar. It was they who good-humoredly devised a ceremony, with candles and promises and music and a gold ring, and all the other features which seem expected by the quaint sort of husband whom their beloved Vanadis had fetched up from the Hall of the Chosen. But her sisters took no part in this ceremony, upon the ground that they considered such public preliminaries to be unheard-of and brazen.

Thus was Donander made free of Ydalir, the land that was above Lærath and the other heavens and paradises: and after Donander's seven hundred years of celibacy, he and his bride got on together in her bright palace lovingly enough. Vanadis found that she too, comparatively speaking, had lived with her five earlier husbands in celibacy.

Chapter LXII

The Demiurgy of Donander Veratyr

Now the one change that Donander made an explicit point of was to fit out in this palace of Reginlief a chapel. There he worshiped daily at the correct hours, so near as one could calculate them in an endless day, and there he prayed for the second coming of Manuel and for the welfare of Donander's soul upon the holy Morrow of Judgement.

'But, really, my heart,' his Vanadis would say, ineffectually, 'you have been dead for so long now! and, just looking at it sensibly, it does seem such a waste of eternity!'

'Have done, my darling, with your heathen nonsense!' Donander would reply. 'Do I not know that in heaven there is no marrying or giving in marriage? How then can heaven be this place in which two live so friendlily and happily?'

Meanwhile, to the pagan priests wherever the Ænseis were adored, had been revealed the sixth and the wholly successful marriage of blue-robed Vanadis: her spouse had been duly deified: and new temples had been builded in honor of the bright lady of Reginlief and of the Man-God, Donander Veratyr, her tireless savior from vain desire and bodily affliction. And time went stealthily as a stream flowing about and over the worlds, and changing them, and wearing all away. But to Donander it was as if he yet lived in the thrice-lucky afternoon on which he married his Vanadis. For, since whatever any of the Ænseis desired must happen instantly, thus Ydalir knew but one endless day: and immeasurably beneath its radiance, very much as sullen and rain-swollen waters go under a bridge upon which young lovers have met in the sunlight of April, so passed wholly unnoticed by any in Ydalir the flowing and the all jumbled wreckage of time.

But it befell, too, after a great many of those æons which Ydalir ignored and men cannot imagine, that Donander saw one of his smaller brothers-in-law about a droll-looking sport. Donander asked questions: and he learned this dark brisk little Koshchei was about a game at which the younger Ænseis were used to play.

'And how does one set about it?' Donander asked then.

'Why, thus and thus, my heart,' his wife replied. Fond Vanadis was glad enough to find for him some outdoor diversion which would woo him from that stuffy chapel and its depressing pictures of tortured persons and its unwholesome fogs of stifling incense.

Then Donander broke away a bough from the tree called Lærath, saying meanwhile the proper word of power. Sitting beside the fifth river of Ydalir, he cut strips of bark from this bough, with the green-handled knife which Vanadis had given him, and he cast these strips about at random. He found it perfectly true that those scraps of bark which touched the water became fish, those which he flung into the air became birds, and those which fell upon the ground became animals and men.

He almost instantly, indeed, had enough creatures to populate a world, but no world, of course, for them to animate and diversify. So Donander destroyed these creatures, and placed one of the lighter weirds upon the beetle Karu. That huge, good-tempered insect fell at once to shaping a ball of mud, and to carving it with mountains and plains and valleys. Then Karu burrowed his way into the center of this ball of mud: and from the hole into which Karu had entered came all kinds of living beings needful for the animating and diversifying of a world; and these began to breed and to kill one another and to build their appropriate lairs, in nests and dens and cities.

This so excited another beetle, named Khypera, that he behaved in a fashion not at all convenient to record; but many living creatures were at once brought forth by his remarkable conduct, and plants and creeping things and men and women, too, came out of the moisture which Khypera let fall.

That was the second demiurgy of Donander Veratyr. Then with a golden egg Donander made another world: and from the entrails of a spider he drew another; from the carrion of a dead crow he made a fifth world; and with the aid of a raven Donander made yet one more. Thereafter he went on, in turn attempting each method that any Ans had ever practiced.

These sports amused Donander for a long while and yet another while. And Vanadis, apart from her natural pleasure in the augmented vigor he got from so much open-air exercise, bright Vanadis smiled at his playing, in the way of any wife who finds her husband occupied upon the whole less reprehensibly than you would expect of the creature. And the sons of Sidvrar also were used, as yet, to smile not unfriendly when they passed where Donander was busy with his toys. Even the sisters of Vanadis only said that really of all things, and that of course they had expected it from the very first.

Sidvrar Vafudir, the Weaver and Constrainer, said nothing whatever. . . . So everybody was content for a long while and yet another while.

And throughout both these whiles Donander was pottering with his worlds, keeping them bright with thunderbolts and volcanic eruptions, diligently cleansing them of parasites with one or another pestilence, scouring them with whirlwinds, and perpetually washing them with cloud-bursts and deluges. His toys had constantly such loving care to keep them in perfect condition. Meanwhile, his skill increased abreast with his indulgence in demiurgy, and Donander thought of little else. He needed now no aid from ravens and beetles. He had but, he found, to desire a world, and at once his desire took form: its light was divided from its darkness, the waters gathered into one place, the dry land appeared and pullulated with living creatures; all in one dexterous complacent movement of self-admiration.

His earlier made stars and comets and suns and asteroids Donander Veratyr began destroying one by one, half vexedly, half in real amusement at the archaic, bungling methods he had outgrown. In their places he would set spinning, and glittering, and popping, quite other planetary systems which, for the moment in any event, appeared to him remarkably adroit craftsmanship. And everywhere upon the worlds which he had made, and had not yet annihilated, men worshipped Donander Veratyr: and in his pleasant home at Reginlief, high over Lærath and every other heaven and paradise, Donander worshiped the gods of the fathers and of all the reputable neighbors of Donander of Évre; and in such pagan surroundings as Heaven out of Heaven's wisdom had selected for him, awaited the second coming of Manuel and the holy Morrow of Judgement.

Chapter LXIII

Economics of Sidvrar

Then of a sudden gleaming Sidvrar Vafudir, the Weaver and Constrainer, came with his wolves frisking about him. He came with his broad-brimmed hat pulled down about his eyes decisively. He came thus to his daughter, blue-robed Vanadis, and he stated that, while patience was a virtue, there was such a thing as overdoing it, no matter how little he himself might care for the talking of idle busybodies, because, howsoever long she might argue, and always had done from childhood, being in this and in many other undesirable respects precisely like her mother, even so, no sensible Ans could ever deny her husband's conduct was ridiculous: and that, said Sidvrar Vafudir, was all there was to it.

'Do not bluster so, my heart,' replied Vanadis, 'about the facts of nature. All husbands are ridiculous. Who should be surer of this than I, who have had six husbands, unless it be you, who as goat and titmouse and birch-tree have been the husband of six hundred?'

'That is all very well,' said Sidvrar, 'in addition to not being what we were discussing. This Donander of yours is now one of the Ænseis, he is an Ans of mature standing, and it is not right for him to be making worlds. That is what we were discussing.'

'Yet what divine hands anywhere,' asked Vanadis, 'are clean of demiurgy?'

'That is not what we were discussing, either. When you brats of mine were children you had your toys, and you played with and you smashed your toys. Nobody denies that, because you all did, from Rönn to Aduna, and even little Koshchei used to be having his fling at such nonsense. Now do you look at the very fine and sober fellow he is, with all his pranks behind him, and do you ask Koshchei what he thinks of that husband of yours! But instead you prefer to wander away from what we were discussing, because you know as well as I do that for children to be playing at such games is natural enough, besides keeping the young out of grave mischief, now and then. Though, to be sure, nothing does that very long nor very often, as I tell you plainly, my Vanadis, for do you look, too, as a most grievous example, at the wasteful and untidy way you destroy your husbands!'

'Donander Veratyr I shall not ever destroy,' replied Vanadis, smiling, 'because of the loving human heart and the maddening human ways he has brought out of his Poictesme, and for two other reasons.'

'Then it is I who will put an end, if not to him, at least to his nonsense. For this Donander of yours is still playing with stars and planets, and setting off his comets, and exploding his suns, and that is not becoming.'

'Well, well, do you, who are the Father and Master of All, have your own will with him, so far as you can get it,' Vanadis returned, still with that rather reminiscent smile. She had now lived for a great while with this sixth husband of hers, who had a human heart in him and human ways.

Chapter LXIV

Through the Oval Window

Sidvrar went then from Vanadis to Donander. But the Constrainer found there was no instant manner of constraining Donander Veratyr into a conviction that Donander of Évre had died long ago, and had become an Ans. People, Donander stated, did not do such things; when people died they went either to heaven or to hell: and further reasoning with Donander seemed to accomplish no good whatever. For Donander, as a loyal son of the Church, now shrugged pityingly at the heathen nonsense talked by his father-in-law. He stroked the heads of Sidvrar's attendant wolves, he listened to the Weaver and Constrainer with an indulgence more properly reserved for the feeble-minded; and he said, a little relishingly, that Messire Sidvrar would be wiser on the holy Morrow of Judgement.

Then Sidvrar Vafudir became Sidvrar Yggr, the Meditating and Terrible. Then Sidvrar fell about such magicking as he had not needed to use since he first entered into the eternal yew-vales of Ydalir. Then, in a word, Sidvrar unclosed the oval window in Reginlief that opened upon space and time and upon the frozen cinders which once had been worlds and suns and stars, and which their various creators had annihilated, as one by one the Ænseis had put away their childhood and its playing.

Among such wreckage sped pretentiously the yet living worlds which Donander had made. These toys, when seen thus closely through the magic of the oval window, were abristle with the spires of the temples and the cathedrals in which they that lived, as yet, upon these worlds were used to worship. In all these churches men invoked Donander Veratyr. Through that charmed window now, for the first time, came to his ears the outcry of his clergy and laity: nowhere was there talk of another god, not even where from many worlds arose the lecturing of those who explained away their ancestors' quaint notions about

Donander the Man-God, the Savior from Vain Desire, the Preserver from Bodily Affliction, and proved there could not be any such person. And to Donander, looking out of the window at Reginlief, all these things showed as a swarming of ants or as a writhing of very small maggots about the worlds which he had made to divert him: and in the face as in the heart of Donander awoke inquietation.

'If this be a true showing,' Donander said, by and by, 'show now that Earth which is my home.'

After a while of searching, Sidvrar found for him the drifting clinker which had once been Earth. Upon its glistering naked-ness was left no living plant nor any breathing creature, for the Morrow of Judgement was long past, and Earth's affairs had been wound up. Upon no planet did anyone remember the god whom Donander worshiped, now that Jahveh had ended play-ing, and his toys were broken or put away. Upon many planets were the temples of Donander Veratyr, and the rising smoke of his sacrifice, and the cries of his worshipers as they murdered one another in their disrupting over points of theology which Donander could not clearly understand.

Nor did he think about these things. Instead, Donander Veratyr, who was the last of the Ænseis to play at this unprofit-able sport of demiurgy, was now remembering the days and the moon-lighted nights of his youth, and the dear trivial persons whom he had then loved and revered. He did not think about the two wives whom he had married upon Earth, nor about his son Maugis, nor about any of the happenings of Donander's manhood. He thought of, for no reason at all, the shabby little village priest who had confirmed him, and of the father and mother who had been all-wise and able to defend one from every evil, and of the tall girl whose lips had, once, and before any other lips, been sweeter than were the joys of Ydalir. And he thought of many other futile things, all now attested always to have been futile, which long ago had seemed so very important to the boy that, in serving famous Manuel of Poictesme, had postured so high-heartedly in one of the smallest provinces of an extinct planet.

And Donander wrung immortal hands, saying, 'If this be a true showing, what thing have I become, who can no longer love or reverence anything! who can have no care for any Morrow of Judgement! and to whom space reveals only the living of these indistinguishable and unclean and demented insects!'

The cry of his worshipers came up to him. 'Thou art God, the Creator and Preserver of all us Thy children! Thou art Donander Veratyr, in Whom is our firm hope! Thou are the Man-God, That wilt grant unto us justice and salvation upon the holy Morrow of Judgement!'

'Is it,' Donander said, 'of Manuel that these little creatures speak?'

'We know not of any Manuel,' the universe replied to him. 'We only know that Thou art God, our Creator and Preserver.'

Then, after regarding again the vermin which swarmed about his worlds, Donander said, like one a little frightened, 'Is God thus?'

They answered him, fondly and reverently, 'How can God be otherwise than Thou art?'

At that Donander shuddered. But in the same moment he said, 'If this be a true showing, and if I be indeed a god, and the master of all things, the human heart which survives in me wills now to create that tomorrow for which these weaklings and I too have so long waited.'

And Sidvrar pointed out, as patiently as outraged common-sense permitted: 'Still, still, you are talking nonsense! How can an Ans create tomorrow?'

Donander asked, in turn, 'Why not, if you be omnipotent?'

'It is because we are omnipotent. Thus in Ydalir there is but one day, from which not even in imagination can any Ans escape. For, whatever any of the Ænseis desires, even if it be a tomorrow, must instantly happen and exist; and so must be today. That ought to be plain enough.'

'It is not plain,' Donander answered, 'although, the way you put it, I admit, it does sound logical. Therefore, if this indeed be the way of omnipotence, and if none may escape his day, and if I be a trapped and meager immortal, and the master only of these things which are today, then now let all things end! For my heart stays human. Today does not know the runes of my heart's contentment. My heart will not be satisfied unless it enter into that morrow of justice and salvation which the overlords of men, as you now tell me, cannot desire nor plan. So now, if this be a true showing, now let all things end!'

Within the moment Donander saw that, while he was yet speaking, space was emptied of life. Down yonder now were no more men and women anywhere. None any longer awaited the oncoming day which was to content one utterly with an assured bright heritage, divined in the dreams which allured and derided all human living endlessly, and condemned the heart of every man to be a stranger to contentment upon this side of tomorrow. That ageless dream about tomorrow, and about the redeeming which was to come – tomorrow – had passed, as the smoke of a little incense passes; and with it had gone out of being, too, those whom it had nourished and sustained. There were no more men and women anywhere. Donander could see only many cinders adrift in a bleak loneliness: and Donander of Évre must endure eternally as Donander Veratyr, a lonely and uncomprehended immortal among his many peers.

'So do you be sensible about it, my son-in-law,' said Sidvrar Vafudir, when he had spoken the word of power which closed forever that cheerless window, out of which nobody was ever to look any more – 'be sensible, if there indeed stay any root of intelligence in you. And do you henceforward live more fittingly, as a credit to your wife's family. And do you put out of mind those cinders and those ashes and those clinkers that were the proper sport of your youth. Such is the end of every wise person's saga.'

Chapter LXV

The Reward of Faith

Thereafter the King and Father of the Ænseis departed, well pleased with the lesson taught that whippersnapper. And Donander also smiled, and he looked contentedly about his pleasant quarters in the everlasting vales of Ydalir.

'Still, not for a great deal,' Donander reflected, 'would I be treading in that old sorcerer's sandals; and it is a fair shame that I should have such a person for a father-in-law.'

For, as a loyal son of the Church, Donander did not doubt that the wonders which Sidvrar had just shown to him could only be an illusion planned with some evil spirit's aid to tempt Donander away from respectability and the true faith. In consequence Donander Veratyr, that had been the Creator and Destroyer of all things except the human heart which survived in him, went now into the chapel of Reginlief. There he decorously said the prayers to which Donander was accustomed, and he prayed for the second coming of Manuel and for the welfare of Donander's soul upon the holy Morrow of Judgement.

Book Ten

At Manuel's Tomb

*'What hast thou here, that thou hast
hewed thee out of a sepulchre?'*
                    ISAIAH, xxii, 16

— Salut, *ami, dit Jurgen, si vous êtes une créatue de Dieu.*
 — Votre *protase est du bien mauvais grec, observa le Centaure,
car en Hellade nous nous abstenions de semblables réserves.
D'ailleurs mon origine vous intéresse certes moins que ma desti-
nation.*

— LA HAULTE HISTOIRE DE JURGEN

Chapter LXVI

Old Age of Niafer

Now the tale is of crippled old Dame Niafer, who had reformed the Poictesme which her husband redeemed, and of the thinking which came upon her in the last days of her life. Until latterly Niafer had not, with at every turn so many things requiring to be done, had very much time for thinking. But now there was nothing more ever to be done by Madame Niafer. Radegonde saw to that.

The gray-eyed minx ruled everything and everybody. That was not pleasant for her mother-in-law to behold, after Niafer herself had ruled over Poictesme for some twenty years, and all the while had kept frivolity and disorder out of fashion. No mother could, in the first place, honestly enjoy seeing her own son thus hoodwinked and led into perpetual dissipation at all hours of the night, by a wife who at thirteen hundred and some years of age, might reasonably be expected to know better. In the second place, Niafer could have managed things, and very certainly poor Emmerick, with immeasurably more benefit to everybody, and to common-sense too.

All that warring with Maugis, for instance, had been a sad mistake. Now, under my regency, the aged Countess would reflect with complacence, there was grumbling here and there – men being what they are, with no least idea as to what is actually good for them – but never any armed revolt. When people were dissatisfied, you sent for them, they came, you had a sensible talk, you found out what was really wrong, and you righted matters to the utmost extent that such a righting seemed judicious; you eked out the remainder with a little harmless soft-soaping, and that was all there was to it. No warrior in his sane senses would go to war with an intelligent old lady who esteemed him such a particularly fine fellow.

Now, if at the very beginning, that poor Maugis – quite a nice-looking child, too, until he lost flesh under that continual plotting and throat-cutting, with parents you had known for years – had been had in to dinner, just with the family, then all that killing and burning and being awakened at unearthly hours by the misguided boy's night attacks upon Bellegarde would have been avoided.

But, Niafer, of course, had been allowed no say in the matter. She was allowed no say in any matter by that woman, who topped off her ill-doing by being always so insufferably pleasant and so considerate of Mother Niafer's comfort. And in this enforced idleness it was rather lonely now that Holmendis was dead. Nearly seven years ago that dependable and always firm friend had gone crusading with St Louis; and the pair of them had passed from the ruins of Carthage to eternal glory with the aid of dysentery. Niafer missed Holmendis a great deal, after the three decades of close friendship and of the continuous intimacy about which people said things of which the old Countess was aware enough and utterly unmindful.

She had her children, of course. It was particularly nice to have Melicent back again, after all these years of never quite really knowing whether the child was managing her abductor tactfully, in that far-off Nacumera. But the children had their own children now, and their own affairs; and none of these possessions they were inclined to let Niafer control, in the Poictesme wherein, for eighteen years, she had controlled everything. For the rest, Dame Niafer knew that a prophecy which had been made to her very long ago by the Head of Misery was now being fulfilled: she had no place in the world's ordering, she was but a tolerated intruder into her children's living, and nobody anywhere did more than condone her coming.

Niafer did not blame her children. She instead admitted, with the vast practicality not ever to be comprehended by any male creature, that their behavior was sensible.

'I would meddle perpetually if they permitted it. I am very often a nuisance, as it is. And so, that part of the prophecy about my weeping in secret is quite plainly nonsense, since there is nothing whatever to weep about, or even to be surprised at,' Dame Niafer stated cheerily.

And so, too, if sometimes, after one or another crossing of her still pertinacious will, the dethroned old ruler of Poictesme would hobble very quietly into her own rooms, and would remain there for a lengthy while with the door locked, and would come out by and by with reddened eyes, nobody noticed it particularly. For she, who in her prime had been the most sociable of potentates, seemed nowadays to prefer upon the whole to be alone. She was continually, without any ostentation, limping away from any little gathering of her descendants. Mother was becoming slightly queer: you shrugged, not at all unfondly, over the fact, and put up with it. Grandmother would be there one moment laughing and talking like everybody else; and the very next moment she was gone. And you would find her, accidentally, in some quiet corner, quite alone, bent up a little, and not doing anything whatever, but just thinking. . . .

Dame Niafer thought, usually, about her husband. Her lot had been the most glorious among the lots of all women, in that she had been Manuel's wife. That marvelous five years of living which she had shared with Manuel the Redeemer was not an extensive section of her life, but it was the one part which really counted, she supposed. It was only on account of her human frailty that she remembered so many more things about Holmendis, who was a mere Saint, than she did about her Manuel. She found it, nowadays, rather hard – and injudicious, too – to recall any quite definite details about her miraculous husband: there was only, at a comfortable remoteness, a tall gray god in a great golden glowing. It was all wonderful, and inspiring, and very sad, too, but noticeably vague: and the tears which came into your eyes were pleasant, without your knowing exactly what you were crying about.

That was the best way in which to think of her Manuel. A prying into particulars, a dwelling upon any detail whatever, was injudicious. Such a perhaps blasphemous direction of your thoughts suggested, for instance, that matters were going to be a trifle awkward, just at first, after that second coming of the Redeemer.

It was not, altogether, that Manuel would be a stranger to her, nor even that omniscience, of course, knew all about Holmendis. In dealing with a liberal patron of the Church it was the métier of omniscience to become a little myopic. For that matter, Dom

Manuel's earthly past was not so far gone out of his wife's memory that he could be the only person to do any talking about natural frailties. No, the drawback would be, rather, that, when her Manuel had returned, in undiminished glory, you would have to get accustomed to so many things, all over again. . . . Niafer hoped that, in any event, at his second coming he would not bring back with him that irritating habit of catching cold on every least occasion: for you probably could not with decency rebuke a spiritual Redeemer for his insistence upon keeping the rooms stuffy and shut up everywhere on account of the draughts, any more than you could really look up to him with appropriate reverence if he came snorting and sneezing all over the place. . . . And if he for one single solitary moment expected to have, in his reordering of human affairs, that Alianora and that Freydis of his established anywhere near his lawful wife. . . .

That mad contingency, however, was not at any time mentally provided against, because at this point Niafer would turn away from this undoubtedly blasphemous trend of speculation. Her Manuel was in all things perfect. He would come again in unimaginable glory, and he would exalt her, his chosen, his one bride, who was so utterly unworthy of him, to the sharing of an eternal felicity which – after you got accustomed to it, and really settled down, with a fresh growth of hair and a complete set of teeth and all the other perquisites of unfading youth – would be quite pleasant. Details could wait. Details, the moment you dwelt upon them, became upsetting. Details in any way relative to those hussies were no doubt directly suggested by the powers of evil.

It was after such considerations that Niafer would go to pray beside the tomb which she had builded in honor of Manuel.

Chapter LXVII

The Women Differ

Now the tale tells that in the spring of the year old Niafer, thus sitting beside her husband's tomb, looked up and found another aged woman waiting near her.

'Hail, Queen of England!' said Dame Niafer, with quite as much civility as there was any need for.

'So!' said the other. 'You would be his wife. Yes. I remember you, that day near Quentavic. But how could you be recognising me?'

'Are there not tears in your old eyes? There is no other person living, since that double-faced Freydis got her just deserts,' replied Niafer, very quietly, 'who would be shedding tears over my Manuel's tomb. We two alone remember him.'

'That is true,' said Alianora. And for no reason at all she smiled a little. 'One hears so much about him, too.'

'The world has learned to appreciate my husband,' Niafer assented. She did not altogether approve of Madame Alianora's smile.

Now the Queen said: 'He was rather a dear boy. And I am not denying that I cared a great deal about him once. But even so, my dear, this wonder of the world that the poems and the histories are about, and that the statues and the shrines commemorate, and that one, in mere decency, has to pretend to remember!'

'I am sure I do not at all understand you, Madame Alianora.' And Niafer looked without any love at this Queen of England who in the old days had been upon terms of such regrettable intimacy with Dom Manuel.

But Alianora went on, with that provokingly pleasant air of hers: 'No, you would not understand the joke of it. You do not properly value the work of your hands and of your imagining. But this legend which you in chief, with the pride and the foolishness of Poictesme to back you, have been quietly and so tirelessly fostering through all these years, has spread through the known world. Our Manuel has become the peer of Hector and of Arthur and of Charlemagne for his bravery and his wisdom and his other perfections. Our Manuel is to come again, in all his former glory! And I, who remember Manuel quite clearly – though I am not denying he has had his successors in my good will and friendly interest – well, in perfect candor, my dear, I find these notions rather droll.'

To this sort of talking Niafer replied, sharply enough, 'I do not know of any reason in the world for you to be speaking of my husband as "our" Manuel.'

'No, my dear, I am sure he took excellent care that you should never know about such things. Well, but all that is over a great while ago. And there is no need for us two to be quarreling over the lad that took his pleasure with the pair of us, and with Queen Freydis too, and with nobody knows how many other women, and who, to do him justice, gave to each playfellow a fair half of that pleasure.'

This exposed unvenerable handsome old Alianora to the gaze of perturbed decorum. 'I do not think, madame, that you ought to be alluding to such frivolous matters here at his tomb.'

'After all, though,' Alianora stated, 'it is not as if he were really buried in this place. You dreaming braggarts of Poictesme had not even a corpse to start with, when you began on your fine legend. No: the entire affair is pure invention; and is very neatly symbolised by this stately tomb with nothing whatever inside it.'

'What, though, if Manuel had been truly buried here, what would this world have been relinquishing to the cold grave?' said Freydis. For Niafer saw that Freydis also was at hand. This Freydis was a witch-woman with whose connivance Dom Manuel had in the old days made unholy images and considerable scandal.

'Nobody knows that,' continued Freydis. 'Not even we who, as we said, loved Manuel the Redeemer in his mortal life knew anything about Manuel. I know that he wanted what he never found. I think that he never, quite, knew what he wanted. But that is all. That is all I know, today. What sort of being lived inside that squinting tall strong husk which used to fondle us? I often wonder about that.'

'My dear creature,' said Alianora, 'do you really think it

particularly matters? I am sure we never used to think about that especial question at the time, because the husk was, in all conscience, enough to deal with. Yes, you may say what you will about Manuel, but among friends there is no harm in conceding that in some respects we three know him to have been quite wonderful.'

It was then that the old Queen of England looked up toward the gleaming statue of the man whom these three women had loved variously. Manuel towered high above them, bedazzling in the May sunlight, serene, eternally heroic, eternally in that prime of life which his put-by spent bedfellows had long ago over-passed; and he seemed to regard exalted matters ineffably beyond the scope of their mortal living and the comprehension of frail human faculties. But wrinkled jovial Alianora smiled up at this superb Redeemer fondly and just a little mockingly.

'You understood me,' Alianora said, 'And I you. But we did not talk about it.'

'I say that nobody understood Manuel,' replied Freydis. 'I say it is a strange thing that we three should be continuing the life of Manuel and the true nature of the being who lived inside that husk, and that we three should yet stay ignorant of what we are giving to the times that are to come. For Manuel has already returned, and he will keep returning again and again, without redeeming anything and without there being any wonder about it—'

Alianora was interested. 'But do you explain, my darling — '

'Dead Manuel lives again in your tall squinting son — '

'Yes — and do you just imagine, Freydis dear, what a reflection that is to any mother, with what Manuel's irregular notions about marriage — !'

' — And in the four children that he had by Niafer,' Freydis continued. 'And in these children's children our Manuel's life will be renewed, and after that in their grandchildren: and Manuel's life and Manuel's true nature will thus go on, in many bodies, so long as men act foolishly by day and wickedly at night. And in the images which I aided him to make and to inform with fire from Audela, in these also, when these are set to live as men among mankind — and to my fancy, no more reasonably than my two elder children, Sesphra and Raimbaut, have lived already — in these also, will our Manuel live. Yes, in all these inheritors of his foiled being, our Manuel will, thus, live many lives — wanting always what he has not ever found, and never, quite, knowing what thing it is which he wants, and without which he may not ever be contented.'

'I see,' said Alianora: 'and your explanation of his second and of, indeed, his two thousandth coming seems to me, I confess, much the more plausible. Yes, I see. Manuel has already returned; and he will return again any number of times — '

Freydis said moodily, 'And to whose benefit and pleasuring?'

'My darling Freydis! You may depend upon it that on each occasion two persons will get a great deal of pleasure out of preparing the way for him. And that,' said Alianora, 'that and whatever else may befall those persons who have Manuel's proclivities and life in them will be but another happening in the Biography of Manuel. We three have begun a never-ending set of comedies in which the life of Manuel will be the main actor. We have, as one might say — among friends, my darlings — collaborated with the dear boy to make an endless series of Manuels, without any special reassurance that to do this was going to give good and pleasure to anybody except — say what you will, my dears — it does always give to a hearty young woman. For we do not know, even now, exactly what sort of a creature this Manuel was and, thanks to our collaboration, will continue to be. Yes, now I see your point, my dear Freydis; and it is really a curious one.'

Again, though, Alianora smiled up toward the statue of Manuel as though there were some secret between them. And Niafer had no patience whatever with the leering and iniquitous old hussy.

'The whole world knows,' said Niafer, indignantly, 'what sort of person my husband was, for my Manuel is famous throughout Christendom.'

'Yes,' Alianora assented, 'he is famous as a paragon of all the Christian virtues, and as the Redeemer whose return is to restore the happiness and glories of his people: and it is upon that joke, my dear Niafer, I was congratulating you a moment ago.'

'He is famous for his loyalty and valor and wisdom,' said Freydis. 'I hear of it. And I remember the tall frightened fool who betrayed me, and whom at the last I spared out of mere pity for his worthlessness. And still, I spare the frightened, blundering, foiled living of Manuel, and I perpetuate and I foster this living, in my children, because it is certain that a woman's folly does not ever perish.'

'Nevertheless, I know how to avail myself of a woman's folly,' said Horvendile – for now, Dame Niafer perceived, that queer, red-headed Horvendile also was standing beside her husband's tomb – 'and of the babble of children, and of the unwillingness of men to face the universe with no better backing than their own resources.'

Then Horvendile looked full at Niafer, with his young, rather cruel smile. And Horvendile said:

'So does it come about that the saga of Manuel and the sagas of all the lords of the Silver Stallion have been reshaped by the foolishness and the fond optimism of mankind; and these sagas now conform in everything to that supreme romance which preserves us from insanity. For it is just as I said, years ago, to one of these so drolly whitewashed and ennobled rapscallions. All men that live, and that go perforce about this world like blundering lost children whose rescuer is not yet in sight, have a vital need to believe in this sustaining legend about the Redeemer, and about the Redeemer's power to make those persons who serve him just and perfect.'

'It is you who are much worse than a rapscallion!' cried out Dame Niafer. 'You are as bad as these women here. But I will not listen to any of you or to any more of your jealous and foul blasphemies – !'

Then Madame Niafer awakened, to find herself alone by the great tomb. But real footsteps were approaching, and they proved to be those of a person rather more acceptable to her than was that jeering Horvendile or were those brazen-faced and thoroughly vile-minded women about whom Dame Niafer had been dreaming.

Chapter LXVIII

Radegonde is Practical

For at this point Madame Niafer was approached by Jurgen, the son of Coth, who came to Manuel's tomb upon a slight professional matter. Jurgen – now some while reformed by the ruthless impairments of middle age, and settled down into tempestuous matrimony with the daughter of Ninzian (by the wife of well-to-do old Pettipas) – had since his marriage brought new life and fresh connections into the business of his nominal father-in-law; and was today the leading pawnbroker of Poictesme. It was thus to Jurgen, naturally enough, that Count Emmerick's wife, Radegonde, had applied in these hard times which followed the long and impoverishing war with Maugis d'Aigremont.

The Countess had been taking of Dom Manuel's tomb what she described as a really practical view. The tomb was magnificent and in every way a credit to the great hero's family. Still, as Radegonde pointed out to her husband, that effigy of Manuel at the top was inset with scores of handsome gems which were virtually being wasted. If – of course without giving any vulgar publicity to the improvement – these jewels could be replaced with bits of suitably colored glass, the visual effect would remain the same, the tomb would be as handsome as ever, and nobody would be the wiser excepting only Count Emmerick and Radegonde, who would also be a good deal the wealthier.

Emmerick had replied, with appropriate indignation, that it would be blasphemy thus to despoil the tomb of his heroic father.

But to the contrary, it was Emmerick, as he forthwith learned, who blasphemed his heroic father's memory in even for one moment supposing that the blessed dead cared about such vanities as rubies and sapphires, and wanted their own innocent grandchildren to starve in the gutter; and, for the rest, would he simply look at that pile of bills, and not be driving everybody crazy with his high-and-mighty nonsense.

Emmerick did look, very briefly and with unhidden aversion, toward the candid smallish mountain of unsettled accounts with which he was already but too familiar. 'Nevertheless,' said Emmerick, 'it would be an abominable action, if the story were ever to get out – '

'It will not get out, my dear,' replied his wife, 'for we will leave the whole matter to Jurgen, who is the soul of discretion.'

'And I cannot afford to have any part in it,' said Emmerick, virtuously.

'You need take no part whatever,' his wife assured him, 'but only your fair half of the proceeds.'

So Radegonde sent for Jurgen the pawnbroker, and asked him to appraise the jewels in Dom Manuel's effigy and to name his best price for them.

It was thus that Jurgen happened to come just then to Manuel's tomb and to disturb the dreaming of Madame Niafer.

Chapter LXIX

Economics of Jurgen

'You,' the fluttered old lady began – oddly enough, it must have seemed to Jurgen – 'you were the last living person to lay eyes upon him. It is strange that you, of all people, should come now to end my dreaming. I take your coming, rogue, as an omen.'

Then Madame Niafer began to tell him somewhat of her dream. And Jurgen listened, with the patience and the fondness which the plight of very old persons always seemed to evoke in him.

Jurgen was upon excellent terms with Madame Niafer, whom, for Biblical reasons, he was accustomed to refer to as the Centurion. 'You say to one man, Go, and he goeth; and you say to another man, Come, and he cometh,' Jurgen explained. 'In fine, you are a most terrible person. But when you say to me, Go, I do not obey you, madame, because you are also a dear.'

Niafer regarded this as sheer impudence, and vastly liked it.

So she told him about her dream. . . . And it was possible, Dame Niafer now admitted, that this dream might have a little misrepresented the deplorable women involved, because that snaky-eyed Freydis was known, since she got her dues from the Druids and the satirists, to be satisfactorily imprisoned in infamous Antan, whereas that hypocrite of an Alianora was now a nun at Ambresbury. But in Madame Niafer's dreaming the hussies had seemed equally free from the constraint of infamy and of the convent: they had seemed to be far more dreadfully constrained by scepticism. . . .

'Madame,' said Jurgen, at the end of her account, 'what need is there, after all, to worry over this little day-dream? I myself had but last month, upon Walburga's Eve, a far more extensive and disturbing dream: and nothing whatever came of it.'

The Countess answered: 'I grow old; and with age one is less certain of everything. Oh, I know well enough that the lewd smirking hussies were very slanderously in the wrong! Still, Jurgen, still, dear rogue, there is a haunting whisper which tells me that time means to take all away. I am a lonely powerless old creature now, but I stay Manuel's wife. That alone had remained to me, to have been the one love and the proud wife of the great Redeemer of Poictesme. Now, at the last, a whispering tells me, time must take away that also. My Manuel, a whispering tells me, was no more splendid than other men, he performed no prodigies, and there will be no second coming of the Redeemer: a whispering tells me that I knew this always and that all these years I have been acting out a lie. I think that whispering talks nonsense. And yet, with age, Jurgen, with age and in the waiting loneliness of age, one grows less certain of everything.'

'Madame,' said Jurgen, with his most judicial aspect, 'let us regard this really very interesting question from its worst possible side. Let us – with suitable apologies to his great shade, and merely for the quicker confounding of his aspersers – suppose that Dom Manuel was, in point of fact, not anything remarkable. Let us wildly imagine the cult of the Redeemer, which is now spread all over our land, to be compact of exaggeration and misunderstanding and to be based virtually on nothing. The fact remains that this heroic and gentle and perfect Redeemer, whether or no he ever actually existed, is now honored and, within reason and within the reach of human frailty, is emulated everywhere, at least now and then. His perfection has thus far, I grant you, proved uncontagious; he has made nobody anywhere absolutely immaculate: but none the less – within limits, within the unavoidable limits – men are quite appreciably better because of this Manuel's example and teachings – '

'Men are happier also, Jurgen, because of that prediction as to his second coming which he uttered in your presence on the last night of his living, and which you brought down from Upper Morven.'

Jurgen coughed. 'It is a pleasure, it is always a pleasure, to further in any way the well-being of my fellow-creatures. But – to resume the immediate thread of my argument – if this superb and most beneficial example was not ever actually set by Dom Manuel – owing to the press of family and state affairs – if this example were, indeed, wholly your personal invention, then you, O terrible Centurion, would be one of the most potent creative artists who ever lived. That, now, I proclaim, as a retired poet, to be a possibility from which you should not take shame, but only pride and thankfulness.'

'Do not be talking your wheedling nonsense to me, young fellow! For, if my life had been given over to the spreading of romances about a Manuel who never lived – !'

Her weak, old, shriveled hands were fluttering before her, helplessly, in a kind of futile wildness. She clasped them now, so that each hand seemed to restrain the other. And Jurgen answered:

'I quail. I am appropriately terrified by your snappishness, and flattered by your choice of an adjective. I venture none the less, to observe that I have encountered, Centurion dear, in the writings of one or another learned author, whose name at the present escapes me, the striking statement, and the wholly true statement – and a statement which was, indeed, a favorite with my saintly father – that a tree may always be judged by its fruit. Now, the children of Dom Manuel have thus far most emphatically borne out this statement. Count Emmerick' – here Jurgen coughed – 'Count Emmerick is learned in astrology. He is noted for his hospitality – '

'Emmerick,' said Dame Niafer, 'would be well enough if he were not led by the nose in everything by that wife of his.'

Then Jurgen's shoulders went up, his hands went outward, to disclaim any personal share in the old lady's appraisement of his present client Radegonde. But Jurgen did not argue the matter.

'Madame Melicent,' Jurgen equably resumed, 'has been the provoker of much gratifyingly destructive warfare oversea, just as Madame Ettarre has been the cause of another long war here at home, in which many gentlemen have won large honor, and hundreds of the humbler sort have been enabled to enter into a degree of eternal bliss appropriate to their inferior estate. Such wars evoke the noble emotions of patriotism, they enable people to become proficient in self-sacrifice, and they remarkably better business conditions, as my ledgers attest. As for Madame Dorothy, while she has incited no glorious public homicides and arsons, she has gratified and she has made more pleasurable the existence of half the gentry of Poictesme – '

'And what, you rogue, do you mean by that?'

'I allude to the organ of vision, without any anatomical excursus. I mean that to behold such perfect beauty makes life more pleasurable. Moreover, Madame Dorothy has incited a fine poem and a hungering and a dreaming that will not die, and a laughter which derides its utterer, too pitilessly – '

Now Jurgen's voice had altered so that the old lady looked at him more narrowly. Niafer had an excellent memory. She perfectly recalled the infatuation of Jurgen's youth, she who had no delusions about this daughter of hers. And Niafer reflected briefly upon the incurable romanticism of all men.

But Niafer said only, 'I never heard of any such poem.'

Jurgen now completed the third of those convenient coughing spells. 'I refer to an epic which stays as yet unpublished. It is a variation upon the Grail legend, madame, and pertains to the quest of a somewhat different receptacle. However! In regard to the other children of Dom Manuel, – concerning whose mothers your opinions, my adored Centurion, do equal credit to your sturdy morality and your skill in the art of impassioned prose – we have Messire Raimbaut, a very notably respected poet, we have Sesphra, who has become a god of the Philistines. Poets befall all families, of course, with nobody to blame, whereas a god, madame, is not ever, as rhetoricians express it, to be sneezed at. We have, moreover, Edward Longshanks, among the most respected monarchs that England has ever known, because he so compactly exhibits in his large person every one of the general defects and limitations of his people. Thus far, madame, we may estimate the children of Dom Manuel's body to have made a rather creditable showing.'

'There is something in what you say,' Dame Niafer admitted. 'Yet what is this nonsense about "the children of his body"? Have men any other implement, unknown to their wives, with which to beget children?'

Jurgen beamed. Jurgen, it was apparent, had found an enticing idea to play with.

'There is quite another sort of paternity, acquired without the need of troubling and upsetting any woman. So, for the perfect rounding off of our argument, we must consider also Dom Manuel's children in the spirit, those lords who were of the

Fellowship of the Silver Stallion, and whose heroism was modeled so exactly after his fine example.'

Niafer replied, a little puzzled: 'They were notable and pious persons, who were sent into all parts of the earth as the apostles of the Redeemer, and who will return again with Manuel. . . . But do you tell me just what you mean!'

'I mean that it was of rough and ungodly fighting-men that Dom Manuel's example made these incomparable heroes. There was a time, madame – a time to which we may now, in the proper spirit, refer without any impiety – when their delight in battle was as vigorous as their moral principles were lax, a time when they jested at holy things, and when their chastity was defective.'

The Countess nodded. 'I remember that time. It was an evil time, with no respectability in it: and I said so, from the first.'

'Yet do you consider what Dom Manuel's example and teachings made, in the end, of his companions in this life! Do you consider the saintly deeds of Holden and of Anavalt, and how Ninzian was for so long the mainstay of all religion hereabouts – '

'Ninzian was a holy person, and even among the apostles of Manuel he was perhaps the most devout. Nevertheless – '

But Jurgen now became more particular. 'Do you consider how but fourteen years ago Donander died a martyr in conflict with the pagan Northmen, proving with his body's loss the falsity and wickedness of their superstitions, when in the sight of both armies Donander was raised up into heaven by seven angels in the same instant that a devil carried his adversary northward!'

'That miracle is attested. Yet – '

'Consider how holy Gonfal also perished as a martyr among the infidels of Inis Dahut, after his chaste resistance to the improper advances of their Queen! There, madame, was a very soul-stirring example for you, because you brunettes are not easy to resist.'

'Get along with you, you rogue! My eyes stay dark and keen enough to see that what hair I have is white in these days.'

'Then also, pious Miramon Lluagor, it is well known, converted many hundreds of the heathen about Vraidex, by the great miracle which he wrought when Koshchei the Deathless, and Toupan, the Duke of Chaos, and Moloch, Lord of the Land of Tears, and Nergal, the Chief of Satan's Secret Police – and several thousand other powers of evil whose names and infernal degrees at this instant evade me – came swarming out of hell in the form of gigantic bees.'

'It is known that such favor was vouchsafed by Heaven to the faith and the prayers of Miramon. Ninzian, indeed, was present at the time, and told me about those awful insects. Each was about as large as a cow, but their language was much worse. Nevertheless – '

But Jurgen was nowhere near done. 'Then Guivric,' he pointed out – 'Guivric of Perdigon, also, in whom the old leaven stayed longer than in the others, so that for a while he kept some little faults, they say, in the way of pride and selfishness – Guivric got wholly rid of these blemishes after his notable trip into the East to discomfit single-handed the signal schisms of the pernicious and sinister Sylan. There was never a sweeter nor a more prodigally generous nor a more generally lovable saint upon earth than all found Guivric after his return from exorcising that heathen heresiarch into a mere pile of bones; and so the dear old Heitman stayed up to the glorious hour of his seraphic death.'

'That is true. I recall the change in Guivric, and it was most edifying.'

'Do you recall, also, madame, how the venerable Kerin went down to teach the truth about the Redeemer in the deepest fastnesses of error and delusion! and how he there confuted, one by one, the frivolous scientific objections of the overseers of hell – with a patience, a painstakingness and a particularity surprising even in an apostle – in an argument which lasted twenty years!'

'That also is true. In fact, it was his own wife who told me about it. Nevertheless – '

But Jurgen was still talking. 'Lastly, madame, my beloved father Coth, as a matter of equally general knowledge, went as an evangelist among the brown-skinned and black-hearted unbelievers of Tollan. He introduced among them the amenities of civilisation and true religion. He taught them to cover their savage nakedness. And, in just the manner of holy Gonfal, Coth likewise subdued the goad of carnal desire and the prick of his flesh – not once, but many times – when Coth also was tempted by such an ill-regulated princess as but to think of crimsons the cheek of decency.'

The Countess said, meditatively: 'You and your cheek – However, do you go on!'

Jurgen now shook a grizzled head, in rather shocked deprecation. 'You ask the impossible. Upon the innumerable other pious exploits of Coth, I, as his wholly unworthy son, may not dwell without appearing vainglorious. That would be most unbecoming. For the modesty of my father was such, madame, that, I must tell you, not even to me, his own son, did he ever speak of these matters. The modesty of my father was such that – as was lately revealed to a devout person in a vision – even now my father esteems himself unworthy of celestial bliss; even now his conscience troubles him as to the peccadillos of his earlier and unregenerate days; and even now he elects to remain among what, in a manner of speaking, might be termed the less comfortable conditions of eternal life.'

'He is privileged, no doubt, to follow his own choice: for his consecrated labors are attested. Nevertheless . . .'

Then for a while Dame Niafer considered. These certainly were the facts as to the lords of the Silver Stallion, whom she herself could remember as having been, in the far-off days of her youth, comparatively imperfect persons: these acts of the apostles were facts recorded in the best-thought-of chronicles, these were the facts familiar even to children, facts which now a lengthy while ago, along with many other edifying facts about the saintly lords of the Silver Stallion, had each been fitted into its proper niche as a part of the great legend of Manuel: and as she appraised these facts, the old Countess validly perceived the strength of Jurgen's argument. . . .

'Yes,' Niafer conceded, by and by, 'yes, what you say is true. These consecrated persons had faults when they were first chosen by my husband to be his companions: but through their intimacy with him, and through the force of his example, they were purged of these faults, they were made just and perfect: and after the Redeemer's passing, they fared stainlessly, and were his apostles, and carried that faith which his living had taught them into every direction and about all quarters of the earth. These are the facts recorded in each history book.'

'So, you perceive, Centurion dear! I can but repeat that, in the axiom favored by my honored father, every tree must be judged by its fruits, The exploits of the Fellowship of the Silver Stallion I estimate as the first fruits of the cult of the Redeemer. Men of the somewhat lax principles to which these apostles in their younger days – I say it in the proper spirit, madame – did now and then, we know, succumb, such men are not unmiraculously made just and perfect. I deduce we may declare this cult of Manuel the Redeemer to be a heavenly inspired and an in all ways admirable cult, since it produces miraculously, from the raw material of alloyed humanity, such apostles. This cult has already, in the holy lives and the high endings of the lords of the Silver Stallion, madame, passed the pragmatic test: it is a cult that works.'

'Besides,' said Niafer, with a not unfeminine ellipsis, and with a feminine preference for something quite tangible, 'there is that last sight of my husband's entry into glory, which as a child you had upon Upper Morven, and the fearful eucharist which you witnessed there. I could never understand why there was not even one angel present, when as many as seven came for Donander. Even so, you did witness very holy and supernatural occurrences with which Heaven would never have graced the passing of an ordinary person.'

'The imagination of a child – ' began Jurgen. He stopped short. He added, 'Very certainly, madame, your logic is acute, and your deduction is unassailable by me.'

'At all events – ' Then it was Niafer who stopped abruptly. But in a while she continued speaking, and in her withered face was much that puzzled and baffled look which Coth's old face had worn toward the end.

'At all events, it was only a dream about those hussies. And at all events, it is near time for dinner,' said Dame Niafer. 'And people must have both their dreams and their dinners in this world, and when we go out of it we must take what we find. That is all. I have not the imagination of a child. I am old. And when you get old it is better not to imagine things. It is better for an old person not to have any dreams. It is better for an old person not to think. Only one thing is good for an old person, and gives to that old person an end of loneliness and of bad dreams and of too much thinking.'

Niafer arose, not without difficulty; and the bent, limping, very aged Countess Dowager of Poictesme now went away from Jurgen, slowly and moodily.

Chapter LXX

All Ends Perplexedly

Jurgen, thus left alone, forthwith ascended the side of the great tomb. He stood now at the top of it, holding to the neck of the horse upon which sat the sculptured effigy of Manuel. The stone face, above and looking beyond Jurgen, when seen at such close quarters, was blotched and grotesquely coarse, the blank eyeballs gave it a repellent air of crass idiocy. But Jurgen was there to appraise not the face but the garments of the overtowering hero, and it was at the gems with which this famous effigy was inset that Jurgen was really looking.

Then, without any deep surprise, Jurgen whistled. To his trained eye it was apparent enough that these gems with which Madame Niafer had prodigally adorned her husband's statue were one and all, and had been from the first, bright bits of variously colored glass. The Countess Radegonde, it appeared, had been by a great many years forestalled in her economics, and in her practical view of the tomb, by the countess who builded it.

And somehow Jurgen was not much surprised. His only verbal outbreak was to utter one of his favourite remarks. He said, 'These women!'

He climbed down to the pavement afterward, with the gingerly care befitting a person of forty-and-something. He cocked his gray head, looking upward with a remarkable blending of the quizzical and of the regretful. Now, seen at an appropriate distance, now Manuel of Poictesme appeared again resplendent and in everything majestic. He sat there, wary and confident and superb, it seemed, perpetually to guard the country which he had redeemed; and to which, men said, he was to return. . . .

Thus Jurgen waited for some while, regarding the vast tomb which was wholly empty, and which everywhere was adorned with a worthless tinsel glitter, and which yet stayed the most holy and, precisely as Jurgen had pointed out, the actually inspiring shrine of the heroic cult of the Redeemer....

Jurgen opened his mouth. Then he shut it.

For Jurgen recalled that only last month he had become involved in a somewhat perturbing experience, on account of having spoken extempore in praise of the Devil; and so, as concerned the Redeemer, Jurgen decided not to commit himself, one way or the other. It seemed the part of wisdom for an aging pawnbroker to keep out of all such extra-mundane affairs.... Even so, a carnival of thoughts now tempted him to play with them, because this was a paradoxical tomb about which, but for the promptings of discretion, one might say a number of fine things. Those tinsel fripperies were, to the eyes of a considerate person, worthy of a reverence undemanded by mere diamonds, because of the deeds which they had prompted: and this emptiness was sacred because of the faith which people had put in it. And that this glittering vacuity could, as a matter of fact, work miracles was now fully attested: for it had reduced Jurgen to silence.

No: you could never, shruggingly, dismiss this tomb as, upon the whole, a malefic fraud which emanated only folly and intolerance and a persecution of the short-sighted by the blind. That was, in fact, a relatively unimportant aspect, in that it was an aspect which need never trouble you personally, if you were careful. And, at forty-and-something, you were careful.

Meanwhile you knew the shining thing to have been, also, the begetter of so much charity, and of forbearance, and of bravery, and of self-denial – and of its devotees' so strange, so troublingly incomprehensible, contentment – that it somewhat frightened Jurgen. For Jurgen, but a moment ago, had been handling – perhaps a bit over-intimately – that really dangerous fountain-head of all the aspiring and fine standards which the aging pawnbroker was used unfeignedly to admire, with a vague, ever-present underthought as to the disastrousness of acquiring them. It would, he felt, be the very deuce if in business life one were ever to find these notions on the wrong side of his counter....

Æsthetically it was, of course, delightful to regard the pre-eminent manifesters of the Redeemer's power and sanctity, in those splendid lords of the Silver Stallion about whom Jurgen had but now been talking. It was an ennobling and a picturesque reflection, that humanity had once risen to such heights; that mere mortal men had, through their faith in and their contact with the great Redeemer, become purged of all faults and carnal weaknesses, and had lived stainlessly, and had even performed their salutary miracles whenever such a course seemed requisite. Jurgen thought it would be rather fun to work miracles. In any event, it was pleasant, and it was non-committally uplifting, just to think about the heroic saints of yesterday, and to envy their lot in life and their assured fine place in history.

Jurgen thought, for example, of gentle and great-hearted old Guivric sharing his worldly wealth in such noble irrationality with all needy persons; and of kneeling Miramon with those seven thousand horrific bees swarming about him – screeching out infernal threats, but powerless to trouble the serene, psalm-singing and unstung saint. Jurgen thought of Kerin facing so intrepidly yet other hideous cohorts of disputatious fiends and cowing their science so-called with decisive Biblical texts; and of the noble shocked figure of virtuous Gonfal holding fast his nightgown about him with one hand, and with the other repulsing the enamored – and they said, quite good-looking also – Queen Morvyth of the Isles of Wonder, when she assaulted his chastity. Performances like these were well worthy to be commemorated in history: and Jurgen regarded them with a warm, gratifying thrill of purely æsthetic appreciation.

For, from any practical standpoint, Jurgen obscurely felt, it would be inconvenient to be quite as perfect and superb as all that. Or, you might put it better, perhaps, that this was not a condition which a really honorable person, with a shop and a wife and other obligations, could conscientiously do anything directly to provoke for himself. Any, as one might say, defenseless house-holder whom the all-powerful Redeemer had explicitly and un-arguably singled out to live in the heroic sanctity of an apostle would be, of course, in a piously different and wholly justifiable case. . . .

And Jurgen was wondering what it was that the child who Jurgen once had been had, actually, witnessed and heard upon Upper Morven. He could not now be certain: the fancies of a child are so unaccountable, so opulent in decorative additions.... Yet the testimony of that child appeared to have done more than anything else toward establishing Dom Manuel's supremacy over all the men that Poictesme had ever known; indeed, when every fostering influence was allowed for, the whole cult of the returning Redeemer had begun with the testimony of that child. And perhaps it was natural enough (in this truly curious world) that Jurgen nowadays should be the only person remaining in any place who was a bit dubious as to the testimony of that child. ...

Anyhow, young Jurgen had brought down from Morven a most helpful and inspiring prediction which kept up people's spirits in this truly curious world; and cheerfulness was a clear gain. The fact that nothing anywhere entitled you to it could only, he deduced, make of this cheerfulness a still clearer gain. ...

There might, besides, very well have been something to build upon. Modesty, indeed, here raised the point if Jurgen – at that tender age and some while before the full ripening of his powers – could have invented out of the whole cloth anything quite so splendid and far-reaching? And that question he modestly left unanswered. Meanwhile (among so many perplexities) it was certain that Poictesme, along with the rest of Christendom, had now its wholly satisfactory faith and its beneficent legend.

EXPLICIT

Compendium of Leading
Historical Events

(Abridged from the computations of Bülg)

1239   MANUEL THE REDEEMER departs from Poictesme, in the September of this year. Last siege of the Fellowship of the Silver Stallion held upon the feast of St Clement the Roman. NIAFER named regent in her husband's stead, pending either the return of DOM MANUEL or the arrival of the twenty-first birthday of their son EMMERICK.

1240   GONFAL goes into the Isles of Wonder. COTH travels to Sorcha, and thence westward. KERIN disappears in the May of this year. MIRAMON LLUAGOR leaves Poictesme.

1243   Execution of GONFAL, on or about the feast day of Tiburtius and Valerianus.

1244   Miraculous birth of FAUXPAS DE NOINTEL.

1245   MIRAMON LLUAGOR acquires, but gets inadequate benefit from, the bees of TOUPAN. COTH imprisoned at Ran Reigan.

1247   COTH reaches Porutsa, and is made Emperor of Tollan. COTH is blown back into Poictesme.

1250   Death of MIRAMON LLUAGOR. Flight of DEMETRIOS the parricide into Anatolia.

1252   ST FERDINAND enters into eternal life. ANAVALT goes into Elfhame, and perishes there.

1253   ORK and HORRIG suffer martyrdom among the Peohtes.

1254   Marriage of DOM MANUEL'S reputed son, PRINCE EDWARD, at fifteen years of age, to the infant daughter of ST FERDINAND.

1255 MÉLUSINE puts a magic upon KING HELMAS, and transfers his charmed castle called Brunbelois to the high place in Acaire. Betrothal of MELICENT to KING THEODORET.

1256 PERION DE LA FORÊT comes, in disguise, to Bellegarde. JURGEN goes into Gâtinais. DOROTHY marries MICHAEL, the son of GUIVRIC.

1257 MELICENT escapes out of Poictesme, and is purchased by DEMETRIOS. JURGEN makes merry with the third wife of the VIDAME DE SOYECOURT.

1258 Ending of DAME NIAFER'S regency in the name of MANUEL; with the formal accession, in the June of this year, upon the feast day of St Peter and St Paul, of COUNT EMMERICK THE FOURTH.

1260 The portrait of QUEEN RADEGONDE becomes a mortal woman, and terminates the intimacy with HOLDEN which began at Lacre Kai in 1237. COUNT EMMERICK marries RADEGONDE. Death of HOLDEN. Death of AZRA.

1261 GUIVRIC goes east to face the Sylan. COTH dies in his sleep. KERIN returns to Poictesme after twenty-one years spent underground.

1262 Birth of EMMERICK'S first son. NINZIAN detected by his nine hundred and eightieth wife, and is visited by LUCIFER.

1263 Rape of ETTARRE, with her prompt rescue by GUIRON. MAUGIS D'AIGREMONT goes into rebellion. DONANDER leaves Poictesme, and is killed by PALNATOKI.

1265 KERIN murdered by outlaws. Continuation of MAUGIS' rebellion.

1268 Death of POPE CLEMENT THE FOURTH, with the resultant accession, in December, of AYRART DE MONTORS. JURGEN visits the Château de Puysange, and there meets the VICOMTE'S wife.

1269   Birth of FLORIAN DE PUYSANGE.

1270   HOLMENDIS leaves Poictesme, and dies in Africa. Edifying decease of GUIVRIC. JURGEN returns into Poictesme, and marries LISA, the daughter by courtesy of old PETTIPAS the pawnbroker. COUNT EMMERICK at odds with the POPE.

1271   Accession to the papal chair of GREGORY THE TENTH. Continuation of MAUGIS' disastrous rebellion, with the partial burning of Bellegarde.

1272   Death of BALTHIS. Disappearance of NINZIAN. Accession of DOM MANUEL's reputed son to the crown of England.

1275   PERION and MELICENT come back into Poictesme. End of MAUGIS' rebellion, with his just punishment by death. Marriage of ETTARRE to GUIRON DES ROCQUES, who in the following year succeeds his brother, as PRINCE DE GATI-NAIS.

1277   JURGEN has a queer dream, upon Walburga's Eve. NIAFER visited by a queer dream during the forenoon of St Urban's day. Death of NIAFER, in the June of this year.

1287   The second rape of ETTARRE by SARGATANET, Lord of the Waste Beyond the Moon, and the beginning of her retention in his domain for 592 years.

1291   ALIANORA dies at Ambresbury, and is interred piecemeal, parts of her being buried in the Benedictine convent there, and the remainder at the Friars Minors in London.

1300   COUNT EMMERICK murdered by his nephew, RAYMONDIN DE LA FORÊT, who seeks refuge in the unhallowed Forest of Columbiers, and there marries MADAME MÉLUSINE the enchantress.